Praise for
The Green Road

A *Washington Post* Best Fiction Book of the Year
Winner of the Irish Book Awards' Novel of the Year

"Gorgeously roving."   —Megan O'Grady, *Vogue*

"Luminous."
                    —Steve Donoghue, *Christian Science Monitor*

"Anne Enright is a novelist of fearless superiority whose genius is maddeningly hard to pin down."
                    —Frances Wilson, *New Statesman*

"Enright's writing is by turns lyrical and aphoristic . . . but she never loses the fine sense of irony that is a thread throughout her work."
                    —Rachel Nolan, *San Francisco Chronicle*

"Enright, newly crowned as the first Irish Fiction Laureate, has her own distinctive voice. She is witty, sharp, profound, perceptive and often very funny as she slyly undercuts her characters' self-deceptions."
                    —Sue Gaisford, *Financial Times*

"*The Green Road* ripples with fierce resentments and glows with tenderness. Anyone who has experienced the Gordian knot of family life will recognize the complex interplay of emotions in these beautifully rendered pages."
                    —Tom Beer, *Newsday*

The Green Road

The Green Road

Anne Enright

W. W. NORTON & COMPANY
Independent Publishers Since 1923
NEW YORK • LONDON

For information about permission to reproduce selections from this book,
write to Permissions, W. W. Norton & Company, Inc., 500 Fifth Avenue,
New York, NY 10110

For information about special discounts for bulk purchases, please contact
W. W. Norton Special Sales at specialsales@wwnorton.com or 800-233-4830

Manufacturing by Courier Westford
Production manager: Louise Mattarelliano

Library of Congress Cataloging-in-Publication Data

Enright, Anne, 1962–
The Green Road / Anne Enright. — First edition.
    pages cm
ISBN: 978-0-393-24821-0 (hardcover)
1. Domestic fiction. I. Title.
PR6055.N73G74 2015
823'.914—dc23

                              2015004414

ISBN 978-0-393-35280-1 pbk.

W. W. Norton & Company, Inc.
500 Fifth Avenue, New York, N.Y. 10110
www.wwnorton.com

W. W. Norton & Company Ltd.
Castle House, 75/76 Wells Street, London W1T 3QT

2 3 4 5 6 7 8 9 0

for Nicky Grene

Part One

LEAVING

Hanna

Ardeevin, Co. Clare
1980

LATER, AFTER HANNA made some cheese on toast, her mother came into the kitchen and filled a hot water bottle from the big kettle on the range.

'Go on up to your uncle's for me, will you?' she said. 'Get me some Solpadeine.'

'You think?'

'My head's a fog,' she said. 'And ask your uncle for amoxicillin, will I spell that for you? I have a chest coming on.'

'All right,' said Hanna.

'Try anyway,' she said, coaxingly, taking the hot water bottle to her chest. 'You will.'

The Madigans lived in a house that had a little river in the garden and its own name on the gate: *ARDEEVIN*. But it was not far to walk, up over the humpy bridge, past the garage and into town.

Hanna passed the two petrol pumps standing sentry on the forecourt, with the big doors open and Pat Doran in there somewhere, reading the Almanac, or lying in the pit below a car. There was an oil drum by the swinging Castrol sign with the bare fork of a tree sticking out of it, and Pat Doran had dressed it in a pair of old trousers with two shoes stuck on the ends of the branches, so it looked like a man's legs waving around in a panic after him falling into the barrel. It was very lifelike. Their mother said it was too near to the bridge, it would cause an accident, but Hanna loved it. And she liked Pat Doran, who they were told to avoid. He took them for rides in fast cars, up over the bridge, bang, down on the other side.

After Doran's was a terraced row of little houses, and each of the windows had its own decoration and its own version of curtains or blinds: a sailboat made of polished horn, a cream tureen with plastic flowers in it, a pink felted plastic cat. Hanna liked each of them, as she passed, and she liked the way one followed the other in an order that was always the same. At the corner of the Main Street was the doctor's, and the little hallway had a picture done out of nails and metallic string. The shape twisted over itself and twisted back again and Hanna loved the way it seemed to be moving but stayed still, it looked very scientific. After that were the shops: the draper's, with a big window lined in yellow cellophane, the butcher's, his trays of meat fenced around by bloodstained plastic grass, and after the butcher's, her uncle's shop – and her grandfather's shop before him – Considine's Medical Hall.

KODACHROME COLOUR FILM was written on a plastic strip stuck along the top of the window with Kodak FILM in bold letters in the middle of it and KODACHROME COLOUR FILM repeated on the far side. The window display was cream pegboard, with little shelves holding cardboard boxes faded by the sun. 'Just right for the constipated child,' said a sign, in groovy red letters, 'SENOKOT the natural choice for constipation.'

Hanna pushed the door open, and the bell rang. She

looked up at it: the coil of metal was filthy with dust while, many times an hour, the bell shook itself clean.

'Come in,' said her uncle Bart. 'Come in or go out.'

And Hanna went inside. Bart was on his own out front, while a woman in a white coat moved around the dispensary, where Hanna was never allowed to go. Hanna's sister, Constance, used to work the counter, but she had a job up in Dublin now, so they were a girl short and there was a testing irritation to the look her uncle gave Hanna.

'What does she want?' he said.

'Em. I can't remember,' said Hanna. 'Her chest. And Solpadeine.'

Bart winked. He had one of those winks that happen free of the surrounding face. Hard to prove it ever happened.

'Have a cachou.'

'Don't mind if I do-hoo,' said Hanna. She fingered a little tin of Parma Violets from in front of the cash register and sat in the prescriptions chair.

'Solpadeine,' he said.

Her uncle Bart was good-looking like her mother, they had the long Considine bones. Bart was a bachelor and a heartbreaker for all the years of Hanna's girlhood, but now he had a wife who never put her foot in the door of the shop. He was proud of it, Constance said. There he was, paying shop-girls and assistants, and his wife banned from the premises in case she laughed at the parish priest's impacted stools. Bart had a perfectly useless wife. She had no children and beautiful shoes in a range of colours, and each pair had its own matching bag. The way Bart looked at her, Hanna thought he might hate her, but her sister Constance said she was on the pill, because they had access to the pill. She said they were doing it twice a night.

5

'How are they all?' Bart was opening a pack of Solpadeine and taking the contents out.

'Good,' she said.

He tapped around the counter top looking for something and said, 'Have you the scissors, Mary?'

There was a new stand in the middle of the shop of perfumes, shampoos and conditioners. There were other things on the lower shelves and Hanna realised she had been looking at them when her uncle came out of the back room with the scissors. But he did not pretend to notice: he did not even wink.

He cut the card of tablets in half.

'Give her this,' he said, handing over a set of four tablets. 'Tell her to take a rain check on the chest.'

That was a joke, of some sort.

'I will so.'

Hanna knew she was supposed to go then, but she was distracted by the new shelves. There were bottles of 4711 and Imperial Leather bath sets in cream and dark red cardboard boxes. There were a couple of bottles of Tweed and a cluster of other perfumes that were new to her. 'Tramp', said one bottle, with a bold slash for the crossbar of the T. On the middle shelf were shampoos that weren't about dandruff, they were about sunshine and tossing your head from side to side – Silvikrin, Sunsilk, Clairol Herbal Essences. On the bottom shelf were puffy plastic packages and Hanna could not think what they were, she thought they must be cotton wool. She picked up Cachet by Prince Matchabelli, in a twisted oblong bottle, and inhaled where the cap met the cold glass.

She could feel her uncle's eyes resting on her, and in them something like pity. Or joy.

'Bart,' she said. 'Do you think Mammy's all right?'

'Oh for God's sake,' Bart said. 'What?'

Hanna's mother had taken to the bed. She had been there for two weeks, nearly. She had not dressed herself or done her hair since the Sunday before Easter, when Dan told them all that he was going to be a priest.

Dan was in his first year of college up in Galway. They would let him finish his degree, he said, but he would do it from the seminary. So in two years he would be finished in ordinary college and in seven years he would be a priest, and after that he would be off on the missions. It was all decided. He announced all this when he came home for the Easter holidays and their mother went upstairs and did not come down. She said she had a pain in her elbow. Dan said he had little enough to pack and then he would be gone.

'Go up to the shops,' said her father, to Hanna. But he didn't give her any money, and there was nothing she wanted to buy. Besides, she was afraid that something would happen if she left, there would be shouting. Dan would not be there when she got back. His name would never be mentioned again.

But Dan did not leave the house, not even to go for a walk. He hung around the place, sitting in one chair and then moving to another, avoiding the kitchen, accepting the offer of tea or turning it down. Hanna carried the cup to Dan's room, with something to eat tucked in on the saucer; a ham sandwich or a piece of cake. Sometimes he only took a bite of the food and Hanna finished it as she took it back to the kitchen, and the stale edge to the bread made her even more fond of her brother, in his confinement.

Dan was so unhappy. Hanna was only twelve and it was terrible for her to see her brother so pent up – all that belief, and the struggle to make sense of it. When Dan was still at school, he used to make her listen to poems off his English course, and they talked about them afterwards and about all kinds of other things, too. This is what her mother also said, later. She said, 'I told him things that I told to no one else.' And this statement was very teasing to Hanna, because there was very little of herself that their mother held back. Her children were never what you might call 'spared'.

Hanna blamed the Pope. He came to Ireland just after Dan left for college and it was like he flew in specially, because Galway was where the big Youth Mass was held, out on the racecourse at Ballybrit. Hanna went to the Limerick Mass, which was just like standing in a field with your parents for six hours, but her brother Emmet was let go to Galway too, even though he was only fourteen and you were supposed to be sixteen for the Youth Mass. He left in a minibus from the local church. The priest brought a banjo and when Emmet came back he had learned how to smoke. He did not see Dan in the crowd. He saw two people having sex in a sleeping bag, he said, but that was the night before, when they all camped in a field somewhere – he could not tell his parents what was the place.

'And where was the field?' said their father.

'I don't know,' said Emmet. He did not mention the sex.

'Was it a school?' said their mother.

'I think so,' said Emmet.

'Was it beyond Oranmore?'

They slept in tents, or pretended to sleep, because at four in the morning they all had to pack up and troop through the pitch black to the racecourse. Everyone walked in silence, it was like the end of a war, Emmet said, it was hard to explain – just the sound of feet, the sight of a cigarette glowing at someone's face before it was whipped away. We were walking into history, the priest said, and when the dawn came, there were men with yellow armbands in their good suits, standing under the trees. That was it, as far as Emmet was concerned. They sang 'By the Rivers of Babylon' and he came back with his voice gone and the dirtiest clothes his mother had ever seen; she had to put them through the wash twice.

'Was it on the road to Athenry?' their father said. 'The field?'

The location of the field outside Galway was one abiding mystery in the Madigan family, another was what had happened to Dan, after he went to college. He came back for Christmas and fought with his granny about taking precautions, and his granny was all in favour of taking precautions, that was the joke of it, her sister Constance said, because 'precautions' were actually condoms. Later, after the pudding was lit, Dan passed Hanna in the hall and he took took her to him, saying, 'Save me, Hanna. Save me from these ghastly people.' He folded her in his arms.

On New Year's Day a priest called to the house and Hanna saw him sitting in the front room with both her parents. The priest's hair had the mark of the comb in it, as though it was still wet, and his coat, hanging under the stairs, was very black and soft.

After this, Dan went back to Galway and nothing happened until the Easter break, when he said he wanted to be a priest. He made the big announcement at Sunday dinner, which the Madigans always did with a tablecloth and proper napkins, no matter what. On that Sunday, which was Palm Sunday, they had bacon and cabbage with white sauce and carrots – green, white and orange, like the Irish flag. There was a little glass of parsley sitting on the tablecloth, and the shadow of the water

9

trembled in the sunshine. Their father folded his large hands and said grace, after which there was silence. Apart from the general sound of chewing, that is, and their father clearing his throat, as he tended to do, every minute or so.

'Hchm-hchmm.'

The parents sat at either end of the table, the children along the sides. Girls facing the window, boys facing the room: Constance-and-Hanna, Emmet-and-Dan.

There was a fire in the grate and the sun also shone, now and then, so they were as warm as winter and warm as summer for five minutes at a time. They were twice as warm.

Dan said, 'I have been speaking again with Father Fawl.'

It was nearly April. A dappled kind of day. The clean light caught the drops on the windowpane in all their multiplicity while, outside, a thousand baby leaves unfurled against branches black with rain.

Inside, their mother had a tissue trapped in the palm of her hand. She lifted it against her forehead.

'Oh, no,' she said, turning away, and her mouth sagged open so you could see the carrots.

'He says I must ask you to think again. That it is hard for a man who does not have his family behind him. It is a big decision I am making, and he says I must ask you – I must plead with you – not to spoil it, with your own feelings and concerns.'

Dan spoke as though they were in private. Or he spoke as though they were in a great hall. But it was a family meal, which was not the same as either of these things. You could see their mother had an impulse to rise from the table but would not allow herself to flee.

'He says I am to ask your forgiveness, for the life you had hoped for me, and the grandchildren you will not have.'

Emmet snorted into his dinner. Dan pressed his hands down on to the tabletop before swiping at his little brother, fast and hard. Their mother blanked for the blow, like a horse jumping a ditch, but Emmet ducked and, after a long second, she landed on the other side. Then she put her head down, as though to gather speed. A moan came out of her, small and unformed. The sound of it seemed to please as well as surprise her so she tried again. This next moan started soft and went long, and there was a kind of speaking to its last rise and fall.

'Oh God,' she said.

She threw her head back and blinked at the ceiling, once, twice.

'Oh dear God.'

The tears started to run, one on top of the last, down to her hairline; one, two-three, four. She stayed like that for a moment, while the children watched and pretended not to be watching and her husband cleared his throat into the silence, 'Hchm-hchmm.'

Their mother lifted her hands and shook them free of their sleeves. She wiped her wet temples with the heels of her hands and used her delicate, crooked fingers to fix the back of her hair, which she always wore in a chignon. Then she sat up again and looked, very carefully, at nothing. She picked up a fork and stuck it into a piece of bacon and she brought it to her mouth, but the touch of meat to her tongue undid her; the fork swung back down towards her plate and the bacon fell. Her lips made that wailing shape – touching in the middle and open at the sides – what Dan called her 'wide mouth frog' look, then she took a sharp inhale and went: 'Aggh-aahh. Aggh-aahh.'

It seemed to Hanna her mother might stop eating or, if she was that hungry, she might take her plate and go into another room in order to cry, but this did not occur to her mother, clearly, and she sat there, eating and crying at the same time.

Much crying, little eating. There was more work with the tissue, which was now in shreds. It was awful. The pain was awful. Her mother juddering and sputtering, with the carrots falling from her mouth in little lumps and piles.

Constance, who was the eldest, bossed them all quietly about and they carried plates and cups past their mother, as she dripped, one way or the other, into her own food.

'Oh, Mammy,' said Constance, leaning in, with her arm around her, to slip the plate neatly away.

Dan was the eldest boy, so it was his job to cut the apple tart, which he stood to do, dark against the window light, with the silver triangle of the cake slice in his hand.

'You can count me out,' said their father, who had been playing, in a tiny way, with the handle of his teacup. He got up and left the room and Dan said, 'Five, so. How am I going to do five?'

There were six Madigans. Five was a whole new angle, as he moved the cake slice through the ghost of a cross and then swung it eighteen degrees to the side. It was a prising open of the relations between them. It was a different story, altogether. As though there might be any number of Madigans and, out in the wide world, any number of apple tarts.

Their mother's crying turned to funny, staggered inhalations 'phwhh phwwhh phwhh', as she dug into her dessert with a small spoon and the children, too, were comforted by the pastry and by the woody sweetness of the old apples. Still, there was no ice cream on offer that Sunday, and none of them asked for it, though they all knew there was some; it was jammed into the icebox at the top right hand corner of the fridge.

After that, their mother went to bed and Constance had

to stay at home instead of getting the bus back to Dublin and she was furious with Dan: she bashed about doing the dishes while he went up to his room and read his books and their mother lay behind her closed door, and on Monday their father went out to Boolavaun and came back home in the evening, and had no opinions that anyone could discern.

This was not the first time their mother took the horizontal solution, as Dan liked to call it, but it was the longest that Hanna could remember. The bed creaked from time to time. The toilet flushed and the door of her room closed again. They got off school early on Spy Wednesday and she was still ensconced. Hanna and Emmet lurked about the house, that was so large and silent without her. It all looked strange and unconnected: the turn of the bannisters at the top of the stairs, the small study with its light bulb gone, the line of damp on the dining room wallpaper inching up through a grove of bamboo.

Then Constance came up and whacked them, and it became clear – too late – that they had been noisy and wrong-headed when they had meant to be cheerful and full of fun. A cup hit the floor, a lick of cold tea spread towards the library book on the kitchen table, a white, patent leather belt turned out to be plastic when Emmet put a bridle on Hanna and rode her out the front door. After each disaster the children dispersed and acted as though nothing had happened. And nothing did happen. She was asleep up there, she was dead. The silence became more urgent and corpselike, the silence became fully tragic, until the door handle hit the wall and their mother burst out of there. She came flying down the stairs at them, hair undone, the shadows of her breasts moving under the cotton of her nightgown, her mouth open, hand raised.

She might throw another cup, or upset the whole teapot,

or fling the broken belt into the flowerbed through the open door.

'There,' she said.

'Happy now?'

'Two can play at that game,' she said.

'What do you think of that?'

She would stare for a moment, as though wondering who these strange children were. After which brief confusion, she would swivel and slam back up to bed. Ten minutes later, or twenty minutes, or half an hour, the door would creak open and her small voice come out of it saying, 'Constance?'

There was something comical about these displays. Dan pulled a wry face as he went back to his book, Constance might make tea and Emmet would do something very noble and pure – a single flower brought from the garden, a serious kiss. Hanna would not know what to do except maybe go in and be loved.

'My baby. How's my little girl?'

Much later, when all this had been forgotten, with the TV on and cheese on toast made for tea, their father came back from the land at Boolavaun. Up the stairs he went, one stair at a time then, after knocking twice, into the room.

'So?' he might say, before the door closed on their talk.

After a long time, he came back down to the kitchen to ask for tea. He dozed in silence for an hour or so and woke with a start for the nine o'clock news. Then he switched off the telly and said, 'Which one of you broke your mother's belt? Tell me now,' and Emmet said, 'It was my fault, Daddy.'

He stood forward with his head down and his hands by his sides. Emmet would drive you mad for being good.

Their father pulled the ruler from under the TV set, and Emmet lifted his hand, and their father held the fingertips until the last millisecond, as he dealt the blow. Then he turned and sighed as he slid the ruler back home.

'Up to bed,' he said.

Emmet walked out with his cheeks flaring, and Hanna got her goodnight beardie, which was a scrape of the stubble from her father's cheek, as he turned, for a joke, from her kiss. Her father smelt of the day's work: fresh air, diesel, hay, with the memory of cattle in there somewhere, and beyond that again, the memory of milk. He took his dinner out in Boolavaun, where his own mother still lived.

'Your granny says goodnight,' he said, which was another kind of joke with him. And he tilted his head.

'Will you come out with me, tomorrow? You will, so.'

The next day, which was Holy Thursday, he brought Hanna out in the orange Cortina, with the door that gave a great crack when you opened it. A few miles out, he started to hum, and you could feel the sky getting whiter as they travelled towards the sea.

Hanna loved the little house at Boolavaun: four rooms, a porch full of geraniums, a mountain out the back and, out the front, a sky full of weather. If you crossed the long meadow, you came to a boreen which brought you up over a small rise to a view of the Aran Islands out in Galway Bay, and the Cliffs of Moher, which were also famous, far away to the south. This road turned into the green road that went across the Burren, high above the beach at Fanore, and this was the most beautiful road in the world, bar none, her granny said – *famed in song and story* – the rocks gathering briefly into walls before lapsing back into field, the little stony pastures whose flowers were sweet and rare.

And if you lifted your eyes from the difficulties of the path, it was always different again, the islands sleeping out in the bay, the clouds running their shadows across the water, the Atlantic surging up the distant cliffs in a tranced, silent plume of spray.

Far below were the limestone flats they called the Flaggy Shore; grey rocks under a grey sky, and there were days when the sea was a glittering grey and your eyes could not tell if it was dusk or dawn, your eyes were always adjusting. It was like the rocks took the light and hid it away. And that was the thing about Boolavaun, it was a place that made itself hard to see.

And Hanna loved her Granny Madigan, a woman who looked like she had a lot to say, and wasn't saying any of it.

But it was a long day out there when the rain came in: her granny always moving from place to place, clearing things, wiping them, and a lot of it useless pother; feeding cats that would not come to her call, or losing something she had just let out of her hand that very minute. There was nothing much to talk about.

'How's school?'

'Good.'

And not much Hanna was allowed to touch. A cabinet in the good room held a selection of china. Other surfaces were set with geraniums in various stages of blooming and decline: there was a whole shelf of amputees on a back sill, their truncated stems bulbous to the tips. The walls were bare, except for a picture of the Killarney Lakes in the good room, and a plain black crucifix over her granny's bed. There was no Sacred Heart, or holy water, or little statue of the Virgin. Their Granny Madigan went to Mass with a neighbour, if she went to Mass at all, and she cycled in all weathers five miles to the nearest shop. If she got sick – and she was never sick – she was in trouble, because she never set foot inside Considine's Medical Hall.

Never had and never would.

The reasons for this were of some interest to Hanna, because, as soon as her father was out with the cattle, her granny took her aside – as though there were crowds to observe them – and pressed a pound note into her hand.

'Go in to your uncle's for me,' she said. 'And ask for some of that last cream.'

The cream was for something old-lady and horrible.

'What'll I say?' said Hanna.

'Oh no need, no need,' said her granny. 'He'll know.'

Constance used to be in charge of this, clearly, and now it was Hanna's turn.

'OK,' said Hanna.

The pound note her granny pressed into her hand was folded in half and rolled up again. Hanna did not know where to put it so she stuck it down her sock for safe keeping, sliding it down along the ankle bone. She looked out one window at the hard sea light, and out the other at the road towards town.

They did not get along, the Considines and the Madigans. When Hanna's father came in the door for his cup of tea, he filled the doorframe so he had to stoop, and Hanna wished her granny could ask her own son for the cream, whatever it was, though she sensed it had something to do with the bright blood she saw in her granny's commode, which was a chair with a hole cut into it, and the potty slotted in beneath.

There were four rooms in the house at Boolavaun. Hanna went into each of them and listened to the different sounds of the rain. She stood in the back bedroom her father used to share with his two younger brothers, who were in America now. She looked at the three beds where they once slept.

Out in the kitchen, her father sat over his tea, and her granny read the newspaper that he brought to her from town, each day. Bertie, the house cat, was straining against her granny's old feet, and the radio wandered off-station. On the range, a big pot of water was coming, with epic slowness, to the boil.

After the rain, they went out to look for eggs. Her granny carried a white enamel bowl with a thin blue rim, that was chipped, here and there, to black. She walked in a quick crouch beyond the hen-house to the hedge that divided the yard from the haggart. She scrabbled along the bushes, peering down between the branches.

'Oho,' she said. 'I have you now.'

Hanna crawled in by her granny's bunioned feet to retrieve the egg that was laid under the hedge. The egg was brown and streaked with hen-do. Granny held it up to admire before putting it in the empty dish where it rolled about with a hollow, dangerous sound.

'Get down there for me,' she said to Hanna, 'and check the holes in the wall.'

Hanna got right down. The walls, which were every-where on the land, were forbidden to her and to Emmet for fear they'd knock the stones on top of themselves. The walls were older than the house, her granny said; thousands of years old, they were the oldest walls in Ireland. Up close, the stones were dappled with white and scattered with coins of yellow lichen, like money in the sunlight. And there was a white egg, not even dirty, tucked into a crevice where the ragwort grew.

'Aha,' said her granny.

Hanna placed the egg in the bowl and her granny put her fingers in there to stop the two eggs banging off each other. Hanna dipped into the wooden hen-house to collect the rest of them, in the rancid smell of old straw and feath-ers, while her granny stood out in the doorway and lowered the bowl for each new egg she found. As they turned back to the house, the old woman reached down and lifted one of the scratching birds – so easily – she didn't even set the eggs aside. If Hanna ever tried tried to catch a hen, they jinked away so fast she was afraid she might give them a heart attack, but her granny just picked one up, and there it was, tucked under the crook of her arm, its red-brown feathers shining in the sun. A young cock, by the stubby black in his tail that would be, when he was grown, a proud array, shimmering with green.

As they walked across the back yard, Hanna's father came out of the car house, which was an open-sided outhouse between the cowshed and the little alcove for turf. Her granny stood on tiptoe to shrug the bird over to him and it swung down from her father's hand as he turned away. He was holding the bird by the feet and in his other hand was a hatchet, held close to the blade. He got the heft of this as he went to a broken bench Hanna had never noticed, which lived under the shelter of the car house roof. He slung the bird's head on to the wood, so the beak strained forwards, and he chopped it off.

It was done as easy as her granny picking the bird up off the ground, it was done all in one go. He held the slaughtered thing up and away from him as the blood pumped and dribbled on to the cobblestones.

'Oh.' Her granny gave a little cry, as though some goodness had been lost, and the cats were suddenly there, lifting up on to their hind feet, under the bird's open neck.

'Go 'way,' said her father, shoving one aside with his boot, then he handed the bird, still flapping, over to Hanna to hold.

Hanna was surprised by the warmth of the chicken's feet, that were scaly and bony and should not be warm at all. She could feel her father laughing at her, as he left her to it and went into the house. Hanna held the chicken away from herself with both hands and tried not to drop the thing as it flapped and twisted over the space where its head used to be. One of the cats already had the fleshy cockscomb in its little cat's teeth, and was running away with the head bobbing under its little white chin. Hanna might have screamed at all that – at the dangling, ragged neck and the cock's outraged eye – but she was too busy keeping the corpse from jerking out of her hands. The wings were agape, the russet feathers all ruffled back and showing their yellow under-down, and the body was shitting out from under the black tail feathers, in squirts that mimicked the squirting blood.

Her father came out of the kitchen with the big pot of water, which he set on the cobbles.

'Still going,' he said.

'Dada!' said Hanna.

'It's just reflexes,' he said. But Hanna knew he was laughing at her, because as soon as it was all over, the thing gave another jerk and her granny gave a sound Hanna had not heard before, a delighted crowing she felt on the skin of her neck. The old woman turned back into the kitchen to leave the eggs on the dresser, and came out fumbling a piece of twine out of her apron pocket as Hanna's father took the chicken from her, finally, and dunked the thing in the vat of steaming water.

Even then, the body twitched, and the wings banged strongly, twice, against the sides of the pot.

In and out the carcass went. And then it was still.

'That's you now,' he said to his mother, as he held a leg out for her to tie with her piece of twine.

After this, Hanna watched her granny string the chicken up by one leg on to a hook in the car house and pull the feathers off the bird with a loud ripping sound. The wet feathers stuck to her fingers in clumps: she had to slap her hands together and wipe them on the apron.

'Come here now and I'll show you how it's done,' she said.

'No,' said Hanna, who was standing in the kitchen doorway.

'Ah now,' said her granny.

'I will not,' said Hanna, who was crying.

'Ah darling.'

And Hanna turned her face away in shame.

Hanna was always crying – that was the thing about Hanna. She was always 'snottering', as Emmet put it. *Oh, your bladder's very close to your eyes,* her mother used to say, or *Your waterworks,* Constance called it, and that was another phrase they all used, *Here come the waterworks,* even though it was her brothers and sister who made her cry. Emmet especially, who won her tears from her, pulled them out of her face, hot and sore, and ran off with them, exulting.

'Hanna's crying!'

But Emmet wasn't even here now. And Hanna was crying over a chicken. Because that's what was under the dirty feathers: goose-bumped, white, calling out for roast potatoes.

A Sunday chicken.

And her granny was hugging her now, from the side. She squeezed Hanna's upper arm.

'Ah now,' she said.

While Hanna's father came across from the cowshed with a can of milk to be taken back home.

'Will you live?' he said.

When she got into the car, her father set the milk can between Hanna's feet to keep it safe. The chicken was on the back seat, wrapped in newspaper and tied with string, its insides empty, and the giblets beside it in a plastic bag.

Her father shut the car door and Hanna sat in silence while he walked around to the driver's side.

Hanna was mad about her father's hands, they were huge, and the sight of them on the steering wheel made the car seem like a toy car, and her own feelings like baby feelings she could grow out of some day. The milk sloshing in the can was still warm. She could feel the pound note down there too, snug against her ankle bone.

'I have to go to the chemist's for Granny,' she said.

But her father made no answer to this. Hanna wondered, briefly, if he had heard the words, or if she had not uttered them out loud at all.

Her grandfather, John Considine, shouted at a woman once because she came into the Medical Hall and asked for something unmentionable. Hanna never knew what it was – you could die of the shame – it was said he manhandled the woman out into the street. Though other people said he was a saint – a saint, they said – to the townspeople who knocked him up at all hours for a child with whooping cough or an old lady crazed by the pain of her kidney stones. There were men from Gort to Lahinch who would talk to no one else if their hens were gaping or the sheep had scour. They brought their dogs in to him on a length of baling twine – wild men from the back of beyond – and he went into the dispensary to mix and hum; with camphor and peppermint oil, with tincture of opium and extract of male fern. As far as Hanna could tell, old John Considine was a saint to everyone except the people who did not like him, which was half the town – the other half – the ones who went to Moore's, the chemist's on the other side of the river, instead.

And she did not know why that might be.

Pat Doran, the garageman, said Moore's was much more understanding of matters 'under the bonnet', but Considine's was a superior proposition altogether when it came to the boot. So maybe that was the reason.

Or it might be something else, altogether.

Her mother saying: *They never liked us.*

Her mother pulling her past a couple of old sisters on the street, with her 'keep walking' smile.

Emmet said their Grandfather Madigan was shot during the Civil War and their Grandfather Considine refused to help. The men ran to the Medical Hall looking for ointment and bandages and he just pulled down the blind, he said. But nobody believed Emmet. Their Grandfather Madigan died of diabetes years ago, they had to take off his foot.

Whatever the story, Hanna walked down to the Medical Hall that evening feeling marked, singled out by destiny to be the purveyor of old lady's bottom cream, while Emmet was not to know their granny had a bottom, because Emmet was a boy. Emmet was interested in things and he was interested in facts and none of these facts were small and stupid, they were all about Ireland, and people getting shot.

Hanna walked down Curtin Street, past the window with its horn-sailed boat, past the cream tureen and the pink, felted cat. It was dusk and the lights of the Medical Hall shone yellow into the blue of the street. She went down on one knee in front of the counter, to get the pound note out of her sock.

'It's for my Granny Madigan,' she said to Bart. 'She says you'll know what.'

Bart flapped a quick eyelid down and up again, then started to wrap a small box in brown paper. There was a shriek of Sellotape from the dispenser as he stuck the paper down.

'How is she anyway?' he said.

'Good,' said Hanna.

'Same as ever?'

Some part of Hanna had hoped she would be allowed to keep the pound note but Bart put out his hand and she was obliged to hand the money over, pathetic as it looked, and soft with much handling.

'I suppose,' she said.

Bart straightened the note out, saying, 'It's beautiful out there all right. The little gentians in flower, maybe already. A little bright blue thing, you know it? A little star, blooming among the rocks?'

He put the old note on top of the pile of one pound notes stacked up in his till, and he let the clip slap down.

'Yeah,' said Hanna. Who was fed up of people talking about some tiny flower like it was amazing. And fed up of people talking about the view of the Aran Islands and the Flaggy fucking Shore. She looked at the soiled little note on top of the pile of crisp new notes, and she thought about her granny's handbag, with nothing inside it.

'All right?' said Bart, because Hanna was stuck there for a moment, her skin was alive with the shame of it. Her father came from poor people. Handsome he might be and tall, but the bit of land he had was only rock and he did his business behind a hedge, like the rest of the Madigans before him.

Poor, stupid, dirty and poor.

That was entirely the problem between the Considines and the Madigans. That was the reason they did not get along.

'Mind her change now,' said Bart, sliding a ten pence and a five pence piece out along the curving plastic of the till.

'Keep it, sure,' said Hanna, airily, and she picked up the packet and walked out of the shop.

Later, in the church, she sat beside her father who knelt forward with his rosary beads hanging down over the rail in front of him. The beads were white. When he was finished praying, he lifted them high and dangled them into their little leather pouch, and they slid into it like water. The Madigans always went to Mass even though you didn't have to go to Mass on Holy Thursday. Dan used to be an altar boy but this year he was in a white alb tied with a silken rope, with his own trousers underneath. And over that was a dress of sorts, in rough cream cloth. He was kneeling beside Father Banjo, helping him to wash people's feet.

There were five people in chairs in front of the altar and the priest went along the row with a silver basin and splashed the feet of each one; young and old, with their bunions and verrucas and their thick yellow nails. Then he turned to Dan to take the white cloth, and he passed it along the top of each foot.

It was just symbolic. The people all had their feet well washed before they came out of the house, of course they had. And the priest didn't really dry them properly either, so they had trouble getting their socks back on, afterwards. Dan inched along, trying not to get his knees trapped in the folds of his dress, looking holy.

On Good Friday there was nothing on telly all day except classical music. Hanna looked at the calendar that was hanging in the kitchen, with pictures of shiny black children sticking their tummies out under print dresses, and the priests beside them were robed in white. Above their vestments were ordinary, Irish faces, and they looked very happy with themselves and with the black children whose shoulders they touched, with big, careful hands.

Finally, at eight o'clock, *Tomorrow's World* came on RTÉ 2 and they were watching this when they heard Dan go in to their mother. He stayed in the bedroom for hours, their two voices a passionate murmur. Their father sat pretending to doze by the range, and Constance dragged the listening children away from the foot of the stairs. After a long time Dan came down – sorted. Pleased with himself.

Their brother, a priest: it was, said Emmet, 'Such a fucking joke.' But Hanna felt momentous and sad. There were no flights home from the missions. Dan would leave Ireland for ever. And besides, he might die.

Later, that evening, Emmet sneered at him.

'You don't actually believe,' he said. 'You just think you do.'

And Dan gave his new, priestly smile.

'And what is the difference again?' he said.

And so it became real. Dan would leave them to save the black babies. Their mother had no power to stop him, anymore.

Meanwhile, there was the small matter of Dan's girlfriend, who had yet to be informed. This Hanna realised after the Easter dinner, with the chicken sitting, dead and very much unresurrected, in the centre of the table; half a lemon in its chest or bottom, Hanna could never tell which. Her mother did not come down to eat with them, she was still in bed. She would never get up, she declared. Hanna sat on the landing outside her bedroom and played cards on the floor and when her mother pulled open the door all the cards got mixed up and Hanna cried, then her mother slapped her for crying, and Hanna cried louder and her mother reeled and wailed. On Tuesday, Dan took Hanna back to Galway with him for a few days. He said it was to get her away from all the fuss, but there was fuss of a different kind waiting for them in Eyre Square.

'This is Hanna,' her brother said, pushing her forward.

'Hello,' said the woman, holding out her hand, which was covered in a dark green leather glove. The woman looked very nice. The glove went up her wrist, with a line of covered buttons along the side.

'Go on,' said Dan, and Hanna, who had no manners yet, reached out to shake the woman's hand.

'Fancy a scoop?' she said.

Hanna walked alongside them, trying to make sense of the traffic and the people who passed, but the city was so busy, there was not enough time to take it all in. A couple of students stopped to talk to them. The girl's check jacket was hanging open over a woolly jumper and the man had big glasses and a scraggy beard. They held hands, even while they were standing there, and the girl shifted and took glimpses at Dan from under her messy hair, like she was waiting for him to say something hilarious. And then he did say something, he said:

'What fresh hell is this?' and the girl fell about laughing.

They parted, a little uncomfortably, from this pair and Dan's girlfriend led them in through a pub door. She said, 'You must be starving. Would you like a ham sandwich?' and Hanna did not know what to say.

The pub was very dark, inside.

'She would,' said Dan.

'And what? Do you want a pint?'

'Maybe she'll have a fizzy orange.'

And so it had appeared, in a glass that flared out at the top, and the surface of it a hush of bubbles that rose and were lost to the air.

'So are you in big school?' said Dan's girlfriend, as she

threw three packets of crisps on the table, and sat in. 'Have they killed you yet, the nuns?'

'Doing their best,' said Hanna.

'No bother to you.'

She busied herself with gloves and bag. She wore a clasp in her hair made of polished wood, and she took this out and settled it back in again. Then she held up her glass.

'Gaudete!' she said. Which was Latin, and a joke.

Hanna was mad about Dan's girlfriend. She was so fine. There was no other word for it. Her voice had layers, she had sentiment and irony, she had no idea – Hanna realised, with an odd, crumpled feeling – what the future had in store.

Dan was going to be a priest! You wouldn't think it as he set down the pint in front of him, and hooked his lower lip over the top to clear it of foam. You wouldn't think it as he looked at this young woman beside him with her cascade of light-brown hair.

'So what's the story?'

'She's well up to it,' she said.

'You think?' he said.

Dan's girlfriend was a tragedy waiting to happen. And yet, those green gloves spoke of a life that would be lovely. She would study in Paris. She would have three children, teach them beautiful Irish and perfect French. She would always mourn for Dan.

'Sorry, what's your name?' said Hanna.

'My name?' she said, and laughed for no reason. 'Oh, I am sorry. My name is Isabelle.'

Of course. She had a name that came out of a book.

After the pub they ran down a lane and were suddenly in a place where everyone smelt of the rain. Dan pulled the coat off Hanna even though she was well able to take off her own coat and when Isabelle came back she had the tickets in her hand. They were going to see a play.

The room they went into did not look like a theatre, there was no curtain or red plush, there were long benches with padded backs and when they found the right row, there were two priests in their way. Actual priests. One of them was old, the other was young and they were dealing, in great slow motion, with programmes and scarves. Isabelle had to push past them, finally, and the priests let them through and then sat down in an insulted sort of way. They stuck their holy backsides out a little, and dipped them on to the leatherette. It was the kind of thing Dan would have laughed at once, but now he said, 'Evening, Fathers,' and Isabelle sat in thoughtful silence, until the metal lights cracked and began to dim.

The darkness of the theatre was a new kind of darkness for Hanna. It was not the darkness of the city outside, or of the bedroom she shared with Constance at home in Ardeevin. It was not the black country darkness of Bool-avaun. It was the darkness between people: between Isabelle and Dan, between Dan and the priests. It was the darkness of sleep, just before the dream.

The play moved so fast, Hanna could not tell you, after, how it was done. The music thundered and the actors ran around, and Hanna didn't fancy any of them except the youngest one. He had eyebrows that went up in the middle and when he ran past, she could see everything about his bare feet, the pattern of hair and the comparative length of each toe. He was very real, he was as real as the spittle that flew from his mouth, though the words that came out of him were not real – perhaps that was why she could not follow them.

The story was about Granuaile the pirate queen, who turned, in the middle of it all, into the other queen, Elizabeth the First. The actress lifted a mask, and her voice changed, and her body changed, and it felt like the bubbles rising in Hanna's fizzy orange, except the bubbles were in her head. Dust moved in the hot lights, the lamps creaked in the rafters. The woman turned, and the mask turned slowly, and suddenly it was all happening inside Hanna and she could feel it spread through the audience like a blush, whatever it was – the play – every word made sense. Then the actors ran off and the ordinary lights came on, and the two priests sat still for a moment, as though trying to recollect where they were.

'Well now,' said the older one. And when it was time for the second half, they did not come back.

In the crowded little room outside, Isabelle said, 'Would you like an ice cream?'

'Yes,' she said, and Isabelle went into the pack of people and came back with a Twist Cup.

During the second half, the nice actor spoke to Hanna. He stopped on stage and levelled his head to say something very quiet, and he was looking at her bang in the eye. Even though he could not see her. Or probably could not see her. And Hanna had a sharp urge to step through to the other side and be with him there – his look an invitation to her, as ghosts are invited in from the dark.

After the play was over, Hanna went to find the toilets, where the women were talking with such carelessness to each other, as they splashed their hands beneath the tap, or pulled some fresh towel down from the roll. Hanna didn't want real life to start again yet. She tried to hold on to the play as they walked through the rainy streets and turned down by a big river; even though the river was exciting in the night-time, she tried to hold the play safe in her mind.

In the middle of the bridge, sitting against the balustrade, was a beggar woman who asked Hanna if she had any spare change, but Hanna didn't have any money at all. She turned to tell her this, then stopped, because the woman had a baby – this old, dirty woman had a real, live baby – under the plaid blanket she used for a shawl. Dan took Hanna's arm to steer her forward, and Isabelle smiled.

'Hold on a minute,' she said, and she went back to drop a coin.

Dan's flat was above a hardware shop. They stopped at a little door and went up the narrow staircase to the first floor, where there was a large room with a kitchenette and a sofa for Hanna to sleep on. The sofa had square steel legs and nubbly brown cushions. Hanna rolled out her sleeping bag and took off her shoes, then she climbed into it, and took off her trousers inside, extracting them up out of the mouth of the bag. She reached down again to get her socks, but it was a bit tight in there, and she ended up just pushing them off with her toes. It was the same sleeping bag of dark blue nylon that Emmet brought to the Pope's Mass and Hanna thought she could smell the cigarettes he had smoked that night. She imagined how jealous he would be of all she had to tell, now.

Hanna got off the bus and made her way down Curtin Street, up over the humpy bridge home. The house looked very empty and she went around the back where Emmet had a den out in the garage, but he wasn't there. He was in the broken greenhouse with a new batch of kittens, the mother cat stiff with fury outside the door.

Hanna told him about the girlfriend.

'So much for that,' he said, getting to his feet.

'It's not like it used to be,' she said. 'They encourage you to date girls, until you take your final vows.'

'Date,' said Emmet.

'What?'

'Date?'

He took her ear and twisted it.

'Ow,' she said. 'Emmet.'

Emmet liked to watch her face when he hurt her, to see what it might do. He was more curious than cruel, really.

'Did she stay?'

'Who?'

'The girlfriend?'

'No, she did not stay. What do you mean, "stay"?'

'Did she sleep with him?'

'God almighty, Emmet. Of course not. I was in *the next room.*'

She did not tell him how beautiful Isabelle was: how Dan sat after she was gone and took off his glasses and squeezed the bridge of his nose.

Hanna went into the house through the back door, along the passage, with its washing machine and coal store and apple store, into the big kitchen, where the heat was dying in the range. She went through to the hall, glanced into the little study, where papers fell out of their piles to make yellowed fans on the floor. There was a shaft of cold air twisting in front of the cracked hearth in the front room that was actually someone's ghost, she thought. The house was its weirdly empty self, with their mother 'sequestered', as Dan used to call it. Horizontal. With her mother dead.

So Hanna went upstairs to tell her dead mother she was home, to ask if she wanted tea and to sit beside her on the bed, and then lie down, while her mother – who was warm and actually, beautifully alive – lifted the eiderdown so Hanna could spoon back into her, with her shoes stuck out over the edge of the mattress. Because Hanna was her baby girl, and she would never make her mother cry, and it was enough to lie there, and let her arm hang over the edge of the bed to stir the books piled up on the floor.

Rain on the Wind

'Not that one,' said her mother. 'It's a bit old for you.'

The cover was a girl with pale lipstick flirting with a man. 'Drama, excitement and romance amid the terrible beauty of Galway's Atlantic seaboard.'

'He has a girlfriend,' said Hanna.

'Does he now,' she said.

'Yes,' said Hanna.

'Are you telling me?' said her mother.

'She's really nice,' said Hanna.

And before Hanna knew it, her mother had the covers pulled back and was off out the other side of the bed. She took off her little jacket of turquoise quilted polyester and sailed it across the bedroom on to Hanna's lap.

'Go on. Out!' she said, but Hanna just slid down between the sheets, while her mother walked around the room doing things she could only guess at. It was so nice, lying there in the darkness as the hairbrush clacked on the dresser top and hair clips made their tiny, light clatter. Hanna heard the shush of a hoisted skirt and, as her mother left the room, the dull sound of something tripped against. A shoe belonging to her father, perhaps. When she was gone, Hanna rose into the bedroom light and checked by the end of the bed. There it was, kicked astray; black and polished, ready for Mass.

'Come on now, Hanna!'

Downstairs, her mother filled the rooms again. There was housework. There was chat: 'Tell me all about Galway, you went to see a play?'

Hanna told her about the pirate queen and about the beggar on the bridge, and her mother had the tea towel for a headscarf, and she was hobbling along saying: 'O, to have a little house! To own the hearth and stool and all'! Hanna joined in with the poem which they had not done together since she was a little girl. Her mother told her the story about the day war was declared and she went to see Anew McMaster play Othello. She was only ten and it was in Ennis, maybe, and he was in blackface, with big hoop earrings and armlets, naked to the waist. You could feel his voice like something pushing against you in the darkness. After this, she looked at the tea towel in her hand and had it suddenly thrown into a corner by the sink, saying, 'God, that was in my hair,' and she wrestled out the big saucepan to boil all the kitchen cloths on the range. Before long, the whole house smelt of cooked carbolic and hot, dirty cotton. Hanna came back into the steamed up kitchen, looking for something to eat, but Constance was back up working in Dublin and the only thing cooking was dirty dish-rags. Hanna lifted the lid and looked at the grey water, with its scum of soap. Her mother was sitting at the table, looking straight ahead.

'I thought I could do some cheese on toast,' said Hanna and her mother said, 'I made him. I made him the way he is. And I don't like the way he is. He is my son and I don't like him, and he doesn't like me either. And there's no getting out of all that, because it's a vicious circle and I have only myself to blame.'

This all seemed, to Hanna, either true or beside the point. But instead of telling her mother this, she said the thing she was supposed to say:

'But you like me, Mammy.'

'I like you *now*,' said her mother.

Later, after Hanna made some cheese on toast, her mother came into the kitchen and filled a hot water bottle from the big kettle on the range.

'Go on up to your uncle's for me, will you?' she said. 'Get me some Solpadeine.'

'You think?'

'My head's a fog,' she said. And when Hanna went down to her uncle Bart's there were new perfumes in the Medical Hall.

Dan

New York
1991

WE ALL THOUGHT Billy was with Greg, though the truth was they had both moved on months before – if they had ever been together. It was hard to put a name on things in the East Village in those days, when everyone was dying or afraid to die, and so many were already gone – the pages of your address book scored through, your dreams surprised by the sweet and impossible faces of the dead.

But if the question was whether Billy was still sleeping with Gregory Savalas, then the answer was that they had barely slept together in the first place. Billy was a blond boy, on the sturdy side, with a thug/angel thing going, so there was a line of sad bastards queueing at his door; half of them married, most of them in suits. And Billy hated the closet. What Billy wanted was big, shouty unafraid sex with someone who did not cry, or get complicated, or hang around after the orange juice and the croissant. Billy was across the threshold and cheerfully out and he wanted men who were basically like him; sweet guys, who lifted weights and fucked large, and slapped you on the shoulder when it was time to swap around. He did not want someone like

Greg – blanked out by the fear of death, neurotic, stalled. There were a lot of neurotic guys in the East Village in those months and years, there were a lot of magnificent guys, and the different personalities that they had are all gone now too.

Greg was the kind of guy who had a hand mirror in the bathroom cabinet so he could check the skin of his back for marks and lesions, and he used this hand mirror, once, twice, six times a day. On two occasions he had to leave the restaurant just before a lunch engagement and run back to work and lock himself in the washroom to strip and check himself over and then dress again and run five blocks so he could arrive at his table on time, sliding along the banquette with a smile while, on his back, the prickle of sweat became the itch of cancer pushing up under the skin.

Of all the signs, the purple bruise of Kaposi's was the one we hated most because there was no doubting it and, after the first mother snatches her child from the seat beside you on the subway, it gets hard to leave the house. Sex is also hard to find. Even a hug, when you are speckled by death, is a complicated thing. And the people who would sleep with you now – what kind of people are they?

We did not want to be loved when we got sick, because that would be unbearable, and love was all we looked for, in our last days.

So Gregory Savalas, art hustler, dealer, executor, smiles and sweats through two courses and coffee, and when he is back in his tiny gallery downtown and nothing new is coming in – except the imagined lesions on his back – he picks up the phone and he dials.

The people who are at home are mostly sick too, and the people who are not sick do not like being called up during work hours, because these are long and aimless calls full of hints and silences and it is hard to take the solid tension that Greg pushes down the line at you. He used to ring Max who worked in his studio all day, but Max was just so arrogant, and then he died. He used to ring a lot of people. His girlfriend Jessie has abandonment issues – or whatever – she is mad as a snake, these days, so Greg rings Billy up because although Billy is a bit normal, sometimes normal is what you need.

'Graphics.'

'Hello, cubicle man.'

'As I live and breathe.'

And Greg is away. First up he tells Billy that Massimo spent the afternoon in Oscar's talking over the lighting for his autumn show and this woman came in with four hundred bags and a boy to carry them, turns out she is the Maharani of Jaipur, which is, like, the Jackie O of all India and she has an emerald on her chest that is bigger than your left eye. The bag boy, it turns out, is an actual prince – as in, turban with a plume at the front – and Massimo has bagged him for dinner Thursday night. Greg says he has offered to do a risotto but he can't find the one everyone liked the last time, the one with the red wine. He says his mother called from Tampa, with an earrings-plus-tracksuit dilemma, and did not mention his father, not once. And when he pointed this out to her she said, 'Oh for Christ's sake, Gregory!'

This is all dangerous talk. Words like 'risotto' pull at Billy like he is back in his boyhood bedroom in Elk County, Pennsylvania: there are years of loneliness in a word like 'risotto'. Billy is working on the news today, writing 'New York Fire Chief in Mattress Hazard Warning' on his Quantel Paintbox. He uhuh's and ahah's and dabs about with his stylus until the risotto effect wanes, while Greg talks and talks and doesn't ever really get there. Finally, after a small silence, Billy heaves it out.

'So, how are you?' and Greg says, 'I have a kind of pain in my lung.'

'Oh?'

'Just, you know, when I inhale.'

'OK.'

'Like a stitch.'

'Well maybe it is a stitch,' says Billy, knowing that this is the wrong thing to say as well as the only thing to say, waiting for Greg to untangle the silence enough to reply.

'Maybe.'

You couldn't put the phone down on a dying man, but in those days we were putting the phone down on each other all over New York, gently, we were extricating ourselves.

'You need an X-ray, maybe?'

We were letting each other go, back to the various rooms and beds in which we would die – but not yet. Not until we put the phone down. Because nobody ever died on the phone.

'Maybe. It's just a kind of catch. Like . . . there.'

'There?'

'You probably can't hear – there! – you hear that? You probably can't hear it over the phone.'

'You want me to come round?' says Billy. And because Greg is so difficult these days, he says, 'Not tonight. I am really behind.'

'Or go out, maybe?'

'I can't go out.'

Of course he can't go out, Greg has lost his looks. How could Billy ask him to come out?

'All right. I'm coming round.'

When he was nineteen years old, fresh in from New Jersey, Gregory Savalas fell in love with a gallerist called Christian whose eyes were the colour of ice when it is blue.

Christian was an actual Dane who tested as soon as there was a test to take, after which he kept trying to kill himself in a deliberate, very Danish sort of way. Greg never knew what he would find when he opened the door to the apartment. Blood everywhere – Christian bleeding into the bathwater, or bleeding into the Brazilian linen sheets; Christian shaking on the bed, the floor beneath him littered with empty paracetamol bottles, his chin gleaming with bile. Ironically, it took him for ever to die from the disease itself. He wasted and wasted. He trembled under the sponge when Greg gave him a bath and his eyes were stone-crazy chips of blue.

They were in St Vincent's, on the seventh floor, with the staff in space suits and six different tubes coming out of Christian, when his mother finally showed. Handsome, of course, her blonde hair shading into silver, she hurried over to her unrecognisable son and leaned over his hospital bed.

'Hey.'

They looked at each other, ice to ice, and whispered in Danish and something happened to Christian. He became human again. He became pure. They gazed at each other for three days straight and then he died.

Greg could recognise, as much as the next person, a moment of grace, but he still thought that death was a big surprise for being the most horrible fuck-up possible. Beyond anything known. Christian was dead and the sight of the living filled Greg with contempt. This was 1986 and the horror was everywhere: your neighbours used a Kleenex to press the elevator button, and strangers shouted 'I hope you die, faggot!' when they passed you in the street. Greg found it hard to remember his lover as a person. He spent a lot of time thinking about the sex they'd had and about all the blood he'd mopped up and touched, but the truth was, it was ages before he'd let Christian inside him, it wasn't really his thing.

That was back in the day, when Gregory the Greek was plump and smooth as a Caravaggio boy. By the time Billy came to town, some years later, on a mission to eat risotto and much cock, Greg was gymmed up and slimmed down, he was almost 'mature'. They hooked up between the shelves of the bookshop on Christopher Street and tricked in the staff toilet. Then they went for coffee, which was sort of the wrong way around, really. A few weeks later, they spotted each other watching some guys make out at the back of Meat on 14th and Billy nodded to say, 'Let's get out of here.' Which Greg immediately did. Of course.

'What were we thinking?' Billy said, when they hit the open air, and he took Greg by the lapels of his jacket and gave him a big, muscular kiss. He was so sexy, Billy. He was as sexy as Greg used to be, when he first came to town. Greg could feel the magic leaving him, flowing, almost, into Billy, so golden and easy against his dark grey sheets. Because Greg used to be the one that everyone wanted; now he was the one who did the wanting. He would be, for the rest of his life, a guy more cruising than cruised. He was twenty-nine years old.

At twenty-nine, Greg had gone to Meat because he was so desperate for a blow job, he thought if he didn't get one he would lie down like an old dog and whine. A bad knee had put a stop to his morning jog and the pain was moving into his hip – also downwards. By the time he and Billy had spun out their last kiss, some six weeks after their first, Greg walked as though there was something trapped under his foot, almost like a limp.

In January 1991, Greg slipped on fresh snow on Third Avenue and he rolled on to his back and just lay there for a moment. It was four in the morning, and his collarbone was broken: he had actually heard the snap. Greg looked up at the falling snow, trying to figure out which flakes would end up on his face and which would not. A surprising number of them missed, then one drifted on to his forehead in a tiny, delayed flare of cold. This was followed by two more – one on his top lip, another on the side of his nose. The pain in his shoulder was intense and Greg could taste fur on his tongue, but he stayed where he was, second-guessing the snow, knowing that as soon as he walked into the hospital his dying would begin.

Max and Arthur came to St Vincent's with him for his HIV results. They talked about David Wojnarowicz who was really fading, and Max shouted about Rothko while they waited on the stackable plastic chairs. Because Max was unflinching, you might say remorseless in the face of the disease; the freaked-out staff were a satisfaction to him. Pity just made him impatient.

'Fuck Rothko,' he said. 'Fuck Rothko.'

'You can't say that,' said Greg.

'I just said it.'

'You can't just say fuck Mark Rothko.'

Arthur said, 'I think Max is uncomfortable with the spiritual aspects of the work.'

'Fuck that. I am uncomfortable with the way he owns a colour.'

'You can't own a colour, you just make a colour.'

Max had a narrow shaved head, like a weasel, and small, surprisingly child-like hands. He sat in a green military trench and jackboots with his elbows on his knees.

'There is nothing but owning. That's all he does. He says, *This colour is mine.* He says, *I am as important as this colour. This is how important I am.*'

'You're ruthless,' Greg said.

'How can I be ruthless?' said Max. 'I'm dying.'

'You are dying in a ruthless fashion,' said Greg, but he was really thinking about Christian, remembering Christian's eyes looking at him from the chair as he moved about the room – not attracted any more, not even jealous. Just crossing him off the list. His young body. His hips. His hands.

Goodbye. Goodbye. Goodbye.

Gregory Savalas was about to die himself, now. And he was not sure he would do it well.

And there was Dr Torres, calling him in to the consulting room. Such a hero, Gabriel Torres, so thrilling and kind. We talked about him endlessly, about how he smiled and what he wore, whether he was happy with our bloods, our retinas, our lungs.

When Greg came back outside, Arthur said, 'How is Gabriel? What did he say?'

It was not Billy's fault he did not know Greg's test results, because Greg did not tell him his results. But Greg managed to resent him for it anyway. They went to a thing at the Fawbush and so many of the men were fading, there was this terrible, dark courage in the room, Greg lost all respect for Billy for being so fucking normal, and it was through gritted teeth he said, 'Well there is a reason I haven't been, you know, fun, recently. There is a reason why I haven't been picking up the phone.'

This was when they were walking back uptown.

'Is there something wrong?' Billy said.

'What do you mean, something wrong? I can't walk that fast, any more.'

'I'm sorry.'

'I am not asking for you to be sorry, I am asking for you to slow down.'

Billy did slow down and then he stopped.

'Greg?'

Greg turned.

'What?' he said.

'Oh my God.'

Billy, to Greg's great surprise, was devastated. He twisted around, and around again, as though looking for a missing chair. He stood in the street and looked at Greg, then he lifted his hands to cover his eyes. He started to cry.

'Oh my God, Greg. Oh my God.'

'Well, what did you expect?' said Greg.

'I don't know,' said Billy. 'I just didn't. I didn't expect.'

They went to one bar, and then another and they got very drunk. At one point, Billy wept and Greg comforted him, looking up at the ceiling as he rocked him briefly in his arms, thinking, 'But I am the one. I am the one who is going to die.'

Through all those years, whenever Greg looked into the mirror at his changing face, he thought about Christian and wondered if his lover would be proud of him now. After he and Billy had finished their mercy fuck (drunk – yes – but careful, so careful) he went into the bathroom and checked his skin for black marks and looked into his own eyes and he remembered just how dead Christian was, after he died. There was no one looking at him in the mirror, except himself.

It was hard to cry when there was no one watching, he thought, then he brushed his teeth and went back to bed.

In the months that followed, they were often on the phone. When Greg lost weight, Billy took him out shopping for smaller jeans. He brought up wine and treats from the local deli which quite quickly turned into ordinary bags of food.

'Just the heavy stuff,' he said, smiling at Greg's door that was three flights up – not even breathless after the climb.

44

'You shouldn't have.'

'I want to.'

And he did. Billy knew that, even if he did not love Greg, even if he had other guys, and other plans for the long term, he would still do this thing. He would help Greg in his last months, or years. And he might resent it but he would not regret it: because this was the thing that was given him to do.

Which did not mean that Greg was easy. The groceries were always wrong, for a start. Billy could never tell what was fun trashy food – like Oreos, say – and what was just trash.

'You call this stuff *cheese*?'

In fact, there was no Indian prince at Massimo's on Thursday evening. There was a very nice risotto, which Billy personally found a bit disappointing.

'It's a bit like . . . rice?' he said.

Massimo's boyfriend Alex was in from the west coast and he brought a rather grizzled Ellen Derrick, who stuck to gin and smoked throughout. Jessie was there, of course, as was Greg. There was a wonderful Dominican boy who said very little and, as Jessie later pointed out, only ate three grains of rice all night. There was Arthur, who had aged so much since Max died. And there was an Irish guy, called Dan, who had sandy hair you might flatter to red and beautiful, pale skin.

Massimo's place on Broome Street was an old sweatshop and its floor was made from two foot wide hardwood boards. He had factory windows that kept nothing in or out – not the heat, the cold, nor the noise of the printworks two floors below – but were beautiful nonetheless, each one of them dividing the dusk into thirty rectangles of fading light. Inside, he had many candles and a table so long and monastic that eight people felt like few. The place had cast-iron columns, Marsalis was on the stereo and a long scribbled piece by Helen Frankenthaler took up an entire cross-wall. After the risotto came noisettes of lamb with roast garlic and a mint-pea purée, which Massimo served with a Saumur-Champigny that was like an elevator in a glass, as Greg said, it brought you to a whole new level. Massimo, with his slow gestures and careful, sing-song voice, was alert to everyone's smallest need; unpushy, prepared.

Greg glanced at Billy, as if to say, 'Watch and learn.'

They tried not to talk about the disease. They went through *Twin Peaks*, they talked about the art scene, what Larry was showing next, how money was wrecking the East Village now, and whatever happened to that guy who used to walk a tightrope and piss, beautifully, in an arc, perfectly balanced, into the East River? No, he pissed on the floor down in that club on 48th Street. Should have been the river. Whatever happened to him? Every name they spoke dragged its own tiny silence after it.

Gone. Gone silent. Alive.

Arthur was positive for six years and he hadn't a thing wrong with him, people wanted to touch him, he was so old now. Arthur remembered things no else remembered. Who could keep all that? Who could hold on to it? His head was a museum. And when he died the museum would be empty. The museum would fall down.

Greg read nothing but the classics now, tender of his eyesight and of his time, he talked about Achilles' dream of dead Patroclus, how the dead man would not touch him but only boss him about, when all Achilles wanted was to feel the guy in his arms. Why is that? That the dead have voices in our dreams but no density. It's just this huge sense of themness, it is all meaning and no words. Because words

46

are also physical, don't you think? The way they touch you.

'Sometimes they do. Use words, I mean,' said Arthur. '"My tree is all hibiscus". Someone said that to me, once.'

No one asked who.

'It's a war,' Massimo said.

Greg said fuck that he never signed up for any damn war. He wanted a civilian's death, he said. A personal death. He wanted a death he could call his own.

Massimo said Gabriel Torres was working out in the Y on West 23rd and the *stir* as he wiped down one machine and went to the next. Gabriel Torres was the most beautiful man you have ever seen.

'Where he gets the time?' said Arthur.

'You know,' said Greg, 'Sometimes I think we'd all be better off with a woman in sensible shoes.'

Dan's face, through all of this, was a thing of quiet attention. His pale skin soaked up the candlelight and he listened so well, it seemed the whole table was talking just for him. Greg lifted his glass and said, 'Look at those cheekbones,' and Dan gave a smile.

'The poet. That Irish poet.'

'Yeats?' said Arthur.

On which, to everyone's amazement and delight, Dan opened his mouth and a ream of poetry fell out. Line after line – it was like a scroll unfurling along the tabletop, a carpet unrolled. And each of us, as we heard it, realised where we were, and who was with us. We saw our shadows shifting on the back wall, the office cleaner across the way in trembling fluorescent tinged with green, the dark city brown of the sky.

Dan finished, placed a hand to his chest and inclined his head. There was applause. Alex told him he had a voice like wild honey. And a face, said Massimo, like some portrait with a red hat, what was that one? In the Palazzo Pitti. Some cardinal, anyway, in a red hat.

Dan said, 'Don't fucking cardinal me. Whatever else you do.' And we all laughed. And then we looked at him. That mixture of shyness and blurting arrogance: he was quite the thing, we thought. And we also thought about his freckled white skin, with the blue veins under it, and about his uncut Irish cock.

'You are so wrong,' said Arthur, 'I'm thinking Dutch. Something direct and entirely austere. Like that wonderful sandy-haired boy in the Met.'

And in fact, Arthur walked up to the museum a couple of days later, going through the rooms until he stood in front of it again, a sixteenth-century boy in velvet black against a green background; oil on wood. It was the honesty of the wood that did it, because the full-lipped young man did not, himself, look especially truthful or sincere. The picture was full of integrity, the boy might be anything at all.

After the lamb they had figs poached in marsala with a mascarpone mousse. Alex took off his jacket to help with the plates, and he and Massimo moved with such synchronous ease, you knew they loved each other still.

Greg lit up a cigarette and contemplated Dan through half-closed eyes.

'So. Ireland,' he said. 'Are you from, like, a *farm*?'

Dan refused the question with a smile.

'I'm *sorry*,' said Greg. He was flirting now.

'Actually, yes,' said Dan, relenting. 'Yes. We have a farm.'

'Billy grew up in Elk County, Pennsylvania but he's not reciting Whitman. Are you, Billy?'

'Why not?' said Dan, looking to Billy. 'Why not?!'

'Just,' said Billy.

'He's wonderful.'

'Is he?'

'I sing the body electric,' said Dan, raising his preacher's hands, and we looked at them; the square bones of his knuckles, the tiny tremble in his fingertips, held open that moment too long.

And we looked at Billy, who blushed in the candlelight.

'What's the next line, Billy?' said Greg. 'You see how dumbass the American education system can be? What's the next line?'

But Billy was too busy falling in love to think about the next line so Alex quietly filled it in. 'The armies of those I love engirth me and I engirth them,' as Massimo set down some glasses for port, and reached to the counter for the platter of cheese.

Later, Greg wondered, if he had not needled Billy then Billy would not have turned to Dan and to all that Dan offered him, there at the table: the guilt and the glory; the pomp and cruelty of his love. And he wondered also if it could have played out in any other way. They made such a handsome couple. It was meant, we all knew it. Dan and Billy, Billy and Dan. It had to be.

After cheese, and more cigarettes, and the offer of whiskey, tequila, more wine, Massimo went over to the window to throw down a key, and a whole bunch of people came up on their way out clubbing: Jerry from the Fawbush Gallery, that landscape gardener who did white plantings all over the Hamptons, Estella who was an outrageous queen and this guy in a Weimar-type leather thing – call it a corset – with a German accent no one believed for an instant and considerable quantities of cocaine. Jessie's arch-rival Mandy was also in the mix, with her glossy trustafarian hair and mid-Atlantic drawl and, years later when Jessie was truly fat and Mandy still wonderfully slim, they met and remembered that evening which went on till dawn, and all the hard work they put in, years of it, helping, loving, mourning these men.

A few weeks after this dinner Greg was admitted to St Vincent's for the first time. It was just a thing, he told Billy, they would blitz him with anti-fungals and let him go. Jessie brought him in a cab, with six pairs of ironed pyjamas and a cotton kimono with beautiful cross-hatchings of indigo blue. Greg had a problem with his mouth and tongue. He also had a haemorrhoid that obsessed him more than it deserved, though Jessie told him her father had a real bunch of grapes hanging out there for a while, and she went off to find ice. She also found a bag of doughnuts to fatten him up, then ate most of them herself, but she sat there for another hour and laughed at every small thing.

Arthur arrived with champagne and they pretended to drink it. He said when Max was first up here in the sevens, just two rooms down, the staff slid his food tray across the floor, and he had to change his own sheets. He said it was so much better now, thank you Dr Torres – how was he, by the way? And Greg said, 'I think he's just exhausted, he's just working so hard.'

The drip went in. Billy did not come and, after a while, the visitors went home.

Three hours later, Greg started shaking. He was cold in places that were new to him, and sweat pooled at the base of his neck. A nurse came in to switch on a bedside fan and fold down his sheet. An ordinary white woman in her fifties, she looked at his terror and acknowledged it, eye to eye. Then she left.

Greg could not catch a breath. He pulled the air into him in tiny, shallow draughts, on and on, his body panicking until his mind snapped free and started to wander

50

around the room – also around the thoughts that were in the room, and the memories that were hiding in the corners and under the bed. There was the occasional hallucination: a woman – who looked like his mother but was not his mother – sat in the chair sewing a long grey smock for him to wear when he was dead. Dr Torres, who might really be there, leaned over him and smiled. There was a panting cat draped across the top of his skull and he was terrified of its claws. This went on all night, until a tray startled him and he realised it was only supper time. The night was yet to come.

Two men died towards dawn: at least Greg was pretty sure that men died. He could hear praying in Spanish, then people weeping and helping each other away. In the morning, a man covered in Kaposi's stood in his doorway and said, 'I just need enough to do it. Don't you think?'

The fever was less on this second day. Greg was able to swallow some Xanax, a big tub of which a tranny nurse called Celeste slapped down on his locker.

'You want a cigarette, honey? You want some tea?'

All day, Greg drifted in and out of sleep, watching the sunlight cross the room, and the shadow following it. He smiled and thought about Billy and Dan, trying to imagine how they were together: he just couldn't see it.

And this was strange, because no one else had any trouble seeing it. They were two beautiful young men up in the big city. One was pale and interesting, the other easy and tan, and Billy flung a friendly arm over Dan's shoulder as they took the ferry over to Fire Island while, back in St Vincent's, the Xanax kicked in.

It was a long, hot weekend.

On Monday morning, Greg woke to see Billy standing in his hospital room.

'Hello.'

There are hours and days that change people, and they both had been changed. They were different people now. After a moment, Billy stepped up to kiss Greg briefly on the mouth. And this was such a nice gesture in that place of death, it was as though Greg's fever had never happened and Fire Island was just a dream – though it was not a dream. Billy and Dan had taken several and various substances, they had danced till dawn: we all saw them, and we liked the way Dan kept his shirt on when everyone else stripped down; the two top buttons undone and his sternum gleaming in there, white as the inside of a seashell.

'Where were you?' said Greg.

'I got a house-share in the Pines,' said Billy. 'Didn't I say?'

'Gold dust,' said Greg.

'I know.'

When Billy came back in to the hospital the next day, Greg was sitting on the edge of the bed, very weak but determined to go home. Billy had to find his pants, and push each leg up over Greg's knees. Then he leaned in for an awkward hug, to lift him up off the bed and slip them up the rest of the way.

'Oh God,' said Greg.

'That's it,' Billy said.

'Oh God. Oh God. Oh God.'

'Good luck with that bitch,' said Billy. 'Is this your shirt? Arm. Shush.'

Greg had started to moan. He moaned incontinently. He dribbled noise.

'Hush, now.'

Billy got Greg's shirt on and struggled with buttons and cuffs. He pulled his belt tight, attempted and abandoned the zipper, then he turned to sit beside Greg and for a moment they were both slumped on the edge of the bed.

'Quiet down, will you? Come on.'

The legs he had just handled were the same legs Billy had once hauled up on either side of himself, while Greg's dark and dreamy eyes looked up from the pillow. They were the same legs, except they were half the circumference. They were the same bones.

After he got Greg downstairs and into a cab and up the three flights to his walkup in the East Village, Billy didn't have the energy to settle him in. He phoned Jessie and left a message on her answering service. Then he turned to Greg, who was collapsed in a chair with his coat still on.

'I think it's working,' said Greg. 'I can feel it lifting.'

He took a deep, shuddering breath.

'You're sure you're all right?' said Billy, setting a hand on his back. Then he left.

Greg sat in the silence after the door had closed and realised it was true. His blood was singing; some weight was gone. So he did not care that Billy was off to see Irish Dan, that they would spend the night together, and the morning also. He did not mind that Dan would twist Billy's love, somehow, and make him sad, because Greg had survived a course of amphotericin B, that bastard. He was still alive.

Dan did not shrink from Billy's arm, thrown over his shoulder on the ferry, but he did not seem to want sex when they arrived at the Pines, or he did not want the sex to be good, or interesting or slow. And this was surprising because no one went to Fire Island just to walk along the beach. The only move Dan made, when they were finally in the house that Billy had organised, all tubular chairs and walnut floors, with its white linen curtains and Billy attractively

53

arranged on the bed, was to unzip his fly. He did not let Billy near his ass, which was a pity, because Billy really wanted his ass. He turned away (which was fine) from Billy's kiss. He might as well have folded his arms. For someone else, this would have been a challenge and a delight – a whole weekend to drag this Irish boy out of the closet, kicking and screaming with raw pleasure and afterthrob. But this was not Billy's style. Billy wanted to talk to Dan. He wanted to put his tongue on the salt corner of Dan's eye, where his eyelid trembled shut. He wanted to make him happy.

He also, personally, wanted to come. But Dan had no manners in that regard and, when Billy ended up doing the honours himself, he seemed to sneer a little, looking down at him from a height. Which was also fine. If sneering turned out to be Dan's thing, there were plenty of guys who liked that too.

You could not say that Fire Island was entirely happy in the summer of 1991, but it was defiant, and happiness was there on the horizon, if you lifted your eyes to the sea. Dan did not seem to notice the sea. He watched the Friday night crowd at the Botel from behind a beer, followed by another beer, while Billy smiled and deflected offers of various kinds of fun.

Dan said, 'They all look sort of identical.'

'I know,' said Billy. Though he was wearing the same short shorts and lace-up ankle boots as two hundred other men out on the dance floor.

Billy, meanwhile, was worried about the house-share, which was through a friend-of-a-friend with no mention of the cost. The beers were outrageously expensive and Dan drank steadily then looked for more. In the middle of his, maybe, third bottle, he turned to Billy and said, 'Tell me. What do you want?'

'What do I want?'

This was such a strange question, there in the middle of two hundred bare torsos, all holding the scent of the day's lost sunshine, that Billy got a bit distracted and had to say it again: 'What do I *want*?'

Later, Dan relaxed a little in the darkness of their room. He did not complain about the double bed and allowed Billy to touch him down his back and legs. But he stayed curled over an undoubtedly steaming erection, and Billy woke early and so horny he had to slip out before Dan knew that he was gone.

'Where were you?' Dan was in the kitchen when Billy came back, he was opening and closing cupboard doors.

'Just took a walk,' said Billy, not mentioning the remnants of the night's dancing he found wandering the dawn; a very pink blond boy who knelt in front of him, and a massive, tripping Blatino he leaned against, who jabbed a finger at his ass, and then got it right in.

'A walk?'

'Just in the woods.'

'Right.'

They went down to the harbour for breakfast, and then walked far up the beach to find a quiet spot. Dan undressed under a little towel, he wriggled into his swimming trunks before he let the towel fall, and Billy thought this was the sweetest thing he had seen in a very long time. It was already hot. The sea was big and languid, dropping slow waves on the sand. They waded right in. Billy splashed about a bit and ran back up to the bags while Dan floated on the swell, watching his toes. Then he reached over into a lazy crawl. A bunch of guys ran out of a beachfront property, shedding flip-flops and shorts and they ploughed into the water, all brown backs and white glutes. Billy could feel their skinny-dipping pleasure as the sea swirled higher, and two of them turned to kiss in the waves. He watched them for a while, then squinted after Dan who was quite far out now, his silhouette made uncertain by sunlight on the water.

Minutes passed. Dan was so small in the distance that Billy could not tell if he was heading out or coming home. He sat there, suncream in hand, waiting for Dan to turn back in and, after a long while, it seemed that he had – definitely, Billy thought – Dan was definitely closer now. The figure switched from overarm to breaststroke; Billy could make out his pale features and his water-darkened hair. It was Dan, of course it was. He was right there, just beyond the breaking waves. He dived under, with a curving bob and scissor kick of his long white shins, then surfaced and lay on his back for a while. Each swell that lifted him set him down closer to shore until he turned to catch a breaking wave, scrabbling as he rode the surf, with his mouth pulled down. He ended up on his hands and knees on the sand and he considered this for a moment, before standing heavily to his full height and walking on to dry land.

Billy shifted on the stripy towel, trying to look indifferent.

'What took you so long?'

Dan, when he sat down beside him, was wet, cold and very solid.

'I was swimming home.'

'Oh my.'

'Just over there – see? Three thousand miles thattaway, that's where I am from.'

'You miss it,' said Billy.

'Fuck no.'

Dan eased his goose-bumped legs straight, then lay down carefully in the sun. His muscles jolted and relaxed and after a while he was still. The wind was warm. The waves arrived one by one on the shore. Dan picked himself up a little and set his heavy, wet head on Billy's chest. Then he moved down to settle his ear in the soft arch beneath Billy's ribs.

Billy lay there looking up at the blue of July. He wondered if he should put a hand on Dan's drying hair and then decided against it. For some reason, he remembered a boy at high school – not good looking as Dan was good looking – a boy called Carl Medson.

'I knew this guy once,' he said. 'Like when I was sixteen.'

'And?'

Carl Medson's sister was slick with lip gloss and his mother flirted with Billy in a truly disturbing manner. She was kind of mad. There was a paper seat on the toilet, and when you opened the refrigerator, everything in there was covered in Saran Wrap, even the cartons and jars. Carl Medson moped after Billy for, like, a year though they never did anything except sprawl around in his bedroom listening to music, until Billy couldn't take the suspense any longer. One day he let his hand drift – joke! – on to Carl's package and the next thing you know – pause, move, pause again – he had Carl Medson out of there and in his hand. And Carl has one of those dicks where the foreskin doesn't roll back – Billy's never seen it before – a little tight ring, like the mouth of a string bag, and tucked in, down there, a sad, locked-in dick. You know? Let me out!! Like you are supposed to stretch it, as a kid, but he had never touched himself, not ever. And Carl just turns away from him, and zips up, and they don't really hang out after that. Married now, and moved to Phoenix.

'So he must have got that much sorted out.'

'Huh,' said Dan.

A little bit later, Dan said, 'I am going to get married,' and he sat up, alert to the sea.

'Oh?' said Billy.

'I am.' Dan kicked the end of the towel and pulled it square on the sand.

'Anyone in mind?'

'Yep.'

He studied the horizon. 'I love her,' he said. 'And I love the look of her and the shape of her, and I love the way her body is, and I just think it feels right. All of that. You know?'

'Great.'

'We have sex,' said Dan.

'I know,' said Billy, who had a queue of sad bastard married men and did not need another one, though this, clearly, was what had washed up, one more time, at his door.

They went back to have lunch at the house, with the other housemates fresh off the ferry, and the friend-of-a-friend was just great; very upfront with them both about the bill. Dan did not say, 'Oh, I don't have to pay because I am not actually gay, you know.' In fact, now they were agreed on the subject of his essential and future straightness, Dan chatted, drank wine and trailed after Billy to their room, where he spent a salty, sunny few hours on the bed with him, and in the shower, and in the chair, followed by a little, last eking out against the cedar-scented wall. He kissed Billy as though he loved him, all afternoon.

Dinner was a giddy occasion, with a couple of high performance housemates and their quiet host, who had carried steak and salad all the way from Chelsea. After which, they all washed and changed, downed a ritual martini in the living room and sailed off down the boardwalk. It was a big party weekend on Fire Island and temptation was everywhere but Billy and Dan danced only with each other; they laughed and even smooched a bit out there on the floor, and when Billy went off to queue for the toilet he came back with a couple of pills. He took one and let Dan lick out the other from the crease of his palm.

Bliss.

We can assume, of course, that Dan went back to his melancholy little apartment and his brave wife-to-be, and held all the beautiful men of Fire Island in great contempt for being helpless to their faggotry when his was so clearly under control. But tripping on Ecstasy under a July moon, he was the happiest queer in New York State. And of course we all knew he wasn't really queer, he was just queer for Billy, because who wouldn't be? It wasn't like he wanted to go down on – I don't know – Gore Vidal. Dan loved Billy because it was impossible not to love Billy, and so we sang that same old sad song, as they touched each other in the trees' moon shadow; as they paused in the ineluctable presence of the other, and inhaled.

We met the brave little wife-to-be later, when she came back from Boston, where she had been doing some kind of MFA. She was nice. Skinny, as they often are. Slightly maverick and intense and above all ethical. She had long hair, a lovely accent, and she was writing a book, of course, about – we could never remember what the book was about – something very Irish. As beards went, she was a classic beard. A woman of rare quality – because it takes a quality woman to keep a guy like Dan straight – throwing her heart away.

Or not.

Who is to judge, meine Damen und Herrrren? At least she had a heart to throw.

This was Dan's fifth year in New York City – he had only intended staying for one. He arrived in the summer of 1986, and moved in with Isabelle, who had been there since

May. A friend got him some evening shifts in a bar over on Avenue A and he spent the days stacking and retrieving shoeboxes in a basement on Fifth. After a few months down in the dark, they allowed him up on to the shop floor and Dan pretended to be good at selling shoes in order to cover the fact that he was really very good at selling shoes. He was a beautiful young man with a cute accent and a terrific eye. By Christmastime, he was dashing over to photo shoots with emergency Manolos, he was bringing boxes to clients in their homes. Some of these clients tried to sleep with him. All of them were rich, and most of them were men.

The first time it happened, Dan was kneeling at the feet of a sixty-year-old multimillionaire in a penthouse just around the corner on Central Park South. He was lacing up a pair of chocolate brown brogues over his skinny ankles and grey silk socks, when the guy said, 'Ireland, eh?'

'That's right,' said Dan, as the multimillionaire settled his crotch an inch or two higher in the large white chair.

'I had a wonderful young friend once who was Irish. Where are you from?'

'I'm from County Clare.'

'Well, that's where he was from. Isn't that a coincidence?'

'Yes, that is a coincidence,' said Dan.

'He was a marvellous young man.'

The picture windows looked over Central Park and Sixth Avenue. The floor was white, the furniture was white, and the old man's dick, in the middle of this great panorama, seemed both intriguing and sad. This is the flesh, Dan thought as he pulled the laces tight, in which such money is contained.

And Dan forgot for a moment that he was a spoilt priest and English literature graduate with plans to go home, after his year abroad, to do a master's in librarianship. He forgot that he was a shoe salesman, or a barman, or even an immigrant. For a moment Dan was an open space, surrounded by a different future to the one he had brought in through the door.

He said, 'I think this is your size. I think this is you.'

Dan joked with Isabelle about the multimillionaire, but mostly he did not mention the men who caught his eye or gave him things, in the bar or on the street. He told her he was desperate to get out of shoe sales, but he did not tell her he had sensed some new ambition in himself while she trudged on, teaching English as a foreign language, not writing her novel. Isabelle wondered if postgraduate work was the answer to the feeling she had of getting nowhere – not in this town, but with herself. Dan wanted to tell her that *herself* was not the project any more. This was New York: the answer was all around her, for God's sake, not inside her head.

Dan kept his eyes open, now. He noticed people's desire. He got a job with a fashion photographer, humping gear around Manhattan. He spent his days carting tripods and bags, getting yelled at, getting cold, running for miso soup, running for hard boiled eggs, black coffee, Tabasco, very dry champagne. The pay was less, but you would not think it to look at Dan, who attracted sample size jackets and many invitations by being very open and a little bit wry. Dan was always surprised by things, but never shocked. And he never put out.

This was the man that Billy fell for, four years later, by which time, Dan was moving into the fine art scene. Billy fell for a man who was discarding his former self before he had found a new one, a man who dabbled in guy sex but who still loved his girlfriend. He fell for a liar and a believer, though what Dan believed in was always hard to say.

So pale and ethereal when he arrived, by the end of the

summer we thought there was something freakish about Dan: this very ascetic head, with proud – savage, almost – cheekbones. He looked liked the wrath of God, Billy told him once, when the light was right. And Dan laughed and said, 'You have no idea.'

If Fire Island was an aberration, then it would be his last because Isabelle was about to finish up in Boston, she would be back in New York at the end of July. When the boys came back to the city they had ten days to kiss and part, which should have been enough, because Billy liked to keep moving and Dan wasn't gay, he was just very visual. In those ten days, they did it all: they found a perfect coffee place off Christopher Street, and a wine bar on Bleecker. They bought Billy a pair of art deco bedside lockers in this beautiful yellow wood that turned out to be English yew. They saw *The Double Life of Véronique* and *The Commitments*, they went to the Frick where Dan stood in front of Titian's *Portrait of a Man in a Red Cap* for the first time. And, when they went back to Billy's place, they had conversations that lasted till dawn. They had bitterness and blame and pointless sex. They had sudden sex. They had sex-while-weeping, and tender sex, and rough sex, and leave-taking sex. And then Isabelle came back to town.

But it was not Isabelle that did for Billy in the summer of 1991, it was the way he could not reach Dan, no matter how deep he fucked him, as though all the gestures of their love were beautiful and untrue. It was not as if Billy was looking for anything long term, but he was looking for something in that moment. Recognition. The feeling that what they were doing was real to Dan too.

Oh Danny Boy.

Of course he was charming. Of course he was beautiful. Of course.

When Isabelle came back, she and Dan took a flight to California, where some friends were staging a wedding in Big Sur. Billy had another offer for Fire Island, but he could not face Fire Island, and he did not go back on the scene. He did have sex with a guy on Saturday night, but coming made him feel like he was reaching for something that melted in his hands. So he visited with Greg, who would not venture too far from his air-con, and they sat around and did not mention where Billy had been for the past few weeks, while Jessie wiped down the counters in the kitchenette and glared at him, for being too easily forgiven when he arrived – so hunky in his wife-beater vest – at the door.

Greg had gained some weight. He didn't do that smacking thing with his mouth any more, as though tasting some residue. He sat in his big lounge chair with a careless leg hooked over the arm, and was enthusiastic now, even about his disease.

'Oh God,' he said, when Billy told him he looked great. Greg said he was so anxious now, all the time, he was tossing down the Xanax, and there was a drug called Demerol, this opiate they doled out, that made him feel just wonderful. He felt as though we were all connected.

It was enough, said Greg, to make you want to go back in there, all you had to do was make it into the elevator and then up to Sister Patricia who enfolded you with love, and then there would be the Demerol to fill you up with love on the inside. He said he had switched allegiances, Dr Torres was a prince but Sister Patricia was the person into whose eyes.

He paused and tried again.

Into whose eyes.

Billy leaned in as though to show his own eyes, faithful unto death, but Greg twitched away and said he was thinking about getting some therapy, though – and he chewed down on the words as he quoted Celeste the tranny nurse saying. 'Nothing makes a girl look more relaxed than a few pints of embalming fluid.'

'No,' said Billy. 'She said that?'

'Oh, you got to love Celeste,' said Greg, and Billy glanced over at Jessie, who forbore.

Billy's heart did not start to break until the day he knew that Dan was back in town after the wedding in California, and that he would not be in touch. And Billy's heart did not break properly for a week or two after that when he realised it was not disappointment he had been feeling, but hope, and that this hope was fading with the turning weather. Soon, soon it would be true. Dan would not have called. Besides, if Dan missed him, then he could just go out and find a guy who looked a bit like Billy, and pull his damn zipper down. And that was supposed to be fine. Because if Dan came out, he would be happy, and every gay man in New York would be happy, and the world would be, by so much authenticity, improved.

But Billy did not care if Dan was out or in, any more. All he felt was the weight of Dan's head on his solar plexus, there on the beach, the waves dumping their heavy load of water, and the sea pulling it back, over and over. And he wanted Dan to meet Greg again, before he died.

But September passed and Dan did not call.

Various things happened. Massimo went off with Mandy to her family bolt-hole in the Caribbean, Billy held a dinner party which was a qualified success. Arthur published his book on Bonnard and wept for Max (who had detested Bonnard: who spat at the mention of Bonnard) at the launch. Then Emily von Raabs came to town and she hosted a large and informal supper in her wonderfully ramshackle house on East 10th. Emily had loved Christian, back in the day, so Greg brought Billy along as a kind of protection from all that, but the Countess had a new favourite young man now, an Irish dealer called Corban, who was the most charming man you could hope to meet. And Corban brought his old friend Isabelle, and Isabelle brought her interesting boyfriend Dan.

Emily Gräfin von Raabs (originally from Ohio, now from everywhere) sat sixteen around an old oval table and kept everything simple. A main course was set, buffet style on a sideboard at the top of the room, salad was passed from left to right; it was very homely and hands-on with just one server topping up the wine.

She had Richard Serra next to her, and he was incredibly handsome and, dare one say, monumental. And Kiki Smith was there, which always improved things. Artists, Greg said, are like wild animals in a room like that; it is like being in a a forest, suddenly, instead of a zoo.

As for the rest of us, the wine went down and the volume went up and the question that idled around the table was: Who has slept with whom? And of course it does not matter, because past sex is not as exciting as future sex, it is just a low hum under the melody of what is yet to come. Billy looked Isabelle over, when they moved through the double doors for coffee: the unreliable little ribcage, with a pair of those flat little triangular breasts like flesh origami: also lumpy bits from waist to hip where her underwear was a bit too pragmatic – she would look better without, he thought, though Isabelle was not the sort of girl who would ever go without. The most surprising thing about her were the shoes, which were black to match the rest of the outfit, but with fabulous, bloody red soles. She walked in them like a child playing dress-up.

Well, each to his own, Billy thought and he met Dan's eye with the easy lack of interest he had learned all his life to show. He said, 'You know Gregory Savalas? Greg does the Clements' estate. And now Max Ehring's, am I right?'

They might as well have never met, never kissed. That was the code.

'Oh no,' said Greg. 'That's legally all very. That will take a while. I'm just, literally, collating what's there.'

'So sad,' said Dan. 'I am one of Ehring's biggest fans.'

'You are? That's nice to hear.'

'I am. I just think the work has such vitality, you know? So hard to believe he is gone.'

'Yes,' said Greg. 'He was a dear friend.'

'I'm sorry,' said Dan.

They stood there. Greg who loved Billy Walker and Billy who loved Dan Madigan and Dan who loved Isabelle McBride. He really did.

And Isabelle, who felt self-conscious for some reason she could not identify, took another slug of wine.

'You know he left hundreds of uncatalogued pieces, just thrown about,' said Greg. 'Of course we left the main studio just exactly as it was.'

'That's amazing,' said Dan.

Billy couldn't stand it. He had slept with both these men, and they were talking horse-shit: they were speaking some kind of non-language to each other.

'I can't help wondering,' he said, 'if dying wasn't the best thing to happen to Max. As an artist, I mean. Is that a terrible thing to say?'

Greg blinked, slowly. He turned to Dan. 'You know, sometimes I think I am in the wrong business,' he said. 'Because I would prefer if Max painted nothing and was still here. Alive, I mean. I would prefer him to be alive. Even if he was just, you know, serving the wine.'

'You do? I mean, you would?' Dan seemed genuinely surprised.

Isabelle, as though used to this slight gap between her boyfriend and the world, reached over and pressed Greg's hand.

'You are so right,' she said.

'Is he?' said Dan, persisting.

'Yes he is,' she said.

And Greg turned aside, briefly, to hide his tears.

It was two days after this encounter that Irish Dan turned up at young Billy's door – ashamed of himself, clearly. They had sex but didn't like each other for it, and afterwards Dan went home.

'Everybody dies.'

This is what he had said in Emily von Raab's drawing room, after Greg had pinched the tears back with finger and thumb.

'You die of something,' said Dan. 'You die young, you die old, it is not the fact that you die that matters. It is what you do that matters. What you make.'

It was not clear who he was trying to convince.

'I didn't know you liked his work so much,' said Isabelle.

And Greg thought about the corpse, laid out on a trestle table in the studio, in his working overalls and boots, how it looked nothing like Max, because Max was all movement and annoyance. Max was a constant pain in the ass.

'I respect the work,' said Dan. 'The work is not beautiful, and I would prefer if it were beautiful. The work is violent and garish and he put everything he had into it, and I respect that.'

'Right,' Isabelle said.

'Also, you know, the work is of the moment. This moment. I like that. I need that. I think if we don't have that we are just travelling blind.'

Dan's hands were in the air, he was making the big gestures, and there he was again, the priest, offering it all, demanding it all: truth, beauty, everlasting life.

Or six months on a wall at MOMA, Greg thought, followed by a thousand years in storage, somewhere undisclosed.

Two nights later, at eleven forty-five p.m., Dan the spoilt priest was outside Billy Walker's door, looking for sex. Again. And sex is what he got. At midnight, he was back out on the street and heading home.

That was the 5th of November. Eight days later, he came back for more. Then a short two days after that. He managed to stay away for another week. On the 21st of November, Billy picked up the intercom and said, 'Fuck you, Dan.' But he buzzed him in anyway. Three nights later, he came down the stairs to the front door, and said, 'Let's walk.'

The streets were wet and the air clear after rain. The boys' winter coats were both open to the mild night, their long scarves hung down, blue and green. Dan said he was fighting with Isabelle. That was one of the reasons she had gone to Boston, they had been fighting for maybe two years. Also she had met someone up there, a guy, who was, incidentally, as queer as all get out, which was not the outcome he had wanted for Isabelle, but it was her choice, so maybe it had been a terrific waste of time, his feeling guilty all those years.

'Have you told her?'

'Told her what?' said Dan. 'I love her. I have always loved her. And I fucked her willingly. And none of that is a lie.'

They ended up kissing up against a chain link fence, in a deserted lot by the East River, hands sliding in each other's come, waiting to be knifed by a passer-by.

So that was it. Dan went home at Christmas a new man and he came back to New York ready for more. He found Billy laid low with a cold and made him a hot whiskey to the Irish recipe with lemon and cloves, and he beefed on about his family, his mother who was the usual nightmare, his sister who was pregnant again and developing a mar-tyred air.

'When do you grow out of it?' he said. 'When is all that *done*?'

Billy sat up in a pair of pyjamas with a stripe of powder blue, his blond hair tousled with sweat and a thermometer sticking out of his mouth. He had been over at Massimo's with Greg the day after Christmas, he said, and Mandy brought one of the Kennedys up – the really handsome one? – they had talked about Castro all afternoon, because, you know, Castro knew.

'Huh,' said Dan, jealous as hell.

Billy said he went to this enormous party on one of the piers for New Year's Eve and met so many people, half of them in drag.

'Drag?' said Dan.

'I was not in drag,' said Billy. 'Though I did – briefly, mind you – sport a fetching white tutu. No I was in my faithful 501s.'

'Well that's good to hear,' said Dan.

'Are you checking up on me?' said Billy, and both of them paused right there. They were not ready for cutesie domesticity. Not yet.

'No,' said Dan.

'Though I did catch this cold,' said Billy. 'So maybe you have a point.'

When Greg rang the next day, Billy was still feeling

unwell – which was the wrong way around for them, really: they did not prolong the call. It was the offer of happiness, perhaps, that kept Dan away. For whatever reason, no one saw Billy for another seventy-two hours, when a passing neighbour heard his door open, and looked back to see him sliding down the side of it, before falling out behind her, into the hall.

In St Vincent's, they took one look at him and sent him up to the seventh floor.

The news spread fast. Massimo rang Greg. He said Mandy was in with that dancer who used to be with Pina Bausch, and she could not believe it, she was walking down the corridor and there was a guy pulling at his breathing tube and trying to sit up and he was making quite a noise. And it was Billy.

'Billy?' said Greg. 'No. Are you sure?'

Mandy had actually gone in to him, he was so agitated, and she you know pushed him back down, tried to soothe him a little, and it was Billy. Full-blown PCP.

'I don't think it could be Billy,' said Greg, who was going through his kitchen cupboard, looking for something.

'Oh Greg, I'm so sorry,' said Massimo, and Greg stopped looking in the cupboard and said, 'Billy?'

He grabbed a coat and took a cab over there and he walked the corridor thinking nothing could be worse than this: beyond the disease, this was the worst thing life could throw at him. He checked one bed after the other, and then he stopped in the middle of the corridor and he thought, *It wasn't me – we were careful. It wasn't me.* After a moment he walked on again, and his mind told him that his own dying would be easier now. Because death is not the worst thing that can happen to you. Everyone dies.

It's the timing that matters. The first and second of it. The order in which we go.

And there was Billy's blond head, and there was his chest, pushed evenly up and let mechanically down again, his mouth crammed with the breathing tube so he could not speak, though the wild look he gave to Greg was more vivid than words. Greg could not let his gaze go, he held on to it as he pulled a chair under himself and sat in by the bed.

Arthur arrived next, and Jessie an hour later – redoubtable, she had somehow gained access to Billy's apartment and brought a bag of stuff for him, his address book was there, thick with Wite-Out, like everyone's address book in those days, and there, surrounded by dancing shamrocks, was the listing: DAN!!

'I'll call him,' she said. Billy understood that too, and he blinked in gratitude, and then he checked back for Greg's eyes and settled into his gaze, after which, he did not look away.

Ten minutes later, she was back in the room.

'You all right?' said Arthur, and Jessie, floating on some new sadness, said, 'He's on his way.'

They sat in silence, broken only by the sad crinkle of a packet of Chee-tos that Jessie found in her bag, and time went by.

Jessie never spoke about the call she made to Dan, how polite he was, and unsurprised. It took her years to figure it out. The feeling she had talking to him, as though Dan knew, had known all along, that there was nothing remarkable – in fact there was something almost satisfying – in the fact that Billy was dying. How did he fool her out of the news, make her feel as though she was forming sounds rather than actual words? How long before she could say the obvious thing?

'I think you should come in.'

'When is visiting time?' said Dan and she said, 'Any time. There's no set time on the sevens.'

'Right,' said Dan. 'I just have to wrap up here,' at which point Jessie was tempted to slam down the phone. The whole conversation was so flat and strange, Jessie put it out of her mind as they sat with Billy for the next hour and another hour after that, all the way past midnight. Greg did not leave the bedside. He did not let go of Billy's hand. He refused food, ignored everyone around him. At ten past three in the morning he started to sing, very quietly, and when Billy recognised the tune he tried to smile up at him, and died.

After that, no one saw Dan for years. We did not blame him. At least, we tried not to blame him. These things are very hard.

Constance

Co. Limerick
1997

CONSTANCE STILL COULD not believe the new section of road, after years of bad corners and blind spots, you just pointed the car and went – it was as though the fields unzipped, to let you straight through.

It used to be so epic, the four children in the back of the old Cortina, watching for a sign the journey was nearly done: a big plane lowering into the marshland at Shannon, then the castle at Bunratty, full of Americans in their broad plaid pants, and Durty Nelly's, the yellow pub, squatting by the bridge.

Now Constance was past it all in a moment. The castle was still beautiful but it looked very exposed to the dual carriageway, and she missed the thrill of the old bridge. Her friend Lauren used to sing at the medieval banquets in Bunratty. It wasn't just her voice, they used to audition the girls to fit the velvet dresses, at least that's what Lauren said, who had to double as a serving wench between bouts of 'Danny Boy'.

'The sight of them', she used to say, because Americans had no table manners, but they tipped like crazy, and all the men made passes, never mind the rotated dress. Her last summer there, Lauren worked on French tours in the Folk Park and now she was in Strasbourg for the EU, she was going to work in Prada trousers. Though maybe they hired the translators to fit the trousers – who knew?

It was a bitter thought, but the blouse she put on that morning was her last good blouse and Constance had to add a scarf to hide the place where the buttons gaped over breasts that had done their time.

They've done their time, she thought, closing the mirror on the wardrobe door.

She would do.

Constance used to be pleased with the body that had given her so many surprises, over the years. There were evenings she lay on the sofa with one child paddling her stomach, another pushing, in a tranced sort of way against the fatty side of her chest. Shauna, her youngest, liked to sit on the floor and pluck at her calf, making it wobble from side to side. And, 'No! Not the belly button!' Their little fingers pouncing, Constance shrieking and wriggling away. *Fun for all the family,* she thought, her body was a fabulous object, even Dessie her husband seemed to relish it. But Constance was fed up with herself. And fat, she knew, was a toxic thing.

The traffic snarled up on the approach into Limerick. Constance saw the broad river to the left of her and remembered, of a sudden, that she had forgotten to take the salmon out of the freezer.

'Damn,' she said, and switched off the radio. She would have to buy something else for dinner, on the way home.

But she was on the right side of the city for Dooradoyle, and the traffic was easy all the way to the hospital. Constance found a parking space not far from Outpatients, and brushed the crumbs from off her last good blouse.

Then she gathered her bag and her coat and pulled herself out of the car into the heaviness of the walking world.

Inside the hospital building, she set her feet to follow the nice yellow arrows on the floor, one after the other, as though she would get marks, somehow, for being on time and good. But, *You eejit,* she thought, as she arrived to find the queue already stretching down the corridor. They called a batch of women for ten o'clock, but they all turned up at half past nine because they knew something Constance had forgotten about Outpatients. This was the price she paid for a healthy life, Constance thought – she had been lucky. The woman after her had come in from Adare and the traffic was beyond belief. Roadworks, she said.

Their files were stacked on a trolley in two slanting rows and the nurse in charge was working hard, keeping up the banter as she passed with folders and X-rays.

'Oh I love the glitter! We're not allowed nail polish, would you believe. I miss it!'

There was no way of telling how long each woman would spend in the room across the corridor. A few came out and headed straight for the exit, but if a woman in a white coat came out first, then they followed the big brown envelope she held to join a new queue on a banquette further down the way. These women wore hospital gowns that gaped at the back and carried their tops and coats in a plastic shopping basket which they set on the ground in front of them. Some of them were quite young. Constance wasn't the youngest there that morning, not by any means.

The woman sitting beside her had very big thighs, one of which pressed against Constance, as it overspilt the narrow confines of the orange stackable chair. The fat was a little cooler than you might expect, but it contained a secret warmth, and was surprisingly pleasant for being so soft. Constance started to doze in the thick hospital air. That smell – whatever they used to clean the floors. Some sweetness in it, like the smell of your own body, after a child is born.

She was back on the road at Bunratty, cutting through the fields – the impossible ease of it – and she remembered the undoing of her own bones as the children were born. Her pelvis opening – there was a pleasure in it, like the top of a yawn – as the baby twisted out of her. It was all so simply done. And the baby was such a force, each time. Donal, with a grumpy look on him, Shauna who came out in a blaze of red hair, and her sweet-natured middle son, Rory, who turned his mother into a bit of dual carriageway herself, at the last, with such a bad tear. He took both exits, as she said to Dessie, at the same time.

'How is all that?' said Dessie a couple of years later. And Constance just laughed.

'How is all that?' she mocked. And then, 'It's all fine.'

Because it was true. It was fine. Her body had been so clever and self-healing. It had been so good to her, and willing to go again.

Or stupid, perhaps. Her body was a stupid thing.

The woman beside reached down into a plastic bag, and found a bottle of water. She was wearing boots with no laces under a large cheesecloth skirt and when she took off the too-tight cardigan you saw that the cuffs of her blouse didn't go around her wrists. She pushed the sleeves up in the hospital heat and unscrewed the bottle of water and, as she did so, Constance noticed some stripes on her forearm: silvery, like the negative of a tattoo, with a faint flush of red along the edges. They were all going across the way and the effect was not unattractive until you realised the stripes were scars and that they were self-inflicted. Some of them were very old and very wide – you could date the things, like the rings in a tree – they spread as she grew. One of these ancient scars had been freshly recut, and Constance felt her own skin tighten at the thought of it. A pain shot the length of her thighs – or not a pain so much as a weakness, a sympathetic jolt. Sudden, and then over. She stirred in the plastic chair and it was gone.

The woman lifted the water bottle, then looked her way. 'One fifty,' she said.

'No,' said Constance, trying to look back at her.

'For water!'

She avoided the woman's neck and chest, hovered along her hairline, before settling on her eyes. It was a lived-in face, ordinary enough. Unmarked.

'They have you every way,' said Constance.

The woman was trying to lose a bit, she said. She had a wedding coming up in England and she had a great outfit she found in Marks and Spencers and she just had to lose a bit to get into the skirt. She could get into it all right, she just had to zip it up. The thing was, she had terrible bloat.

She looked across the corridor as she talked about the weight, her head swaying slightly from side to side like a boxer's.

'What you need is, you know, a Playtex thing,' said Constance.

'Huh.'

'Some kind of elastic knickers, anyway. Pull you right in.'

The woman glanced round at her, suspicious.

'You know the ones,' said Constance.

'Oh yeah right.'

The woman did not have breast cancer, Constance thought. Clearly not. Or if she had it would just be coincidence.

A double tragedy. The woman was a hypochondriac, she was someone who liked to queue. You could not cure her because there was nothing wrong with her. Apart from everything, of course. Everything was wrong with her. And then, what do you do?

Her own hand was on her breast now, before she was even aware of it, at the place where it merged with her armpit; she could feel the lace of her bra, and under that a softness, and under that again vague knots.

But she really wanted the woman to enjoy her day out. She thought she deserved that much. Not to look stupid in a stupid skirt that she should not have bought in the first place, because it did not fit.

'Have you got a hat?' she said.

'You know, I don't?' she said. 'I am that desperate.'

'What colour?'

'I wanted red,' she said. 'With the spotty netting and the feathers? But they don't do red.'

'No,' said Constance, thinking there was a good reason for that. 'Have you considered black?'

But before she could dismiss the idea out of hand, the nurse called: 'Margaret Dolan!' and with much rummaging and bag gathering the woman collected herself and got up out of the chair. At the grey door, she turned back to say, 'Wish me luck.'

'Good luck,' said Constance. And the woman looked suddenly passionate, destined, before she turned again and was gone.

'She has a wedding coming up,' Constance said to the woman from Adare. And they both settled back in for the wait.

The women were in there two at a time, one with the radiologist, one getting undressed in the changing room outside, so Constance did not know how Margaret Dolan had fared by the time she was called through the door. She faced the back wall of the little curtained cubicle and took off her cardigan, then her blouse. She put them in the basket with her coat and bag and she inserted her arms into the sleeves of the hospital gown, then she sat on the little bench and waited again, facing the curtain. Now that she was private, she lifted the gown and felt her breast properly, looking for the spot. The thing moved like it was full of liquid, or gel, with odd densities in its depths, most of them anchored to her chest wall. She did not, the GP told her, have especially lumpy breasts, but Constance did think it was a bit porridgy in there, and though she liked the look of breasts – even her own, indeed – although she saw something elegant in the orb of them, she wondered what men wanted when they wanted to push a woman's chest around. Her fingertips tested each little lump, check-ing for sensation, and then they found the place: a small, slippery mass like a piece of gristle, that moved around and did not answer her touch. This was the thing to look for: a part of you that could not feel. Just a tiny part. And the reason it could not feel was that it was not you.

Constance did not have cancer. It was just a cyst or duct, some change since the children. She was thirty-seven, for God's sake. She had three children and a husband to look after, not to mention her widowed mother. Constance did not have the time for cancer.

She would be fine.

But it was hard to keep steady, all the same. She was about to blurt something to the nurse who pulled the curtain back; something mad. *Who will look after the chil-dren if I die?* But of course she said nothing.

The nurse invited her out on to a chair and went over her details: Constance McGrath, address, date of birth, next of kin.

'Dessie McGrath,' she said. 'Same address.'

'Contact number?'

Constance gave her Dessie's mobile number, which felt like an oddly intimate thing to do. 'But don't call him, all right? This kind of stuff gives him the flu.'

'Ah,' said the nurse.

Constance felt a twinge of betrayal, though it was true that Dessie went a bit peculiar whenever she was sick. There was no escaping it: he spent all night checking his pulse and ended up with multiple sclerosis. Which was just funny, really. She knew it was because he cared.

'Any medications?' said the nurse.

Constance was on a little something that was nobody's business but her own. 'No,' she said.

Then the nurse made a few more marks on her file, and left. She came back to call Constance through the final door, where a woman waited beside a big white machine. It was the radiologist, and she gave Constance a smile: a woman in her thirties with beautiful highlights and lowlights, she seemed kind. The hair was expensive, mind you; about a hundred and fifty quid, right there, growing out of her head.

'You can slip off the gown for me,' she said, because people were always 'slipping' in and out of things in hospitals, no one ever just took off their clothes. But the cotton felt light as it left her: Constance put it on a chair and turned around.

There was no trace of the scarred woman in the room, but the recent fact of her made Constance grateful, as she walked up to the machine, for the lesser disaster of her bare torso at thirty-seven, thinking, This is the chest my husband loves and my children will love for a few years yet, and I never loved it, not much, why should I?

Not that she would wish them gone.

'And where is the area of concern?' said the radiologist as she scooped a breast up on to the glass-covered platform.

The radiologist did not wear gloves but her little hand was so easy and expert that Constance felt almost soothed by it. The last person she had touched was the woman with all the scars and Constance tried to imagine what all that looked like, or felt like, up close. She wanted to know about the cutting and where, on her body, did it stop. So many different people, and the stories their bodies held. She wondered how many times a day the radiologist lifted this part of a woman on to the ledge of her machine, and pressed the top plate down to the point of pain. She judged it well, at any rate. At just the moment Constance drew in a sharp breath, she disappeared behind the control panel and its protective window; there was a buzzing, then a beep, and the machine, as though shocked at its own behaviour, let her go.

All the time, there was chat, which would annoy you, if you were the type to be annoyed.

'Oh I love the Aran Islands,' she said, as she lifted Constance's arm up over the top of the machine.

'Now I know that feels a little too high, but just bear with me. No, I went there on a school trip, would you believe, and I loved it. At sixteen.'

The Perspex descended as the radiologist worked Constance into position and she was gone behind the desk before Constance could say how much she too loved the Aran Islands, their peaceable flatness that made them at one with the weather.

'If you like it wet,' she said, as the machine beeped, and took fright, and let her go.

'Oh indeed.'

'I'll just put a little biro mark on, if you don't mind,' she said. 'Just to say.' Though say what she did not clarify and, when Constance looked down, she saw four dots in a neat square marking the place where she thought the lump might be.

Everything seemed to happen very fast.

Before she knew it, the radiologist was looking up at a screen, and pressing buttons in a definitive way.

'Can you see anything?' Constance said.

'Em. The doctor will have a look for you. That could be. It could be the kind of thing you could just work out. I could just work it out for you.'

This made no sense at all to Constance, who said, 'You can't see your hand in front of your face, some days, when the mist comes in.'

'You can slip on your gown for me now,' said the radiologist, and she checked that Constance was decently covered before opening a door to a side room.

'Bríd will bring you up to the ultrasound, all righty?'

And there was the technician in the white coat, holding the envelope. At least Constance assumed she was a technician because the coat was not the cleanest and she was a little unkempt, but she could be head of the department for all Constance knew.

'I wish I was there now. Don't you?' said the radiologist. She was talking about the Aran Islands.

'Anywhere but here,' said Constance. It was supposed to be a joke but her voice sounded a bit sudden and aggressive, and both the hospital women seemed saddened by this. It was not their fault that people got cancer. If anything, the opposite was the case. It was hard to be so misunderstood.

Constance followed the technician, her eyes on the big brown envelope, her gown barely fastened at the back, and she sat beside Margaret Dolan on the banquette.

'My God,' she said.

'Well that's that bit done,' said Constance.

'Dear Jesus God almighty,' she said. 'I thought I was in for my womb.' Then she talked about her bloat again. There was no stopping her. Something had been unleashed by their shared experience of the big white machine.

'Oh dear,' said Constance. 'Oh dear,' sneaking her fingers under her sleeve, to check her little wristwatch. Half past twelve.

No one knew she was here. Not Dessie, who had clearly forgotten what day it was. Not her mother. Not her friends who were were all scattered now. Eileen in America, Martha Hingerty in London, and Lauren in Strasbourg – the last to go. They were so rarely home. By the time Constance caught up with them, all her news had gone stale.

And what was her news?

She had cancer. Or, she did not have cancer.

But that wasn't the point, exactly. Constance realised it was for the girls she had been saving the details: the radiologist's highlights, the unhygienic look of the technician's coat, the woman who thought she was in for her womb. There was no use telling Dessie, who would not see the connection between the cost of a haircut and the lump in your breast. Only the girls could run with the ironies, the 'Oh my God' of it all. They had been a gang since school.

Eileen Foley, Martha Hingerty, Lauren O'Dea. When they finished their Leaving cert they all went up to Dublin together, while Constance stayed back a year to repeat her exams and work behind the counter in the Medical Hall. And it was the loneliest year of her life. Constance was supposed to study Pharmacy, but she couldn't get into Pharmacy, and when she failed for a second time there was much weeping and gnashing of teeth in Ardeevin. Her uncle Bart finally took pity on her and swung her a job in a big chemist's on Grafton Street so she should learn about the business side of things before coming back home. But Constance had no intention of coming back to the Medical Hall. Eileen Foley was saving for New York and, at nineteen, Constance was going there too.

She arrived at the flat in Baggot Street with a huge and tatty suitcase and, after all the shouty, funny letters, she discovered the place was indeed a kip and the others were rarely around. Constance suffered much tension about the rent which her friends did not seem to share; Lauren turning up one Saturday morning with a stained cheque saying, 'Did you not get this?' as though it was Constance who had let things slide. But it was worth it for the wildness of being with the girls unleashed – Lauren especially, who went through the men they met like the world was on sale and they were a rail of clothes.

Awful!

Hmmm.

Nothing was right.

Look, oh he's gorgeous, Oh no! He doesn't fit.

Constance could never figure out what the problem was – either they were too keen or they didn't call – but there was no persuading people about such things, you can't order someone to fall in love.

Constance wasn't sure what she liked herself, when it came to men, though she knew what she wanted. She wanted to have sex on Irish soil. Her virginity, she declared, was not getting on the plane with her to JFK. Constance was working in Dublin city centre and every customer who walked in the door came in with a look on their face and a prescription for condoms folded four times. They came in to town so their local chemist would not know. It was like working in a porn shop, she said. They bought hundreds of the things. Ribbed for extra pleasure. They bought lubricant from behind the counter, where it sat between suppositories and steroidal creams. Some of it was flavoured.

'Stop!'

'Oh no!'

Lauren said that lubricant was a sign of an old or a frigid wife. Though the girls all took a tube, when Constance offered them around, along with many illegal packets of Durex, both plain and multicoloured.

Despite the fact that Constance was living in sex central, the men who came up to her till ran away from her. It wasn't just that they would not flirt, they wouldn't even look her in the eye. It was all so unthrilling. She went out for a couple of weeks with a Malaysian guy from the College of Surgeons she met at a medical do. Constance would have done anything he asked, but he didn't ask, and then, somehow, he was gone. To cheer her up, the girls went for cocktails in the Coconut Grove with some suburban rugby types who were all chasing Lauren. They ordered from a drinks menu and the men paid and they clinked glasses and laughed before Constance was roughly deflowered in the back seat of a car by a man whose big fingers had grown around the signet on his pinkie and also around his wedding ring. When Constance threw up afterwards, it came out blue. The guy, whose manners were impeccable, put her in a taxi home.

'Make sure she gets in safe,' he said, and pressed some notes into her hand to cover the fare. He even rang a few days later to ask if he might see her again. Constance, standing by the payphone in the hall in Baggot Street, suffered a moment of absolute confusion. Like maybe she was in some sort of parallel universe, and this guy was in the real world. He certainly sounded real.

'Yes,' she said. 'Lovely. Where?'

In the end she stood him up. She lay face down on her bed and hung on to the mattress, as though it might start to spin and throw her off. She imagined him under Bewley's clock in his sheepskin jacket, standing in the rain.

It was rape, she thought now, or it would have been, if she had known how to say no. Not a word she was ever reared to use, let's face it: *What do you mean, 'No'?* And the men who bought lots of KY but no condoms were probably gay, that was another thing Constance realised, many years later. And it seemed to her a raw business, penetration – at least in those days, when the body was such a stupid place: when her skin was the most intelligent thing about her, for knowing how to blush, and she could not even name herself below the waist.

'I'd say that one's got bad news.'

'Sorry?'

'She's been in there for ages,' said Margaret Dolan. 'She's in a very long time.'

'Has she?'

Constance listened for tears or wails from the ultrasound room.

'Maybe they're on a coffee break.'

'Huh.' Margaret reached behind her and put a scratching hand in through the gap in the gown.

'They saw us coming,' she said.

Constance still liked Ireland, the way you could talk to anyone. It would not be the same in America, she thought, and tried to remember why she failed to get on the plane. Mostly it was the price. The ticket cost maybe £200, which was a huge sum of money in those days. And though Constance saved like crazy, it was hard to save much when you were out having a good time – even when it wasn't such a good time, because the guy in the sheepskin jacket knocked something out of her, too, some carelessness.

Constance lost her taste for adventure for a while, after the Coconut Grove.

If she had gone to New York she would not be worried about cancer now. She would have been jogging for years, living on wheatgrass, she would have a yoga 'practice', maybe even a personal trainer, and her children would be – she could not imagine what her New York children would have been like – whiny, at a guess, that mixture of anxiety and entitlement you saw in city kids. Her children would be fewer. Her children would not exist. Their souls would call to her from the eyes of strangers, as though they'd found some other way into the world. She would turn in the street to look at them twice: *who are you?*

She went last year with Dessie. On a shopping trip, no less. Constance told everyone about it – her hairdresser, the man who delivered eggs, the other mothers at the school gate. 'We're going on a shopping trip. To New York', and they got on the plane at Shannon as though it was a perfectly simple thing to do. This was the place you went to get a whole new life, and all she got was a couple of Eileen Fisher cardigans in lilac and grey. Not that this was a terrible thing. They were really useful cardigans. She and Dessie stayed with her brother Dan on a fold-out bed in his apartment in Brooklyn, and it was quite a large apartment, apparently (Dessie did not mention the 4,000 square feet he was building out in Aughavanna). It was also just around the corner from 'the best ever cherry ice cream', Dan said, because for Dan, in his New York mode, things were always 'amazing' or 'just the best'. The ice cream confused Constance slightly, the cherries were delicious but the full fat cream left a greasy coating in her mouth.

'Isn't it the best?' said Dan. 'Isn't it incredible?'

'Lovely,' she said. Thinking, *Is it for this you left? Was it for the ice cream?*

She thought that Dan was a bit of a hypocrite for liking things so wildly, or pretending to like them. And she started to feel inadequate to the menu in her hand. They went to a kind of brasserie that served a modern take on Jewish food, all gefilte fish and matzo balls, and that was supposed to be 'amazing' too. But it was just *food*. It was a long way to travel, she thought, for dumplings. Her enjoyment was soured, Constance knew, by the years she had spent yearning to go, and not going, selling condoms to men who did not want to sleep with her – the Baggot Street years, time she spent pretending to be a student, when she really wasn't a student, she was a shop-girl, which was to say, a girl who was waiting to get married. Four years out of school the waiting (which had been dreadful) was over. Constance was courted by Dessie McGrath every time she went down home and she ended up going down home more often, just to feel his arms about her.

And she still liked the feel of them. Balding, blunt-spoken Dessie McGrath. Three children on, he had moved sex to the mornings – even this morning, indeed – because it set him up for the day, he said. Constance would sleep again afterwards while he went down to his little office and some time later, whistling in the afterglow, he might get the children up and out for school. Constance liked stretching between the sheets to the sound of their chatter, only to pause and remember what she and Dessie had been up to, a couple of hours before. She kept the memory of him inside her all day. It was there now, if she wanted to think about it, washed as she was, with her underarms scraped for the doctor, and naked to the waist under her hospital gown. Who would have thought? Constance was not a fabulous looking woman, and Dessie was not a fabulous looking man, and that was the laugh of it, really. They were lucky. Because what was the point of looking sexy if you never got any sex, as happened often enough. Even to Lauren, who was always turning men down.

Constance remembered telling her about Dessie, the way she sort of hooted.

'Dessie? Dessie McGrath?' Then later she said, 'He's really nice.' And she meant it. And she sounded sad.

On the other side of the corridor, the technician in the white coat came out carrying an envelope and the woman who followed her ducked her head as she turned towards the next queue on the banquette. She lifted her fingers to her breastbone, with her head inclined, like some painting of the Virgin Mary that Constance remembered. She tipped herself lightly there as though to say, *My life is not my own.*

'So who's getting married?' Constance said to Margaret Dolan.

'Sorry?'

'The wedding.'

'Oh, the wedding. My daughter.'

'My goodness,' said Constance. 'Mother of the bride.'

'Hah,' she said. She leaned forward, so her bare back swelled out of the open gown and she rubbed her hurt hands together.

'I have a girl,' said Constance.

But the woman did not hear. She was talking about the bridesmaids, who would be in lilac to match the bride's black hair. She was worried about her daughter's asthma, the way her sinuses blew up on her whenever she was stressed.

'Oh dear,' said Constance.

Other people's children can be very dull, her own mother liked to say. And it was sort of true. Constance remembered Lauren the year she moved to Strasbourg, sitting in the kitchen with a big glass of white, talking about ski trips and restaurants and skinny French women with their horror of plastic surgery. One child teething and the other going behind the sofa for a quiet poo, and Lauren sort of elaborately unsympathetic to all this, talking about the difference between a pink tinted foundation and one that was a bit more yellow.

'What age is Rory, again? Three?'

Even her own mother listened without listening.

'Oh, I can't remember,' she would say, when there was some little problem. 'It's a long time ago.'

But it was not a long time ago for Constance, who was still in it. Whose children were coming up to teenagers now, with no gap – or none that she could discern – between breast-feeding and breast cancer, between tending and dying. Who did not know what else she could do.

'Do something!' said her mother.

Rosaleen believed a woman should be interesting. She should keep her figure, and always listen to the news.

'Like what?'

'Take up horse riding.'

'Right,' said Constance. Her mother had always wanted a daughter who looked good on a pony, or a daughter who did ballet, like a daughter in a book. Rosaleen always had a paperback on the go, opera on the radio, cuttings rooting in pots on the windowsills and overflowing on to the floor. Which was hardly the McGrath style – living, as they did, in bungalow bliss down the road.

'You are so lucky,' she used to say. Meaning something else entirely.

But she was also right. Constance was lucky. Trips to New York were just the tip of the iceberg, Constance was spoilt with tickets to Bruce Springsteen and the Galway Races, a leg of lamb brought home on Friday, chocolates if she wanted them or No chocolates! As soon as they could afford it Dessie found a girl to help with the housework, and if one sister-in-law went to Prague, the other went to Paris, because in the years she had known them the McGraths did well and then better yet. There was no stopping them. If Constance got her chairs reupholstered, some other Mrs McGrath would discover minimalism, and a third would be into shabby chic and, somehow, she would have to start all over again.

'They are driving me nuts,' she would say to her mother and the pair of them would laugh at the jumped-upness of the McGrath clan, the auctioneer, the quantity surveyor, the builder and even Dessie himself, who made pergolas and fences for gardens all the way to Galway.

'So pretty,' said Rosaleen.

Constance had not told her mother about the mammogram. And that was fine. There was no need. But it was on days like this she missed her girlfriends, who had their own lives and their own troubles in distant towns. Because Constance had two sons who told her nothing and a husband who told her nothing and a father who told her nothing and then died. And, of course, Dessie had forgotten about the lump. Incredible as that might seem. He forgot she was in for tests this morning, because he always forgot about things like that. They made him too anxious. At 5 a.m. they slipped into the bathroom and then got back into bed – and this would be the last time they made love, Constance thought, before she was diagnosed with cancer or told she was in the clear. It was particularly tender, life and death sex: it was very fine. Then, while she was stuffing lunches into the children's schoolbags and he was pulling his keys off the hook, he said, 'What are you up to?'

'Sorry?'

'Today?'

'Why?' She kept her voice careful, just to be sure.

'No reason. I'm away to Aughavanna, is all, to check things over this afternoon, so I might be back a bit late, if that's OK.'

'Off you go,' she said, and he kissed her, and goosed her, and was out the door.

A couple of years ago, Constance got her wisdom teeth out, and she must have said it a hundred times, she needed a lift home because they wouldn't let you drive after the sedation. When the day came Dessie said, 'What?' He said he would rearrange everything, he would do it right away, and he started panicking and going through bits of paper until Constance told him not to bother. She just drove herself over there, and got the teeth out without the drugs. It was painful all right, but not exactly a disaster.

'I like to know where I am,' she said to the dentist, who promised to stuff her with local anaesthetic. Then she got up out of the chair, her jaw banging like a gong, and she got into the car, and drove back home.

Her mother was outraged.

'You should have called me,' she said. But Rosaleen liked to say things like that, when the opportunity to help was gone.

'He cares too much,' Constance said. 'That's the problem. He loves me too much,' listening to her mother's silence on the other end of the phone.

There was, of course, a fair amount of boasting in the complaints she made to her mother. Dessie's caring was legendary, and Constance herself was indestructible: those two things were well known.

'God you are indestructible,' said Rosaleen. She made it sound like an insult.

Because Rosaleen was actually depressed, Constance

thought, there was no other word for it. She was two years a widow and Constance felt her mother leaving, now, all the time.

'So smug,' she said, when Constance rattled on about the kids – which admittedly, she did non-stop.

'So smug.'

Her own grandchildren.

Oh all your geese are swans.

And why not? Why not have children who were wonderful?

Everyone was so disappointed, these days, Constance thought, it was like an epidemic. Lauren was clearly disappointed with her life in Strasbourg, her Prada trousers notwithstanding. And Dessie viewed his fortieth birthday as a personal insult, he couldn't understand it was happening to him – never mind the trips to New York and the Galway Races, and the house he was finishing now, out in Aughavanna with more space than Constance wanted or could fill. He had one of those little cherry blossoms already planted; big, solid pink pompoms on this little sapling in the middle of the lawn. Horrible. Her mother clearly thought it was all vulgarity rampant.

'How lovely,' she said to Dessie. Driving him up the wall.

When Constance told her mother she was getting married, Rosaleen said Dessie was 'an eccentric choice', which was an odd thing to say, because Dessie was just the opposite, really. Twelve years on, they were very thick.

'Have you had enough, Desmond?'

Sometimes Constance felt she was actually in the way.

'Cut him another slice of that cake, Constance. Will you have another slice of cake?'

Her mother would put her hand lightly to Dessie's forearm, she would glance over her shoulder at him, with some backward-flung piece of charm. It was a hoot to watch the pair of them. Two drinks and they'd be off laughing in a corner: Dessie buttered up, plumped up, lifting the jacket on to her shoulders from the back of the chair, 'You have to hand it to her', as though Rosaleen was an opponent worth considering, for a man like Dessie. Then, as soon as he was through his own front door, saying, 'That woman', because she had played him, yet again.

Though she managed it less and less, it had to be said, since her own husband died.

Constance was very worried about Rosaleen. She was still out in the old house in Ardeevin and it was still letting in the rain, she had a hundred small things wrong with her, none of which you could name. This had always been the way with Rosaleen, but she went to some new quack in Ennis who told her not to eat broccoli, or to eat lots of broccoli, Constance could never remember which. The GP, meanwhile, said her bloods were coming back fine, so Rosaleen was fighting with the GP whom she had never liked – nor his father before him, she said. Everything was off. She was tired all the time.

The stupid thing was that if you agreed that there was, clearly, something wrong with her, Rosaleen would snap that she was perfectly fine. Or if, in the middle of some intense medical discussion, you suggested she get a scan of the offending organ, whichever one it was, then Rosaleen would look quietly affronted, because of course the thing that was wrong with her was not the sort of thing you could just see with a machine.

'Oh, I don't know,' she would say, turning to look out the window, and a small smile would come, as though she enjoyed being so misunderstood.

Constance did not think there was a cure for grief, but she did think an anti-depressant might cut the worst of it. She was on a little Seroxat herself, since her father got sick and she wouldn't be without it, but it was not something you could ever suggest to your mother.

Daddy said he felt fine.

'I feel absolutely fine,' he had said. Twelve months and two courses of chemo later, he was dead. So a healthy man was in the ground, and a woman who felt mysteriously unwell was driving about the countryside, switching on the windscreen wipers every time she wanted to turn left. Coming home, then, to a house that was falling down around her ears.

Dessie wanted to develop a site out at Boolavaun, that was one of the things Rosaleen teased him about, he had some scheme. He would get the cash to her, and Rosaleen would sign the land over – he would buy it, in effect – and the money would plug the holes in her roof and keep her in nice skin cream. But Rosaleen seemed to like the holes in her roof. She seemed to like saying, 'What will I do? I don't know what to do.' She liked panicking with pots and buckets and having them all run around for her, calling Constance every time it rained. Calling Constance when the mousetrap went off, saying, 'I think it's a rat.'

Constance who had cancer. Or who did not have cancer.

What was the word she was looking for?

'No.'

What do you mean, 'No'?

'No, I am busy. No, I have more important things on. No, I will not do this for you now. No.'

'Margaret Dolan!'

The woman beside Constance lunged towards the floor to gather her basket and her bag and her empty water bottle, and her gown opened to show her back, which was creamy and huge. Constance had the urge to touch it. She wanted to lay her head on the expanse of it, say, 'Stop.

Hush.' And when Margaret Dolan paused, she would reach down to take her scarred and pudgy hand, and feel her own hand squeezed in return.

'OK,' said Margaret Dolan and she heaved herself, with some difficulty, up off the seat.

'Well,' she said, turning slightly to Constance. 'Here goes nothin'!'

'Take it easy now,' said Constance.

The empty space she left behind was still occupied by the sharp, peculiar smell of her sweat.

'Keep drinking the water!' said Constance, at the last minute, just before the door closed, and the woman from Adare shot a small glance her way.

It was true.

All Constance wanted to do was to make people happy. Why was it her job to fix them? Not one of the people she cared so much about knew where she was, right now. There wasn't a sinner to remember that she had a mammogram today, or enquire how it had gone, and a terrible sharp desire came over Constance to be told the lump was malignant, so she could say to Dessie, 'You know where I was this morning?' and tell her mother, 'Yes Mammy, cancer, they saw it on the scan', then wait for the news to filter, finally, through to Lauren, Eileen, Martha Hingerty: who would then be obliged to call, 'Why didn't you tell me? I just heard.'

There it was.

She was in the room and there it was: a picture of her breast was pinned on to a light-box on the wall and, on her breast, which was a network of white lines and inter-sections, was a lump: it looked like a knot, a snarl of light. And everything around it – the exterior line of the breast, the map of ducts, or veins, perhaps – was very beautiful,

96

like a landscape seen from space, one of those pictures of the earth taken at night.

But there might have been an arrow pointing to the thing. There might as well have been a big stick-on piece of cardboard with the word CANCER written on it in red marker, because even Constance could see it, there was no doubt it was there. It was a while before she could look away from it and listen to what the doctor was saying.

'You're a bit old for one and a bit young for the other, if you know what I mean.'

Was that good?

Constance was lying on the couch. The doctor, who was a woman, had the sonic pen Constance remembered from her pregnancies, and she thought she heard the liquid boom of a baby's heart through the Doppler machine. Then she realised it was the sound of her own blood, rushing in the flesh of her ears.

The doctor looked to the picture on the light-box, and felt – unerring – for the lump. She moved her index finger around it, while her other hand brought the pen into play and the screen beside Constance jumped into life. The picture was in black and white, and this time the inside of her breast looked like marble, it was mottled in exactly the same way. It was marbled the way a steak was marbled, she thought, because what she was looking at was fat. Before she knew what was happening, the woman had a needle in there – too fine, almost, to hurt, she could see it on the screen reaching into a blob of darkness, and she looked down in real life as it was taken out, and she realised a nurse was holding her by the shoulders so she would not make any sudden movement. As soon as the needle was gone she wanted to sit up and take a breath, and this is what she did. She was wiping the jelly off her skin with some rough green paper towel, she was reaching for the basket of clothes as the doctor said, 'Hang on.' Then the doctor repeated what she had just said. Some word like 'adenoids' or 'carcinoma' and then: 'I think – hang on – So I am ninety-five per cent – OK? – ninety-five per cent sure this is what it is. And you are a bit old for it, but you're a bit young for the other, all right? With your history, and what I am seeing here on the screen.'

Constance still couldn't understand a word of it. This is why everyone took so long in this room. It was because everyone was stupid, like her.

But the doctor didn't say the word 'stupid'. She rubbed her hand along Constance's arm.

'All right?'

The arm thing was a gesture she had decided on; she did it a hundred times a day. But it felt nice, all the same.

'All right,' said Constance, and she shuffled out of the room: her gown flapping open at the back and the plastic grocery basket that held her clothes clutched in both hands.

She was guided up a set of back stairs into a proper hospital ward.

'Mr Murtagh will be along to you soon.'

This time, the women waited on beds, and each bed was surrounded by curtains, so Constance could not tell where Margaret Dolan was, or if she had already left. Some time later, she heard the woman from Adare go to another stall – she could tell who it was by the sound of her shoes. And while she waited – it must have been the stress – she drifted against the softness of Rory's skin and the thickness of his unwashed curls. She was like some sea creature among the kelp, grazing the side of her face against his older brother, the moving, small bones of his white shoulder, the sweaty insides of his hands paddling against her as she turned and passed, and pulled herself down into the perfumed depths of Shauna's red hair. When she woke – minutes later, or half an hour – she was panicking about the salmon in the freezer, thinking, *What will I buy for the dinner, if I have cancer?*, and then, *Fuck. Fuck. Fuck it. How am I even going to drive myself home?*

Out on the other side of the screen, Margaret Dolan was saying, 'I can't do it next week, I have a wedding,' and a man's voice said, 'Who's getting married?'

'My daughter. I have a daughter.'

'A daughter?' The man was a fool. There was no need to sound so surprised.

'Adopted,' said Margaret, by way of apology, then rallied with, 'She found me. She was adopted and she found me last year.'

'Right,' and his voice had an extra 'oh shit' in there. 'OK. And when is the wedding again?'

'It's in Birmingham.'

'OK.'

'Doctor, do I not have it in my womb?'

And Constance started to cry for Margaret Dolan, quietly, in her cubicle: the tears ran down. Crying too for her own selfishness – how utterly, utterly selfish she was. Constance McGrath sat on the bed where the starched sheet was folded over, feeling abandoned and small. Because she had everything, more than everything, her life was overflowing and Margaret Dolan had so little to call her own. Constance wanted to put her head through the curtain and look her in the eye – to say what? 'I'm so sorry for your trouble. Would you like a lift home?'

But the nurse was already leading her to another room.

'Now Margaret,' she was saying. 'Good woman. You're all right. Good woman.'

*

99

They arrived through the curtains in a team: the folder nurse and the ultrasound woman and two children in white coats who must be students, all of them following a small man with very piercing eyes. This was Mr Murtagh.

Mr Murtagh placed his hand on her breast briefly, but he wasn't much interested. He sort of shoved it away. The way his eyes scanned her, Constance had a sudden panic that she had not shaved under her arms.

'We are very happy with you,' said Mr Murtagh.

He did not seem happy, he seemed a bit impatient but, *That is because I am well,* Constance thought, I have been wasting his time with my robust good health, I have been wasting everyone's time! Her clever body had been doing a great job. Complex. Microscopic. Quiet. The map of light that was her left breast was not frightful but beautiful, and the marbled black and white of its sonic depths was lovely too.

'I'm clear,' she said.

'Yes.'

Clear.

'You can slip your clothes back on for me now,' said the nurse, as though Constance might run out to the car park in her gown, jumping up and banging her heels together in the rain. Constance dressed to her overcoat and pushed the curtain back, exposing the bed to an empty ward.

'Thank you for everything,' Constance said to the nurse who liked glitter nail polish but was not allowed to wear it. She was finishing Constance's notes on a steel clipboard at the end of the bed.

'Now you heard what Mr Murtagh said. You know where we are. Any worry at all.'

'Thank you so much.'

'Safe home, now.'

The air outside the hospital doors was amazing, so packed full of oxygen and weather. Constance could not remember where she had parked the car but she did not mind walking through the spottings of rain, pulling the sky into her lungs. Sipping at the world.

Constance put on the windscreen wipers as the rain set in. She held and turned the wheel with care and the darkness under her left arm flowered and began to fade. A few miles from home, the sun came out. She passed the latest McGrath house – Dessie's brother the auctioneer, who had built a bungalow, high off the road. The slope of raw clay had been ablaze, when her father's hearse passed along that way, with red poppies and with those yellow flowers that love broken ground. Less of them came the next year, and this year fewer again, as grass took over and the cut land healed.

She remembered Emmet, helping him down the stairs in Ardeevin. He wasn't in great shape himself, Emmet. He was back from Africa, or wherever, with a scraggy beard and a hundred yard stare. But he kept his father company through his last months and they were silent and easy with each other, as though dying was like having a glass of stout or watching the news on telly. It was a funny romance, Constance thought – father and son. The chat about politics or scientific advances, because women were fine but prone to foolishness, and why fuss when you could sit on a spring evening and solve the problems of the whole, wide world? Before you die.

The same way her own boys chatted to Dessie, coming up the path, back from hurling on a Saturday. The light clear voice of Donal, who was the spit of his father, he was his father all over again:

'What happens to gravity in the middle of the earth, Daddy?'

'Good question.'

'I mean, if you went through the earth, and you were in the middle of the earth, you wouldn't weigh anything.'

'I don't know. You might weigh even more.'

'Or you might just get very small.'

'Certainly. Certainly. That too.'

It was June. In a few weeks' time she would bring the children down to the sea when the turf at Fanore was fragrant with clover. She could lie down on it – the low aromatic carpet of green that covered the land behind the dunes – and this year she would learn all the names. Sand pansies she knew and, further inland, the meadowsweet and woodbine, but there was a tiny yellow thing like broom that was also scented, and even the tough little succulents behind the marram called the bees through the salt air by their surprising, sweet perfume. This year she would bring a book of names and instead of sitting on the sand while the children played she would walk the turf with her head bowed. That is what she would do.

'How did it go?' said Dessie.

'How did what go?'

'The thingy.'

'You knew?'

'Of course I knew. I mean, I remembered. Sorry.'

'Oh you remembered.'

'Sorry. I'm really sorry.'

'So you should be.'

'What thingy?' said Rory, who was her middle child and the most considerate of the three.

'It was fine,' she said.

'Of course it was fine,' said Dessie.

'There's no "of course" about it,' said Constance, who was starting to rattle the pots and pans now.

'What thingy?' said Rory again.

'Nothing. Everything's fine.'

'But you knew that, didn't you?' said Dessie. 'That's what the GP said.'

'Did he?'

'Yeah. He did. Remember, he said the way it moved around, that was the good thing. I mean, you're a bit young.'

'Am I?' said Constance.

'Well. That's what he said.'

'Oh, dear God,' said Constance. 'Oh dear Lord give me patience,' and Rory slipped out of the room.

'Honestly,' she said. 'No really. Fuck you! The lot of you.'

And they let her blow and stomp, they let her weep and rail, and stagger, weeping, off to the bedroom, after which Dessie went out and got fish and chips for dinner from the takeaway in town.

Later, Donal came in to read her his comic, and Rory lay behind her and stroked her hair. When they left, Dessie came in with a cup of tea and Constance said, 'Did you save me some chips?'

'Oh, sorry. Did you want any?'

'Chips!?'

'Did you want some? I can get some more.'

'You're all right,' she said.

Dessie stood looking at her from the end of the bed.

'There was a woman in front of me,' she said. 'And she had it.'

'Right,' he said, and showed willing by sitting on the edge of the mattress. But it was no use.

'She was very big,' said Constance. 'I mean, *big*.'

'She was probably on the medical card,' said Dessie.

So Constance abandoned one version of her day, and

told Dessie instead about the pain she had felt when she had looked at the woman's scars, the feeling that shot down the length of her thighs. She did not know if other people felt this kind of thing; it was not something she had ever heard discussed. She said, 'Do you ever get that? You know if you see something terrible, if one of the kids is hurt, or that time your man nearly lost the finger, with the knuckle sticking out of it – you remember? – and the whole thing dangling by a piece of skin.'

'Run that by me again?'

'Do you ever get that pain in your legs? Quite a sharp pain. Like, Oh no!'

'Em. I get that, you know. That scrotum-tightening thing.'

'Sympathy.'

'Protection maybe. Like, hang on to your lad.'

'Great,' she said.

'Or sympathy. Yeah. Maybe that's what it is.'

And he kissed her.

'Maybe,' he said.

When she got up later, she hugged the boys and went to look for Shauna and found her outside, lying on the trampoline, looking at the stars. Constance clambered up there to join her, the pair of them in each other's arms. Constance said sorry for shouting and Shauna said, 'It's not that. It's not that.' Then she had a little cry: some friend being mean to her, they could be very bitchy already, at eight and nine.

'Never mind,' said Constance. 'Never mind.'

The cold webbing of the trampoline dipped and rose under them, Shauna's hair flung back across it, fanned out by the static.

'She's just horrible,' said Shauna. 'She's thinks she's like the bee's knees.'

The wind drifted up through the mesh and cooled them from below. They lay on the black expanse that rocked them lightly as they moved, and her daughter was comforted. Constance could do that much, at least. She could still do that much. And Constance was also comforted, lying on the trampoline under the stars, with her daughter in her arms.

Emmet

Ségou, Mali
2002

THREE MONTHS AFTER Emmet moved in with her, Alice found a dog in the marketplace, or the dog found her and followed her home. It was a short-haired street dog with a dirty white pelt and a blunt face, and there was a dry, pink cyst growing from the corner of its left eye. She must have encouraged it. Emmet imagined her smiling over at the dog, then flinching when it turned to look at her. Or starting forward, her hands pressing into her cotton skirt as she crouched to talk to the dog; then reaching out to touch it, pulling back its ear to examine the bad eye.

Alice was drawn to suffering, which is why she lived near the marketplace and not on the edge of town. Emmet, too, was drawn to suffering – it was, after all, his job – and he was drawn to Alice. He did not ask why she had spoken to a dumb animal in a language that was foreign, even to the passers-by. It was her nature. And it was the dog's nature to follow her, with one dog-brown eye more pathetic than the other.

It was the dry season and Emmet was often on the road, so he did not know how long it took him to notice the creature lying in the street outside the house, or to realise that it was always there when he opened the front gate. He seemed to forget the dog each time, and when he stepped around the stretched and panting thing it was with the sense of something he had left unsaid.

'Stop by the dog,' Emmet would say to his driver, meaning, 'Don't run over the dog.' He assumed – if he ever gave the thing a thought – that the dog belonged to the street vendor on the corner, or that the vendor tolerated it: because street dogs don't belong to anyone, they just desperately want to belong. So there it was – each time Emmet came back, dusty and hot, and hoping that Alice had sourced a decent Dutch beer. The dog lay on the ground like a dead dog, with its legs straight down, and its nose straight out, and only when you came close could you see the quick motion of its belly's rise and fall. The creature did not belong in the heat, Emmet thought, any more than they did themselves: the flabby corners of its mouth pulsing pink inside black lips, the eyes squeezing painfully shut against the dust and – one of them – around the slowly expanding balloon of the cyst. Wincing, winking, squeezing tight. This difficulty gave the dog a salty air.

'Eh, yeah,' it seemed to say every time he passed. 'Eh, yeah, I dunno about that.'

One day, Emmet kicked something on the way in through the gate. He looked down to see a china bowl with a pattern of roses, like something you might use back home. What was that doing there? He said it to Ibrahim, when the front door was opened.

'What is the crockery doing in the street?'

Ibrahim never answered a direct question, and you had to respect that. Even so, there was a kind of yearning, in their talk, for the thing that could not be said.

'Mister Emmet, sir?'

His eyes rested, liquid and compassionate, on Emmet's passing sleeve.

'The bowl outside the gate.'

Emmet dumped his bag on the hall table and turned to look, as the watchman ducked out and then back in through the gate under Ibrahim's contemptuous eye. And there was something about this scene that kept Emmet in the doorway for a moment too long. It stayed with him as Alice came from the darkness of the living room to kiss him and recoil a little from the sweat. Something was wrong. He had seen this a hundred times before. The trick was not to ignore it. Or, when you dismissed something – and there was always something tugging at the corner of your eye – to notice your dismissal. You took note.

'What's the shouting for?'

'What shouting?'

'Ib.'

'Is he?'

There were a couple of Tuaregs about the place. Emmet could never tell them apart, their faces were wound about with turbans of white cloth, but they were a proud people and handy in a fight, so he was surprised to see Ibrahim actually push the guy away from the front door to send him round the back of the house. Emmet had sensed it a hundred times before. Something was wrong.

'Which one of them is that?' he said.

But Alice just widened her eyes.

'How are you anyway?' he said. 'Any beer?'

Most of the time it was nothing: the thing that was wrong. It was a clan thing or a sum of money, some mark of respect that had been denied.

'Fridge is down,' said Alice.

'You in long?'

He started to undress, passing her on his way through to the shower, which was just a baffle of low walls, tacked on to the side of the house. The sun blazed into it, and the showerhead was rusted shut. Emmet filled a bucket and slung his clothes over the dividing wall, while Alice turned towards him in the gloom.

'Mozzies!' she said, and he pushed the door shut, imagining how he looked to her eyes – sunlit – his narrow white shanks, the tractor tan. Emmet was so long in the heat, the exposed skin was a different age to the hidden parts of him; he had sixty-year-old knees and the belly of a young man. He scraped the water off with the thin towel and bared his gums in the scrap of mirror. He pushed his nose one way and then another to check for cancers, then he reached, still naked, for his hat. The top half of his forehead was white.

There was a fresh sarong waiting for him on a low stool, though he had not seen Ib open the door to leave it there and, when he went inside, the house was deserted. He made his way upstairs and found Alice lying under the mosquito net, thinking.

'All clean?' she said, which was all the invitation he needed to get in beside her, and spoon until his hat fell off, and make love, the sweat breaking out, first on him and then on Alice, so the pat-pat of his body against hers turned to slipping and silence.

Afterwards, his thoughts turned to the bowl and the scene at the gate. Emmet hated problems with the staff. You could be saving lives all day and be undone at the end of it by a plate of beans and bad lard. Literally saving lives. Because wars you can do, and famines you can do and floods are relatively easy, but no one survives when the cook scratches his arse and then decides not to bother washing his hands.

The swamp cooler in the window came to and Emmet rolled towards its blessed tedium. The electricity was back.

There was a shift in the night air, the sound of voices outside, the smell of woodsmoke and cooking. Alice, dozing in the tangle of thin sheets, gave a faint smile as Emmet bent to kiss her before swinging his legs off the bed. He went back down to the shower stall where he filled another bucket and threw it over himself one more time, and scraped his skin with the same meagre towel, now completely dry.

Ibrahim was busy with the dinner, so he got his own beer from the recently revived fridge. A squat, yellowing thing with a pull handle you don't see at home any more. There was nothing but beer in it. Emmet was earning good money that year but there wasn't a whole heap to buy unless you went to the Western supermarket – which Alice was loath to do. Besides, he was too busy to need much. And Alice was always busy. And it was always hot.

She came down from the bedroom, clean and dressed in white.

'Well now,' she said.

There was a burr in Alice's voice that made her sound teasing and drunk, on the permanent brink of a joke. She was from Newcastle. 'Oh that explains it,' Emmet said, when they first met. He was not a natural flirt. But there was something easy and terrific about the light in her eye, and it was with some new sense of difficulty that he walked away from her that evening. Her first year in the field, with her corkscrew curls going mad in the heat, it was two months before she cracked, necking rum babas at a UNICEF do, giving out about the photocopier blinking in the corner. 'How much did that fucking cost?' she said.

She had just broken up, she told him, with a Swedish guy in Bamako, who was too busy saving the world to save poor Alice. The affair wasn't so much brief as 'very very brief', she said. She was fabulously drunk. Emmet did not complain.

He didn't, in fact, say very much as he walked her back to her guesthouse under a sky thick with stars, while the locals slept or listened in tactful silence to her white woman's carry-on. Halfway home, she sat down on a stone and wept. She was, she said, deeply disillusioned. Deeply, deeply disillusioned. With herself, really. The idea that she could help anyone, change anything, get the smallest thing done.

Emmet pulled her back to her feet, and hummed that she was doing fine, just fine, she would be fine. And she kissed him as soon as they got inside her door, lifting her foot up behind her, like a girl in a romantic comedy.

She was good at all that.

Unlike other women he had known (and, in fairness, there weren't that many), Alice did not excel at the preliminaries and then freak out in the bedroom. Or freak out in the morning. Or freak out, two days later, for no reason he could fathom. The dramatics were not a diversion. Alice followed through.

She was a talented lover.

Emmet did not suppose he was – not particularly – though he did have his moments, and Alice was most certainly one of them. He lay awake, that first time, considering his wild good fortune and the sadness that came with it. He worried about his heart, took comfort in the fact that affairs in the field were not built to last.

A week later, he found Alice an old colonial house that she loved but couldn't quite afford. Then he moved in with her.

'Don't worry,' he said. 'It's only temporary.' Which was not, he thought, a lie.

'Here's to you,' he said, and lifted, in her direction, the dregs of his bottled beer.

'Mud in your eye,' said Alice.

Alice had decorated the house with hangings from the market: she hung wind chimes in the doorframes, and a ritual mask on the bedroom wall. They sat on cushions and she ate Ibrahim's plate of fried fish without cutlery, taking the bones out a little awkwardly with her right hand and balling up the rice. Emmet still liked a fork, if there was a fork to be had. Newbies did nothing but talk about the squitters, like it was a joke. Emmet did not think diarrhoea was a joke. He had seen too many people die of it.

Not, in fairness, that any of them had been white.

So he plied his fork like an old man and remembered the leaky corpses he had seen in one place or another, then he put the corpses out of his mind while Alice clinked her elegant bangles over her plate.

The computers had finally arrived, she said.

'Oh yeah?'

'Two of them.'

'No shit.'

'Telling you.'

'Do they work?'

'Up to a point,' she said. They were mains powered, so they couldn't switch them on until the generator was sorted, and when this happened, some time in the middle of the afternoon, they had discovered one of them was Windows 97 and the other was Windows 95. It was not that they were antiques, it was that they were differently antique. You could move stuff from the older to the newer software but not the other way around. And there was no modem.

'I mean, what's the fucking point?'

'Training?' he said, but Alice had already started to cry.

'It's not just the computers,' she said.

She cried the way she always cried in the evening: vague tears. Her face was simply wet.

'I know.'

Alice was working on child mortality. Children were hard.

'You should stay in the office more,' he said.

It sounded like a joke, but he meant it. She should focus on delivery of mosquito nets and stop gazing at malarial babies, while they died.

'Maybe,' she said.

Good, sweet, kind-hearted Alice. Endlessly sweet. Endlessly kind. Emmet had to oblige himself to stay seated and to continue eating and to smile back at her. He was thirty-eight years old, beyond confusion. He was lucky to have her. But he was not yet sure that you could call it love.

The next trip took him beyond Mopti. They drove along the wide Niger, then east along a scratch in the dust that was the road inland. Seven hours out, they saw the shadow where locusts had stripped the land, the edge of it faint but cruelly precise, a secret map that shifted across the paper map, like the landscape's own weather. This was the line they travelled for the next ten days, with wind-up radios and pesticide packs. When he arrived back at the house Alice washed him, and he washed Alice, and this tenderness was as much as either of them could muster. Alice sat cross-legged inside the mosquito net while he lay behind her on the bed. She said, 'I have fifteen bites.'

'Fifteen?'

She said, 'Active bites. I have five fading. I can, you know, sense them. I find each one, with my eyes closed. I find it, and then I breathe slowly, letting it go. Letting the itch go.'

There was silence.

'And how is that working out for you?'

'I thought you'd never ask,' she said. And then, 'How was the road?'

'Good. Fine.'

'And what did you see?'

'You know.'

'Did you have some meetings?'

'I did.'

'And were these meetings held under a convenient tree?'

'They were,' he said.

He asked her did she ever, when she was a child, break the top off a fuchsia and suck the nectar out, just where the skirts of the flower began.

'Oh dear me,' she said. 'I don't think so. No.'

He noticed the bowl again, when they went out that evening. This time it was inside the house, on the hall floor. He was going to mention it to Ibrahim but it was a Thursday and Ibrahim was anxious to be gone. He let the driver go too. Emmet could not get back into the Land Cruiser, he was tired of Hassan driving like a bastard, shaving past some old woman so the pot wobbled on her head. So many women unkilled by so many white four-wheel-drives in the various countries where he had been driven by men like Hassan, a little more crazy, or less.

'Mind the pot!'

Thousands of miles on dust roads, and gravel roads, and potholed tarmac: roads that turned into rivers, or forest, or crowded marketplaces; roads you drove beside because the road was so bad.

Total kill, he told Alice, as they walked along the river, one goat, a few chickens, something that flew like a pheasant and shattered the windscreen in Bangladesh, and many small bumps that felt, when you thought about it, a bit soft. The biggest was a tiny antelope in the Sudan, suspended mid leap for an endless moment in front of them, before a rear hoof caught the bonnet, and it was upended under their front fender.

'Bam! Back broken.'

They were walking over to a party, slapping themselves idly, or waving the mosquitoes away with a bit of palm leaf.

'Oh no,' she said.

'Somebody got dinner,' he said.

'For sure.'

He didn't mention the small child in Mozambique, who cracked off the side of the car, sailed in an arc, and seemed to bounce off the ground, he was up so fast and running – also smiling – the little bag of peanuts he was trying to sell still held high. Bit of a limp. They wanted to stop, but the driver threw some coins out the window and put the foot down. And:

'No, no!' said the nice aid workers. 'Stop the car!'

'So what was it like?' said Alice.

'What?'

'The Sudan.'

People always wanted to know about the Sudan.

Two thousand people sucking water from the same patch of mud. Thirty water pumps stuck at the airport, and every piece of paper shuffled and lost by the bastards in Khartoum. What did she want to hear?

'There was a lot of paperwork,' he said.

He wanted to tell her that starvation does not smell sweet, the way death smells sweet. There's a chemical edge to it, like walking past the hairdresser's at home.

Alice took his arm in the silence.

The streets were very quiet: a few scooters, the distant sound of trucks coming up from the riverside. Through open doorways, families could be seen, murmuring and eating or sitting against the wall. There was no metal cutlery to bang or clatter, the children did not shout, and no baby was crying, anywhere. From an open window, they heard the pop-pop-popping sound of a paraffin lamp that was newly lit. The woman tending the flame wore a green headscarf, elaborately wrapped, and the light, as it grew, seemed to pull her face out of its own beautiful shadows. Emmet could hear the squeak of the little screw, as they passed.

The party was a desultory thing; with one bottle pretending to be Johnnie Walker and a fetid punch. The next morning they woke to the sound of the muezzin and the relief of a house that was empty of everyone except themselves. They spent the morning catching up on work then packed their togs for an afternoon swim in the tiny pool at the Lebanese hotel. Emmet heated the lunch that Ibrahim had left for them. He was just about to serve up, when he heard Alice open the front door.

'Come on!' she said.

There was a noise on the tiles like a scattering of small beads and Emmet thought something had spilt – her necklace, perhaps, had broken. But when she came into the dining room her necklace was intact, and the small noise continued.

'Lunch,' he said, a little foolishly, with the pot of stew – it was goat – held in both hands. As he set it down on the low table, he saw the dog.

It was the whiteness of the dog that disturbed him first and, after that, the wan look in its good eye.

'Oh Christ,' he said.

'What?'

'Things are bad enough.'

'No they're not. Are they?'

'I mean in Africa. Things are bad enough *in Africa*, without bringing a dog into the house.'

'It's only a dog,' she said.

'Eat your lunch,' he said, ladling the stew on to her plate. But Alice took the plate and scraped half of it into the bowl – which he now realised was the dog's bowl – on the floor. It had been the dog's bowl for some time.

'Eat your lunch,' he said again.

'What are you, my mother?'

Emmet took the pot back out to the kitchen and came back in and sat down and started to eat in what he hoped was a companionable silence. The stew was excellent. The dog liked it, too. Alice said, 'Good boy, Mitch. Good boy.'

The dog ate, then clicked across the tiles to offer its nervous love to Alice, feinting and fawning as her hand found the top of its head.

'Poor guy,' she said. 'There you go.'

A whine of pure emotion escaped the dog as it plonked its chin on Alice's thigh, and looked up into her eyes. Alice ate with one hand, while the other hand scratched under and around its head until the dog collapsed on to the floor and rolled over, paws dangling, back legs agape and her hand worked its way down its ribs and on to the hairless belly.

Every piece of shit in town was stuck to the dog's under-carriage, a fact that did not seem to bother Alice despite the hand-washing campaign she ran for the new mothers of Ségou. Because hand washing – there was no doubt about it – saves lives. On the plus side, Emmet decided, the dog did not have rabies. And if he did, Emmet was up to date on his shots.

He said: 'You know, Ibrahim has first dibs on the left-overs. Usually.'

Alice paused and then scratched on.

'Poor Mitch,' she said.

He said, 'It's just a pain, when they start to pilfer. The staff.'

She looked up. 'Ib is stealing stuff?'

'That's not what I said. No.'

But she was back to cooing at the dog. And Emmet needed to think, so he just shut up for a while.

They walked over to the hotel. On the last stretch of road, Emmet saw a woman afflicted with tiny lumps. They covered her from head to toe. Even her eyelids were lumpy, even the insides of her ears. Emmet had seen her before, and she always greeted him with the sweet, sad smile of a woman who is happy you have not thrown a stone at her. It was hard to know what the problem was. The lumps were under the skin, so they weren't warts, and there was no sign of infection so you couldn't – even in your own mind – dose her with antibiotics and sleep contented. It was a parasite, perhaps, though not one he had ever encountered. It was a syndrome. An autoimmune thing. It was a biblical plague of boils. It was something genetic, because poverty wasn't enough of a curse, clearly, you had to have your own extra, personal curse, just to make you feel special.

And the street was a medical textbook, suddenly. People with bits missing. The bulge of a tumour about to split the skin. The village idiot was a paranoid schizophrenic. A man with glaucous eyes was sweating out a fever in a beautiful carved chair, his head tipped back against the wall.

Emmet fell into the cool of the hotel foyer.

'Good to see you Mister Emmet,' said Paul the receptionist. 'Ms Alice. Very happy.'

'Yes,' said Emmet. 'Hot enough out there!'

The small pool was so warm, it was like swimming in a bowl of soup. Emmet did a few short lengths, keeping his face dry and clear, then he hauled himself out beside the sun loungers where Alice had set their bags.

He ordered a mojito.

'Local?' said the waiter, meaning the alcohol, and Emmet said, 'Imported.'

Alice looked at him. The drink was obscenely expensive and, when it arrived, full of sugar.

'Mud in your eye,' he said, remembering his manners after the first gulp and lifting the glass.

'Here's to you,' said Alice, who was taking the ice out of her cola with doggy hands, and throwing it in to melt in the pool.

The next morning, Emmet woke into the tender hour before the hangover hit and he sat to meditate for the first time since he had moved in with Alice. He crossed his legs and shifted a cushion under the bones of his backside and sighed his way through each breath. Sadly the air entered him and sadly it left as he counted to three on each inhale, and then to four, and then stopped counting. The town was quietly awake. The drinker's morning dread came to tap him on the shoulder. And then it left. Emmet watched his thoughts, which were all, for the moment, about dying. A man falling out of a Portaloo in Juba, half cooked. The used tissues on his father's bedside. A girl in Cambodia with her ribs showing and her little pubic bones jutting out. Then, after a while, his thoughts were not about dying. He was swimming in Lahinch. He was walking the land in Boolavaun. He remembered the taste of fuchsia, when you suck the nectar out. He remembered the taste of Alice.

Just before sunrise, she opened her eyes.

She said, 'I was dreaming about the river.'

There was a noise downstairs, as Ibrahim opened the front door and their eyes locked. Where was the dog?

Emmet was halfway down the stairs when he remembered letting the creature out of the house before making his way to bed the night before. Which meant that only the watchman knew what company they had kept the previous evening. In which case, everyone knew: Emmet and Alice had a dog.

Sort of.

Dogs are unclean to Muslims, as Alice well knew – she had done that course at college – so she also knew not to bring him inside when the help was around.

Still.

'Look at him,' she had said, when they arrived back from their hotel swim and the dog met them in the yard. Emmet looked. The dog's tail was hooked under a shivering rump, that dabbed low and began to swing.

'Hello! Hello!' said Alice, and her fingers kneaded the loose hide of his neck.

'Look into those eyes,' she said to Emmet, and her own eyes, when she turned her face up to him, were happy. Ardent.

Emmet obliged. He looked at the dog and the dog looked quickly away, then back at him. The red lump was not a cyst, he decided, it was a membrane that had popped out somehow.

'He has an old soul,' said Alice.

Emmet ducked around the corner of the house and retrieved a bottle of Bushmills from its hiding place under the outhouse rafters. Then they went inside – all three of them – and shut the door.

They sat and drank in the living room with the dog curled up on the tiles, snout to the floor: every shift or move they made questioned with a gather of its white brows, a forward twitch of the ears.

'Bless,' said Alice.

After a while, she said that Ibrahim was not the most devout Muslim you could meet. They had never seen him roll out a mat to pray, for example, and he had been known to take a beer – not in the house, but in a bar by the market. He was also very keen on mobile phones, and on ringtones that sounded like a woman having an orgasm – which was something she just had to pretend she wasn't hearing, really; even so, she volunteered to keep the dog away from rooms where food was eaten or prepared.

Emmet poured another drink.

'I don't know if it is a food thing,' he said.

'You think?'

'So much as a ritual thing? I mean the dog being "unclean". It's not a question of hygiene the way we think of hygiene, in the Western sense.'

'Right.'

'But of, you know, things being sacred, or defiled.'

'Absolutely.'

'Ritual cleanliness is, I think, not so much about what you put into the body, as what comes out of the body. Shit. Semen.'

'All right,' said Alice. She would only bring him inside in the evening, when Ibrahim had gone home.

They sat in silence.

'Are you coming to bed?' she asked after a while and Emmet lifted his drink and looked down into it. He said, 'I think I'll just stay here for a while. With the dog.'

The next morning, he came tearing down the stairs, to find the animal, as he remembered, no longer inside the house, and Ibrahim sublimely indifferent to whatever had gone on, or not gone on, the night before.

On Sunday evening, they sat and worked in the living room listening to the World Service from the BBC, and the dog sat there too. When Alice finished her paperwork, she joined Emmet on the bamboo sofa and they lay against each other, for as long as the heat allowed. It made their relationship feel strangely normal, having a dog in the room.

Alice leaned back from him and rearranged his hair lightly with her fingers. She asked, in a lazy way, about previous girlfriends.

One or two lasted a while, he said. The rest, not so long. 'Though they felt pretty epic at the time.'

'Oh really?'

'Nothing like a quiet upbringing to make you feel the thrill and the shame of it.'

The dog slept on.

'Ah,' she said.

In fact, the dog slept a surprising amount of the time.

'At home, or where?'

Emmet looked at her; her head rolled on to the back of the sofa, the teasing fingertips picking at his hair. He wondered where it came from, this unreachable pain she had, that made her so sweet and wild.

'What?' she said.

'Nothing.'

'What?'

Later, after he had taken the discussion upstairs, so to speak, Alice told him that her mother spent every Easter in hospital. It was just her time of year. It started with the daffodils, she pulled them out of every garden on the road. Alice would come home from school to find the house shouting yellow, and welts on her mother's hands where she had ripped the stalks out of the ground. The neighbours she robbed said nothing. And, for two or three weeks, they had the best time ever. They had so much *fun*. By Easter Sunday, her mother would be sitting in hospital like the bunny who ran out of battery, not able to lift the fag to her mouth, and Alice is facing the next however many weeks looking after things at home.

'What age?' he said.

'Whatever. I could work the washing machine at nine.'

This was why Alice wanted to help people. This was also why she was so much *fun*.

'Well I think you're great,' he said.

'You think?'

'I do,' he said. 'The way you turned it all to the good.'

Alice, lying on her back, began to laugh: a delicious gurgle that Emmet thought might get out of hand, there was so much hurt in it. Then she stopped and said, 'Well, that's all right then, isn't it?'

After a long while she turned in to him like a child, with her two arms out. By the time he could see her eyelashes in the darkness they had settled in sleep.

Emmet lay there, jealous of her repose. The heat was worse at night – there was no shade, because it was all shade. In the dark, the heat was the same and everywhere, it was like drowning in your own blood-temperature blood.

He tried to remember the freshness of an April day at home, the cool inside of a chocolate Easter egg.

He remembered Geneva airport, a place where he had, after a tough sixteen months in the Sudan, experienced an overwhelming urge to lie down on the clean, perfumed floor. Shop after shop of leather goods and fluffy toys, chocolate shops and Swatch shops, Cartier, Dior. Emmet went into each one of them, trying to buy something for his mother. He looked at this beautiful obscenity of stuff, bags of fine leather and silver chains that turned out to be made of platinum. He ran fifty silk scarves through his shaking hands, trying to imagine what she might like about each one. He ended up with a box of Swiss chocolates, stuck them in his stinking canvas bag, with the red dirt of the Sudan still rimed along the seams. Through security, up into the overhead bin: his father was too sick by then to meet him at the airport, so he carried them on to the bus and walked them up over the humpy bridge home.

'Oh no!' Rosaleen said, because she was on a diet. 'Oh, no! Chocolates!'

Emmet had more than his mother to forgive, of course. He had a whole planet to forgive for the excesses of Geneva airport. For the frailty of his father. For the shake in his own hands that he thought was giardiasis but turned out to be his life falling apart. His mother had a lot to answer for, but not this.

Emmet was sitting on the side of the bed now, with his feet dangling below the net. Outside the bedroom door, he heard the soft scritter-scrat of the forgotten dog. Then the sigh of a furred body sliding down the wood. Then silence.

'Here, Mitch!'

Alice had a 'special' voice for the dog that annoyed Emmet no end. She put strings of beads around his neck, and held a biscuit between her lips for him to snaffle with his mouth.

Something about Emmet's tone, meanwhile, just brought out the whipped cur in Mitch. If he lifted his hand, the dog backed away from him in a palsy of hind limbs.

'You're all right. You're all right.'

If he stepped any closer a shrieking yelp would come out of the dog.

'What did you do to him?' said Alice, the first time it happened. 'What did you do?'

It was a tough cycle to break. The more the dog dragged its belly on the floor, the more it tried Emmet's patience and Alice became increasingly suspicious of Emmet, as Mitch trembled against the wall. Sex was off, that much was clear. Love me, love my dog. Emmet ended up courting the creature with biscuits, which he set in a line on the floor. Every evening, the dog came a little closer, until finally he took the biscuit from Emmet's fingers. Then he pushed his narrow skull up under Emmet's hand and whined.

'Bingo,' said Alice.

After a moment's delay, Emmet patted the dog and scratched behind his ears.

'There you go.'

The delay interested him, for being chilly. The delay was nice.

'You can see the temptation,' he said. 'To give him a kick.'

'I'm sorry?' said Alice.

'You know what I mean,' said Emmet. But she really didn't know, and called Mitch to her. 'What's he saying?' she said. 'What is he talking about?'

'Oh for God's sake,' said Emmet.

And Alice looked up at him and said, 'No, actually. No.'

Alice wanted to get antibiotic drops for the dog's eye, but the cyst-thing was weeping clear and Emmet did not think this was the way to go. Besides, the town was not exactly brimming over with antibiotic drops. So she boiled up some saline instead and squirted it from a blunt syringe she took from the maternity clinic and after a week the weeping stopped. Once this happened they saw how sleek the dog was getting. Its baldy, pink hide was filling in with white hair. Its tail uncurled out from between its legs and swung level, sometimes even proud.

It might have been worse. It might have been a child.

Emmet fell in love with a child in Cambodia, his first year out. He spent long nights planning her future, because the feel of her little hand in his drove him pure mad: he thought if he could save this one child, then Cambodia would make sense. These things happen. Love happens. There are things you can do, if you have the foresight and the money, but there isn't that much you can do, and the child is left – he had seen it many times – the aid worker cries on the plane, feeling all that love, and the abandoned child cries on the ground, because they are damaged goods now, and their prospects worse than they might have been before.

Better a dog.

Ibrahim knew, by now. There was no hiding it, though it was unfortunate he discovered the dog's stool before he discovered the dog – a dry enough turd that Mitch had deposited in a small room off the kitchen. Emmet arrived in to find all three of them looking at it, Alice and Ibrahim and Mitch. The watchman, when he thought about it, had been unusually dignified about opening the gate.

'Bonsoir, Monsieur.' Emmet did not even know the guy spoke French.

Ib was not at the door to take his things. At first he thought the house was empty, then he heard Alice's voice and made his way through the kitchen to find them all crouched over the thing.

'How was the office?' said Alice, with a flare of the eyes to tell him that things were under control, and he said, 'Fine.'

Emmet did not look at Ibrahim so much as feel his silence, over dinner. And his silence felt OK. The food was good, the service almost meditative. If he was angry, Emmet could not locate it, even when Alice fed the dog with her hands from her own bowl. After that, the dog slept inside, on a bed of rags pushed up against the living room wall.

'I think they like each other,' she said. She thought there was a genuine connection. Ib, for example, called the dog by name.

'Which is more than you do.'

But it was clear that Alice felt herself humiliated by the scene in the pantry, and by Ibrahim's silken looks in the days that followed. She saw the edge of his contempt, or imagined she saw it, and was ready at all times to take offence. The more careful he was, the worse it got. Water was poured so beautifully, crockery laid with such utter grace and tactfulness, that she thought she would actually give the man a slap.

'He creeps me out,' she said, and 'You never know where he is in the damn house.' She started stripping the sheets off the bed herself, after sex, and leaving them in a clump on the floor.

It was a relief to go down to the capital for a week-long traffic jam, and a bit of compound living with the government boys and the UN boys and the boys from the FAO. Bamako was not exactly Geneva airport, but still it was a shock. Sometimes, Emmet thought he wanted a nice air-conditioned office with Nespresso coffee and Skype on tap, but then he thought a nice air-conditioned office was an open invitation to his nervous breakdown. Emmet and his breakdown spent some quality time together after the Sudan, when his father was dying and Emmet sat about the house waiting for his own meds to work. How long did it take? Three months? Five? One way or another, that whole year was fucked.

He was fine now. Ten years on. He and his breakdown had kept a respectful distance in various steaming, stinking towns from Dhaka to Nampula, though he did not underestimate it, or consider it gone. Lying on the clean sheets of the Bamako Radisson, Emmet felt it in the ducts, like Legionnaires'.

On his last morning, Emmet made contact with a guy who knew a guy in Vétérinaires Sans Frontières and set up a meeting for him in the Radisson bar. The vet turned out to be a woman from Nebraska called Carol with a tough little body and a nice line in clean khakis. She listened to the problem of the dog's eye in rapt silence, then said, 'First off, let's get another drink.' When it arrived, she said, 'OK, let's fix this little guy,' sending Emmet back north with the good news that the dog's cherry eye could be massaged back into place. 'Unless it has insurance, in which case, it's a three-man job under full anaesthetic.' She pushed her fingertips up under her own eye to demonstrate, and then under his, saying, 'Hey, he has urethritis, you get to do this to his dick.' After which, Emmet could not extricate himself until she'd had far too much to drink. But it was worth it, to bring something of value to Alice; sweet, soft-hearted Alice, with her passion for micro finance, and her body of medieval whiteness under the revolving fan.

He also brought a twelve-pack of Andrex toilet paper back with him, three boxes of Twinings tea bags, and a jar of Nutella. He entered the house, laden, and went from room to room until he found her upstairs with Mitch, both of them under the mosquito net, on the bed.

'Well hellooooo,' she said.

Mitch lifted his tail for a surprising wag that pushed out the netting like some vague stump. Then Alice climbed out from under it, and Emmet knew at once that something was wrong.

'Where's Ib?'

The house was too silent, for a start.

'Sick.'

'How sick? How are you? Look! Look what I got!'

'Nutella!'

And Emmet held it high, making her fight for the jar.

Down in the kitchen, he said, 'What's wrong with Ib?'

'He sick.'

'Like what?'

'He siiiick. Went home on Thursday.'

People here were always siiiick, always waving vaguely over bits of themselves. Pain in your back, pain in your head; it amazed Emmet that people who could barely scrape a meal together had time to notice their frozen shoulders or acid reflux, but they really did. They thought everything was about to kill them. And sometimes they were right.

'Did someone come?'

Alice said a boy stuck his head out of the kitchen, without so much as a by your leave, put his hand out for money and said, 'I shopping.'

'And?'

'And he shopped,' she said. 'Whoever he is.'

Later, over a cobbled-together dinner that was just an excuse for a Nutella dessert, she said, 'I went over to see him this afternoon.'

And now Emmet thought there was something really wrong with Ibrahim, she had waited so long to mention it.

'Is he all right?'

'Just the malaria coming back at him.' She had brought over some Malarone and paracetamol, found Ibrahim shaking under six blankets, the sweat pouring out of him and 'everybody in the room', she paused for the right word. 'All the kids and the wife.'

'Scat,' she said. Mitch was mooching for food, and Alice pushed him away. He nuzzled back in and she gave him a proper shove, 'I said, get off!'

Mitch gave Alice a hurt, sidelong look, but she did not apologise. She just watched him slope away.

'Maybe we should turn vegetarian,' she said. 'You think dogs can be vegetarian?'

'What happened?'

'Nothing.'

'Something happened.'

'It's just stupid,' she said. And she tried to swallow the annoying small smile, that happened in her mouth and would not go away.

After she left Ibrahim's she was followed down the track by the usual posse of children and when she tried to wave goodbye, one of them started to make a noise. One of Ibrahim's. A little guy with big solemn eyes. She didn't know what he was doing and then she realised he was barking.

'And then they all did it,' she said. Six, maybe ten, little children all barking at her and rubbing their bellies.

A passing woman started to laugh at the white lady, who could not get free of the barking children. Open derision – like the time she had to crap out in the bush and everyone fell around the place because she got someone else's shit on her foot, and it was like, 'I am here to save your babies' *lives*, you bastards.' Anyway, there was much mockery and pointing from the passers-by, and she backed away from the pack of children like a bad B movie, and then she turned and fled.

'The thing was,' she said, 'I thought they wanted to eat the dog.'

Emmet realised that he was allowed to laugh now.

'I thought they wanted to eat Mitch.'

'I really don't think that was what they wanted,' he said.

'No.'

They wanted to eat the dog's food. Alice had realised, by the time she got home, that Mitch ate more meat than Ibrahim's children got in a week. Which wasn't exactly news. She just hadn't . . .

'Bang the bread,' said Emmet.

'What?'

'Weevils. Bang it.' You could tell that Ibrahim was off sick, the bread was full of moving black dots.

'No such thing as vegetarian bread in this town,' said Emmet. He slammed his hard bit of loaf on to the floor, shouting, 'Die, you bastards!' while Alice picked up hers and peered into it.

'Ew.'

He flung the bread against the wall.

'Out! Out!' while Alice squealed and fumbled her piece on to the table, flapping her hands in alarm.

Emmet got up to retrieve his and was distracted by a gentle sound that became, as he noticed it, dreadful. They both listened, then looked to Mitch, to see a pool forming at the end of one shivering hind leg, the other leg nervously half cocked.

'Oh no,' said Alice.

The pool did not spread so much as swell, until the tension gave and a runnel of piss broke across the floor.

'Mitch! Stop it!'

Alice said, 'Sit down! What are you doing?'

'What am I doing? Look what he's doing.'

'Why are you shouting? He is doing it because you are shouting.' She was shouting, herself, now. 'Why are you like this?'

Mitch was cowering against the wall, eyes locked on Emmet. When Alice moved to comfort him, a last pathetic gout of liquid came out on to the floor.

'Jesus,' said Emmet.

There was nothing for it but to be nice to the dog, which Alice did, and to clean up the piss, which Emmet did, using up many valuable sheets of Andrex two-ply classic white.

After which, they sat back down to finish their dinner.

'Right,' said Emmet.

Mitch lay in a swoon of reconciliation beside Alice, who fed him and stroked him as they ate in silence. After a while, with the slow air of a woman who doesn't even know that she is looking for a fight, Alice said she had decided to give Ibrahim a raise.

'Great,' said Emmet.

'Seriously.'

'Sure. By all means. Let's give Ibrahim money. Lots of money. I have no problem with that.'

'You're just mean,' said Alice.

'Check your guidelines,' he said.

'You are,' said Alice. 'You're a cold bastard.'

They ate on.

'Let me try something,' he said. 'Can I try?'

Emmet petted the dog and said, 'Don't worry, we're not going to eat you, Mitch.' He took the dog's muzzle in both hands and glanced up at Alice. Then he applied a gentle thumb to the dog's bad eye.

Mitch pulled back and scrambled to his feet, but Alice put her arms about the dog's ribcage and held on while Emmet took his head in his hands again and circled his thumb round the eye's inner corner. He pressed the balloon of flesh down into the orbital socket, closing his own eyes, the better to sense the lump beneath the dog's trembling underlid. He could feel it flatten and go, as though the air had been let out of it, and when he released Mitch for a look, the dog blinked, clear and aggrieved. Then he blinked again. Mitch braced his front legs and turned his head from side to side. Then he shook himself, with violent precision, from top to tail. He lolloped off to his rag bed in the corner, where he turned and turned, and lay down. Then he was up again, pouncing on a cushion as if it was a small animal that had moved.

'It might pop out again tomorrow,' said Emmet. 'In which case, we do it again, apparently.'

'Good trick.'

He was a shallow creature, really – just in it for the sex,

Emmet thought, as he looked at Alice's face made hazy by delight.

'Nutella?' he said.

In the middle of December, Alice went home. She left like a schoolgirl, with folders of notes for head office and an implausible, chunky-knit, black and white scarf.

Emmet tried to imagine her wearing something so uncomfortable and hot. He saw her in a kitchen filled with unlikely daffodils; the mad mother, the two brothers 'who never said much'. The colonial house was empty of tat. Alice had brought it all back with her; the mud-cloth hangings, the Dogon masks; it was all sitting in a suitcase on that seventies lino in Newcastle, smelling of camel shit. Emmet went around the stripped-down rooms like a visitor, and did not know where to sit. Ibrahim, too, was more serious now they were alone: dutiful and male, he acted as though they had an understanding. Which they had, sort of. The dog stayed outside, for a start.

He barked every evening. Confined to the space between the house and the wall, he called the sudden sunset, as though doubting the dawn.

On the 24th, Emmet went on the road, leaving instructions that Mitch should be fed in his absence, though he did not expect him to be fed much. He topped up the bowl before he left. And it was something, when he came back after a week, to be welcomed with doggy joy; a little dashing about.

'Hiya! Hiya!'

Though, when he looked into the dog's clear eyes and the dog looked into his, they were both thinking of Alice.

'Back soon, boyo. She'll be back soon.'

In the middle of January, she rang from Bamako. Emmet went out to buy beer and soap, and brought Mitch back inside.

'Don't tell, eh?' It had only been a month, but the dog seemed confused. He walked from one place to another as though he did not recognise the rooms. Then he went back to the front door, and scratched to be let out. When Emmet opened the door, he sicked up on the front step.

'Shit,' said Emmet. He tried to tempt him in with a biscuit, but Mitch did not seem interested in biscuits and Emmet had to pull him inside, finally, to his rag bed. He called to Ibrahim.

'Monsieur Emmet, sir?'

They looked at the dog, who was panting where he lay. Every breath was a rasp in his throat.

'He sick,' said Ibrahim.

'Yes.'

They stood for a moment.

Emmet said, 'You know, Ib, I never gave you your Christmas box.' Then he palmed the guy ten bucks and left it at that.

By the time Alice got in that evening, the dog was bleeding from the nose. This she discovered when he left a trail across her cargo pants and her homecoming turned, on the instant, from gladness to disaster. She was barely in the door.

Mitch was bleeding from somewhere and heaving with unidentifiable pain. Alice felt around his belly, which was swollen and, as he nuzzled under her palm, he cried, like a baby gone wrong. Alice, still in her blood-smeared travelling clothes, sat beside him and lifted his head on to her lap. Ibrahim came in with newspaper and old cloths, and left quietly for home.

'Did somebody hit him?' she said. 'He must have been hit by a motorbike. Or a car.' But Emmet said – and he was pretty sure it was true – that the dog had not been beyond the gate. Alice was deep in panic. She sat beside Mitch, who cried for another while and then slept. He barked in his dreams, and that strange, uncompleted sound was like crying too. There was more blood.

Emmet tried Carol, the vet from Nebraska, but her African SIM made funny noises and the Bamako office was, naturally, closed.

'Did you get her?' said Alice.

'I think she's gone back home.'

'Let's see,' she said, gesturing for the vet's business card, stained (though Alice was not to know this) with Jack Daniel's.

'What time is it in America?' she said, pushing the numbers into her little slab phone and Emmet was so angry, suddenly, he had to turn away.

An hour later, as though continuing where they had left off, Alice suddenly said, 'What are you even here for?'

He said, 'Come to bed.'

'I mean, if you don't believe in anything? Really. What are you doing here?'

He did not remind her that he was the one who fixed the dog's bad eye; that, although he did not love the dog, he had helped the dog. He said, 'Come on.'

And she dragged herself upstairs for an hour or two, rummaging in her bag first to find her little box alarm.

Emmet watched Alice in her sleep, the imperceptible rise and fall of her breast, the slopes of her body under the white sheet. Downstairs the dog gave a peculiar brief whistle on the top of each inhale and Alice looked indifferent to it, almost happy. Emmet thought about work. His next trip would take him out beyond the Bandiagara escarpment – one hundred and fifty kilometres of cliff, stuck with mud houses like the nests of swifts. Mankind, living in the crevices. Sometimes Emmet thought it was the landscape he loved, the way it stretched as you travelled through it and the hills unfolded. The pleasure of the mountain gap.

When he woke, Alice was back at her post downstairs, sitting against the wall beside Mitch. There was blood on the floor, in a mess of brushstrokes from his muzzle. He was almost still.

When he heard Emmet, the dog opened his eyes and looked for Alice's eyes, and she bent down, offering her face to lick, encouraging his pale tongue to find her chin and mouth. The dog's teeth were very dark, the gums almost white. She let the dog's head gently down on the floor and tilted her own head sadly back against the wall. Mitch coughed. The blood that came out was scarlet, and it spattered her pale forearm. Alice looked down at herself, indifferent.

'I'll make some tea,' said Emmet.

He went outside to the privy and looked up at the fading stars, while he stood to pee. The licking was fine. You can't get TB from a dog and anyway, the dog did not have TB. It was the blood on her arm that disturbed him, and the dog's dark teeth. Some feeling he could not identify. And then he did.

It happened just as he finished pissing, whatever that did to you. A darkness pouring down his spine. He had to turn and sit on the toilet, so as not to fall. Emmet's elbows were on his knees and his hands were out in front of him, and there it was. The forgotten thing, indelibly back. A dog in Cambodia, with a woman's arm in its mouth.

It was up near the Thai border, his first year out. The area was full of minefields and the medics did fifteen, twenty amputations a day. They threw the remains in a heap outside the hospital tent and, if she had a moment, one of the nurses shot at the scavenger dogs. They put pit teams together, but there were latrines to be dug, and the dogs were not fatal, the way diarrhoea is fatal. So it was hard to believe, but it became true, that for a fortnight at least their only defence against this desecration was a crack-shot nurse called Lisbette from the Auvergne, who took a pistol with her when she stepped outside for a fag.

Then, very quickly, it became ordinary. Not pleasant, of course. Just normal. A dog with a human arm in its mouth.

Now, sitting like a fool on a toilet in West Africa, it wasn't normal any more.

Emmet braced his hands against the breeze-block walls, listening to his body, thinking, *This is how you die.*

When he finally got out of there, a wreath of dawn bites around each ankle, Alice was still in her place by the bottom of the stairs. Blood was coming out of the dog's back end now, and he was nearly dead. She didn't ask about her cup of tea. She just cried and cried.

Ibrahim let himself in to the house just as the sun came up. He paused at the bloody scene in the dining room then ducked into the kitchen. There was silence. Emmet imagined him in there, steadying himself against the sink.

'It's going to get hot, Alice.'

Alice gave a tiny answer, that sounded like 'Yes'. She stirred herself and picked vaguely at the cloth of her trousers, where the blood had dried.

'Have a shower.'

He took her hand and pulled her to her feet. She trailed upstairs and Emmet went to the kitchen where Ibrahim was standing stock still, holding his bag, ready for the market.

'All right, Ib?'

'I pain,' said Ibrahim.

'Have you? Little one?'

'Yes. Little bit sick.'

'Right. Well off you go. Don't worry about the dog, Ib. I'll sort that. N'inquiètes-pas du chien.'

'Non, Monsieur. Merci, Monsieur.'

When he was gone, Emmet texted Hassan. He stood listening to the light, erratic footfalls in the bedroom above and looked at the dog's little teeth, exposed in the snarl of death.

'Oh man,' said Hassan when he walked in. 'So dirty this thing. Blood. Dead fucking dog. I can't touch this thing, man, or I spew. You know? For this I spend three weeks in hell.'

'Come on, Hassan my friend. Come on.'

'It's like you ask me to dirty my soul. I love you Emmet, but no way I can do that disgusting thing.'

'How much?'

'How much, my soul? OK. OK. Put him in something. OK. I'll come back.'

And in surprisingly short order, he did. He brought a small, stocky-looking 'Christian man', who helped Emmet roll the dog into a square of hessian then shouldered the body so that the white plume of Mitch's tail was hanging down his back. They were just about set when Alice appeared at the top of the stairs.

'Where are you taking him?' she said.

Emmet looked at her.

'Can you clean that up?' he said, pointing at the blood on the floor, but Alice did not even pretend to hear.

'Bury him,' she said. 'I want him properly buried.' She looked very proud, standing there.

'Yes, Madame,' said Hassan.

Outside the door, Emmet said, 'Don't throw it in the fucking river, Hassan. People drink that stuff.'

He had his roll out. Hassan said, 'Three bucks.'

'Three?'

'No commission.'

He fumbled out the notes, and they left, the Tuareg opening the gate with great ceremony. But instead of going to the Land Cruiser to put the dog in the boot, the 'Christian man' walked away from them, without a word, down towards the market and the river.

Emmet watched him go.

'Give me half an hour,' he said to Hassan.

Hassan let a big laugh out of him. 'I love you, my man,' he said. 'I'll kiss you when you're clean.'

That night Alice said it was Ibrahim who had poisoned Mitch.

'Rat poison. He gave him rat poison. He had internal bleeding. That was how he died.'

'Ib's a good guy.'

'Is he?'

'Yes, he is.'

'So I am supposed to live with this man. I am supposed to eat his food?'

'Yes. Yes you are. Yes.'

She started to weep.

Emmet had a fair idea, by now, who had poisoned the dog, but he wasn't about to get a different man fired. He said, 'Can we draw a line under this one?'

'Draw a line?'

Emmet steadied himself.

'Alice,' he said. 'It's only a dog.'

And that, he knew, was the end of them.

After sex that night, she lifted one short white leg and looked at it in the dim light, turning her foot this way and then the other. Stefan, the Swedish guy, said she had an 'old-fashioned body', which she thought just meant 'fat', but then he said she wasn't fat, she was just 'pre-war'. What about Emmet, did he think she was fat?

'Certainly not,' said Emmet.

'I saw him down in Bam,' she said.

'Oh yeah?'

'Yeah,' she said.

Within a week, she had stopped speaking much, and there was nothing else for it – late one night, Emmet said, 'I love you, Alice. I think I am in love with you.'

She paused where she was, and then walked on.

The next evening, which was Thursday, she had too much to drink and said, 'You always leave it too late, don't you? You wait until it's all over and then you say you're only starting. And then it's like, Oh but I love you, and why are women so mean to me, and why can I never settle down?'

Emmet said nothing.

He was wrapping things up anyway. Alice, too, would be moving on. So there was no reason to hate her the way he seemed to hate her now. He wanted to yell at her. Hit her, maybe. He wanted to tell her to go home and rescue some fucking gerbils, because she was about as much use as a chocolate teapot, she would end up killing more people than she ever helped. And it was all very well, he wanted to say, it was all very nice *as a feeling*, but love was no use, at the end of the day, to man or beast, when there was no fucking justice in the world.

He also wanted to tell her that she was lovely and eternally right and that he, Emmet, was a failure as a human being.

'I'm sorry,' he said.

She was gone when he got back. There was money on the desk, for rent, which made Emmet sad, and a note on the bed he really did not want to read. Alice had the kind of handwriting that put little circles over the i's, and sticky-out puppy tongues where the full stop should be. Alice's handwriting made him feel like a child-molester. The note was a single sheet of paper, inside which she had written the verse everyone quotes, by Rumi:

Out beyond ideas of wrongdoing
and rightdoing there is a field.
I'll meet you there.

Emmet did not take a shower. He shoved the hat back on his head and went downstairs, calling, 'I'll be back late,' and Ibrahim, who had not emerged from the kitchen since he had arrived, called back, 'OK, Monsieur Emmet. *Bonsoir!*'

The Tuareg at the gate was wearing a new cloth of indigo blue, freshly dyed; for a wedding, perhaps. Original blue. The veil across the bottom of his face had stained the man's cheeks – what Emmet could see of them – with years of dye. It occurred to Emmet that the Tuaregs came and went, that there might have been many different men at his gate, and this was why he never knew which one he was talking to and which one had poisoned the fucking dog.

Poor Mitch. Poor bastard.

Emmet went to a shebeen on the side of the marketplace and cracked a beer, watching out for the mad, sweaty guy on his left, nodding at the young lads drinking cola at the low table, and then turning, with the heels of his boots hooked on to the cross-bar of the stool, to watch the world go by.

It was all as it should be. The market was a sea of tat that nobody seemed to buy, and the vegetables were laid out on decorative cloths, like handmade things.

After a while, the bumpy woman came by; the one who was covered in tiny lumps, from the top of her head to the underside of her heels. She turned, as she passed, to level at Emmet a smile of great sweetness and sympathy. Emmet gave her a wan smile back and she continued on, gravely smooth, as though there was a pot balanced on her head.

Rosaleen

Ardeevin
2005

IN NOVEMBER OF 2005 Rosaleen decided to do her Christmas cards, which were few enough, and most of them local. Not, she thought, that she would be getting many back this year, as people died off, or their habits died off, through forgetfulness or the neglect of their families who would not think to go down to the post office and buy them a book of stamps.

The cards were small and square shaped with 'Merry Christmas' written in copperplate writing across the top. All of them were the same design: a block of red, and on it a brown dune, with little camels and kings drawn on the sand in black ink. Above them was the Christmas star, long – like a crucifix with added rays bursting out from the crux of it. The light of the star was made with the white of the paper itself. The printer just left a gap.

The cards were very simple but they were good cards. The red was very satisfying; not so much a sky as a background, like something you would see in a Matisse. Vermilion. Rosaleen closed her eyes in pleasure at a word she had not expected and at the memory of Matisse: a red room with a woman sitting in it, from a postcard or a library book, perhaps. Years since she had given it a thought, and there the woman still sat in her head, waiting to surprise her for never having left. Waiting for her moment, which was an ordinary moment – half past four on a Thursday in November, the sun about to set, sinking towards New York and, below New York as the world turned, all of America.

Straight across the ocean.

'As the crow flies,' said Rosaleen, only to hear an embarrassment of silence around her. The radio dead. Not even a cat, curled up in the chair.

'Oh, little Corca Baiscinn,' she said, also out loud, and looked to the darkening window where her reflection was beginning to shadow the pane. Or someone's shadow. An image thin and insubstantial, like something that happened in the camera once, her dog superimposed on the view of St Peter's Square, after her mother died, when they went to Rome. And the dog, who missed them terribly, came through the photographs, running towards them on the green road beyond Boolavaun.

Rosaleen looked to the window and stood to her full height.

'Oh, little Corca Baiscinn, the wild, the bleak, the fair!
Oh, little stony pastures, whose flowers are sweet, if rare!'

Her voice worked perfectly. Rosaleen set the cards on the table and sat down to write.

The kitchen was the easiest room in the house, with the heat of the range and two windows, one facing south and the other west. But it was November, and there were days when she filled a hot water bottle just to make it down the hall. Outside, she had a winter flowering cherry set against the silhouetted winter branches, but it would not bloom for many weeks yet. Meanwhile, she had no evergreens, for being too depressing, and every November she thought about a blue spruce, or those needle-thin Italian pines, and every November she decided against. It was an Irish garden. A broadleaf garden, except for the monkey puzzle at the front of the house. Straggly now – there were dead and half dead branches for fifty feet or more, but it was her father's tree and nothing gave her more pleasure. The monkey puzzle was allowed, as Dan used to say.

'That's allowed.'

Ah. But was talking aloud *allowed*?

Rosaleen smiled. She picked up one of the cards and saw it again through Dan's eyes. Because it was Dan – of course it was – who sent the postcard of the woman in the red room. It had lived on the fridge door for years. Dan, she thought, would like the little red Christmas card, that made no claims, that was innocent and tasteful enough. For an utterly pretentious boy, he was very set against pretension. Much fuss to make things simple. That was his style.

And it was also her style. Rosaleen opened the card to check. 'Beannachtaí na Nollag' the greeting said, in Irish, which was all lovely and just right for an American mantelpiece, whatever his mantel looked like these days. Granite, perhaps. Or none, the fireplace a simple square cut in a white wall. Rosaleen set the card flat and lifted her pen with a flourish – a special gel pen she had bought in the new supermarket.

'My darling Dan,' she wrote, and then she paused and looked up.

After a moment she saw what her eyes lingered upon: a shelf for the radio and for bills, and above that, a clock stopped these five years or more, the face sticky with cooking grease. The wall itself was a dusty rose, a colour which was unremarkable most of the day and then wonderful and blushing as the sun set. Like living in a shell. Under that was the 1970s terracotta, Tuscan Earth it was called, up on a chair herself, coat after coat of it, to cover the wallpaper beneath, fierce yellow repeats of geometric flowers that kept breaking through. And under the wallpaper? She could not recall. The whole place should be stripped and done properly or – better yet – the wall turned to glass, dissolved: it would be a kind of rapture, the house assumed into heaven. Like who? Our Lady of Loreto, of course. Her house flying through blue Italian skies. The patron saint of air hostesses everywhere. Because Everywhere is the place that air hostesses like to be.

There was nothing that lifted Rosaleen's heart like the sight of a plane in the summer sky.

She looked down at the white paper on the table in front of her, and the writing on it – her own writing. 'My darling Dan'.

Dan would love a glass wall at the back of the house. Dan would strip back the old paper, he would paint the place 'winter lichen' or 'mushroom'. When he worked in a gallery they painted the place every six weeks he said. He would get professionals in to do it, so the lines would be true.

Rosaleen picked the paper up and turned it over again. It was his Christmas card and he would like it. Dan liked simple things. He would be over forty now. He would be forty-four in August. Her son was forty-three years old.

Rosaleen tried to think what he might look like, this very minute, or how he looked the last time he made the trip home, but all she could remember was his smooth eight-year-old cheek against her cheek. Her blessed boy. He was so happy up against her, never pulled away. And he smelt of nothing, not even himself. Leaves, maybe. Rust. Boys were easy, she always thought. Boys gave you no trouble.

'I think of you often,' she wrote. 'And just as often I smile.'

They were another planet. Surrounded by their own sense of themselves; their faces englobed, she thought, in their boyhood beauty. They wore their maleness as a gift.

What did you do today? *Nothing.* Where did you go? *Nowhere.* Though that was more Emmet's style. Dan told you everything except the thing you needed to know. The schoolmaster's shoes with the secretly stacked heels, the local woman gone up to Dublin to be in the audience for *The Late Late Show.* Dan was a master of irrelevance.

'I miss your old chat,' she wrote.

Dan's eyes, Emmet's eyes, as they looked at their mother, playful and impenetrable. Two sets of green, flecked with black. Stones under bright water.

She could still see them asleep, each in their beds as she passed their bedroom doors. Emmet under a hundred blankets. Dan sprawled, agape, a kind of push in him, even then, as though dreaming impossibilities. He slept like a shout. And as soon as he got the chance, he was gone.

The whole night long we dream of you, and waking think we're there, –

She indulged herself a moment, pictured him sitting across the room from her, with a newspaper, perhaps, a cup of tea. It gave her a pang, just to catch the edge of it. An imagined life. Dan and herself somehow together in this house with their books and their music. The old style.

Vain dream and foolish waking, we never shall see Clare.

The world she grew up in was so different it was hard to believe she was ever in it. But she was in it, once. And she was here now.

Rosaleen Considine, six years old, seventy-six years old.

Some days, it wasn't easy to join the dots.

She had not redecorated the bedrooms, upstairs. They were still the same. The same quilt on Dan's bed. It was there now, if she cared to go up and look at it. The side lamp he found all by himself down in the local hardware, coming home excited, at what age? Eleven. Excited by a lamp. A print by Modigliani of a naked girl leaning on to her hand. And, in Emmet's room, a big map of the world, the countries pink, green, orange and lilac. Yugoslavia. USSR. Rhodesia. Burma. When they grew up, Dan went everywhere, and Emmet, she liked to say, went everywhere else. But Dan always sent a message home.

'All my love,' she wrote. And then looked at what she had written. She underlined the word 'All' with a strong stroke of the pen: once, twice, a little wiggling tail on this second line, trailing down the page.

'Your fond and foolish Mother, Rosaleen.'

The card went into its envelope. She tucked the flap in, turned it, pristine, and smoothed it down before writing 'Mr Dan Madigan' on the other side. Then she propped the envelope up against the little stainless steel teapot. His address was on a piece of paper in the drawer. Toronto. That was where he was. Or Tucson. One or the other. She did not know how he lived, but there were always rich people around him. At least that was the impression he liked to give. That he was thriving in some way that was beyond her understanding.

Which, indeed, it was.

'Oh rough the rude Atlantic.'

Rosaleen spoke the poem a little out loud as she fumbled about in the drawer full of old papers, and what did she come across, only the postcard of the woman in the red room. The woman was dressed in black, and her face was carefully inclined over a stand of fruit that she set on the red table, and you could tell by the tilt of her head that she thought the fruit was beautiful. A widow, perhaps, or a housekeeper. The pattern on the tablecloth moved up on to the wall behind her and it was both antique and wild. Rosaleen turned the card over and there was Dan's grown-up writing: 'Hi from The Hermitage, where the security guards all look like Boris Karloff and are ruder than you can imagine. Love! Danny.'

Did he come home that time? There were trips when he flew right over the house, or might have done, and did not set foot on Irish soil.

A silver dot in the summer sky, her own flesh and blood inside it. Dan opening a magazine, or glancing out the window perhaps, while she caught at the gatepost to steady herself and squint skyward, 20,000 feet below.

Rosaleen had to close her eyes, briefly, at the thought of it. She put the postcard back in the drawer and tried to swallow, but her throat seemed to resist it and she was sitting back at the table when she realised she had not found Dan's address, after all – Constance would have to sort it out for her. The next card was open in her hand. Rosaleen looked at the whiteness of it, that gave her no clue as to what to say.

'My dear Emmet.'

Something was wrong. Perhaps it was the card. She turned the thing over to check the back and it was as she had suspected – the charity was one that Emmet did not like, or probably did not like – not because they fed the starving of Africa, but because they fed the starving in the wrong way. Or because feeding the starving was the wrong thing to do with them, these days. Rosaleen could not remember the particular argument – she did not care to remember it. All Emmet's arguments were one long argument. Those babies, that you saw on the TV, the women with long and empty breasts, their eyes empty to match, and Emmet's own eyes full of fury. Not passion – Rosaleen would not call it passion. A kind of coldness there, like it was all her fault.

Which, of all the wrongs in the world, were her fault, Rosaleen would not venture to say, but she thought that famine in Africa was not one of them, not especially. Not hers more than anyone else's. Rosaleen had not said boo to a goose in twenty years. She didn't get the chance. Her life was one of great harmlessness. She looked to the window, where her face was sharper now on the dark pane. She lived like an enclosed nun.

Her books, the poetry of her youth, Lyric FM. These were the scraps that sustained her. Mass every morning – and Rosaleen had no interest in Mass – for the chance of company; each parishioner more decrepit than the next and Mrs Prunty, this last twelve months, smelling of wee. If she'd had the choice, Rosaleen would have been a Protestant, but she didn't have the choice. So this is what she was reduced to. Resisting bingo on a Saturday night. Waiting for the tiny bursts of pink on her winter flowering cherry. Deciding against yew and spruce, one more time, for the last time. And yet it seemed every child she reared was ready with one grievance or another. Emmet first in the queue, for telling her she was wrong. No matter what good she tried to do with her widow's mite. Wrong to give it to this charity or to that charity and wrong to give it to fly-blown babies and big-bellied Africans: she'd be better off throwing it in a hedge.

'Happy Christmas. Keep up the good work! Your loving Mother, Rosaleen'.

There would be no problem with his address this year. Emmet was home now – not that this made much difference to her routine. A phone call every week, a visit one Sunday in every month. Emmet was saving the world from a rickety little office in the middle of nowhere, and he had a girlfriend, no less. A drab looking Dutch thing, with good manners and clumpy shoes. She would do well to hang on to him, Rosaleen thought. He was a hard man to pin down.

And, not for the first time, Rosaleen wished her son some ease. The boy with so many facts at his disposal: that politeness edged with contempt, even at four, even at two. *Yes Mama, whatever you say.* The moment he came out of her, he opened his eyes and met her eyes and she felt herself to be, in some way, assessed.

Absurd, she knew. The power of the moment. The first baby she had seen right after birth, his eyes opening, whoosh, in the middle of the purple mess of his face, and those eyes saying, *Oh. It's you.*

What did you do today? *Nothing.* How was school? *Good.*

He had a job in the civil service – a proper job – and he left it in 1993 for the elections in Cambodia, came back with stories of bodies in the paddy fields. And he was thrilled by these stories. Delighted. These dead people were much more interesting, he was at pains to point out, than his mother was, or ever could hope to be. And after Cambodia, Africa, places she had barely heard of. And then, unexpectedly, home.

He sat, for the year his father was dying, in the front room, like his own ghost. Rosaleen would come across him and get a fright at this unkempt man who had arrived one day to live in her house; a chemical tang that lingered after he used the toilet as bad or worse than the smell of chemotherapy from his father. Rosaleen thought he was taking pills of some sort. And one day, after he had cleaned up and made a new start of himself, she saw him at the desk of the old study, and it was her father all over again: the same size – Emmet had wasted to an old-fashioned weight – the same focus, and fury, and clammy sense of sanctity. It was John Considine.

A man she had always adored.

Oh Dada.

Oh, little Corca Baiscinn, Rosaleen in a green silk dress that shushed as she walked, hairband of Christmas red, black patent shoes. Rosaleen in her ringlets on the hearthrug in the good front room, saying her piece for Dada.

> *Oh, little Corca Baiscinn, the wild,*
> *the bleak, the fair!*

Oh, little stony pastures, whose flowers
are sweet, if rare!
Oh, rough the rude Atlantic, the thunderous,
the wide,
Whose kiss is like a soldier's kiss which will
not be denied!
The whole night long we dream of you, and
waking think we're there, –
Vain dream, and foolish waking, we never
shall see Clare.

Where did the time go? It was ten o'clock, and she had not eaten yet. She wasn't even hungry, though it was now fully dark – the only thing between herself and the night was her image on the windowpane. Rosaleen straightened up. The same weight as ever. She walked. Every day she drove out in her little Citroën and she walked. She was the old woman of the roads. But she had legs like Arkle, her husband used to say, by which he meant that she was a thoroughbred. Rosaleen recognised, in her reflection, the good bones of her youth. She never lost it. From a distance, if you keep the hump out of your back, you might be any age at all.

She was doing a Christmas card for Emmet. A man who blamed her for everything, including the death of his own father. Because that is what your babies do, when they grow. They turn around and say it is all your fault. The fact that people die. It is all your fault.

Rosaleen put the card in an envelope, then took it out again to see if she had signed the thing. There it was, in handwriting that was unwavering. 'Your loving Mother, Rosaleen'. Four words that could mean anything at all. She read them over but could not put them together, somehow. She could not put them in a proper line.

She had lost her son to the hunger of others.

She had lost her son to death itself. Because that is where your sons go – they follow their fathers into the valley of the dead, like they are going off to war.

Rosaleen sealed the envelope with a careful, triple lick, lapping the edge of the envelope so as not to get a paper cut on her tongue. She had to pause then to remember who it was for – Emmet always managed to upset her, somehow. She wrote his first name in strong letters on the envelope, and maybe that was enough for now, Constance could finish the rest.

'To Hanna,' the third card was started, before she even had time to consider it. 'Happy Christmas. We will be seeing you, I hope, this year.' She turned the last full stop into a question mark, ' We will be seeing you, I hope, this year?' but that looked too querulous, she thought, and she scribbled the question mark out. Then – of course – the thing was not fit to send.

And it was not ten o'clock, because that clock had been stopped for years, maybe five years. It stopped some time after Dan went. And by Dan she meant Pat, of course, her husband. The clock stopped some time after her own true love Pat Madigan died. It was nice to think he would have fixed it for her, if he had not died but, to be honest, death made very little difference to all that. His mother's house was always tended and tarred, there were boxes of nails and guns full of mastic out at Boolavaun. But nothing of that nature ever got done in Ardeevin unless she begged him. Rosaleen had to nag like a housewife, she had to get down on her knees and wring her hands and even then, it might not happen – a new washer in the toilet cistern, a couple of slates on the roof – she might weep for them to no avail. The trick, of course, was not to want it. If she managed this for a year or more, if she actually, herself, forgot the tile or the slates or the stalled clock then it might get done. Or it might not. By this man she loved more than sunlight or rain. Pat Madigan. A man whose face she watched as he himself watched the weather.

And when the weather was right, off he went, to the land in Boolavaun. The few scrubby fields he had there, the little stony pastures, Rosaleen had planted them with pine trees, since, for the few thousand they brought in a year. Dessie McGrath organised it for her, the man who married Constance. Ugly dark trees in their serried ranks and rows.

Dessie wanted to build out in Boolavaun. He had an idea for a half-acre at the end of the long meadow, on the rise that looked out to sea. The sea view was everything these days, he said. The home place didn't have one, of course, it was in a dip with its back to the cold Atlantic. Surrounded, these days, by the dark timber, it looked like a shed in comparison with the other places out that way. Popcorn houses, Rosaleen called them, because they went – pop, pop, pop – to twice the size they had been the week before. Pop! a second storey and Pop! some dormer windows and Piff! the outhouse turned into a conservatory: rooms painted Dulux peach, and, under the glass roof, a couple of dead pot plants from the supermarket, together with some cheap wicker chairs. Rosaleen knew well what Dessie McGrath had in mind with a half an acre of the long meadow, and he could whistle for it. Or he could wait for it. He could have it when she was gone. Because that is what they were waiting for. They were all waiting for Rosaleen to be dead.

'Oh oh oh,' she cried, and she hit her weak old fist on to the tabletop.

It was not ten o'clock. Rosaleen had no idea what the proper time was and the card on the table was spoilt. They were all gone from her, there was no one to help. 'We will be seeing you, I hope, this year? ' Typical of Hanna to make her mar the thing, she was always an accident-on-purpose sort of child. Hanna lived in mess, her life was festooned in it; her side of the bedroom was like a dirty protest, Constance said once, and she was right. The girl was a constant turbulence, she was always weeping and storming off. Constance said maybe it was pre-menstrual but Rosaleen said that child was pre-menstrual her entire life, she was pre-menstrual from the day she was born. Hanna Madigan, who seemed to require a surname at all times, because she would not do a single thing she was told.

Get in here, at once, Hanna Madigan.

No she would not start a new card for her, she had not the energy. What time was it anyway? Rosaleen looked to the clock and then to the darkness outside. She was not even hungry. Her whole life on a diet and now there was no need.

Rosaleen caught the sound of mischief upstairs and looked to the ceiling. But there were no children up there any more, she had chased them all away.

'To Dessie and Constance, Donal, Rory and.'

Rory was her pet. The clearness of him. She would remember the little girl's name in a minute. A little strap of a thing, with blotched red cheeks and orange, tinker's hair. Rosaleen had no problem remembering the child's name, but her heart failed her suddenly. Something was wrong. She felt a shadow fall through her – her blood pressure, perhaps – some shift in her internal weather.

'Oh,' she said again, and slapped her hand on to the tabletop, then she checked the tremor, silenced by the blow. As soon as she moved, it started again. There were days she would shake the milk out of the jug. She knew a man called Delahanty, who was fine except for a little trouble with the buttons on his shirt. Less and less he was able to do them, and one day not at all. And that was how the Parkinson's came to him, he said. The buttons were the sign.

Rosaleen left her hand palm down on the tabletop, where it buzzed a little and came to rest. Something was wrong. The turf subsided behind the metal door of the range in a sigh of ash and Rosaleen would get up to put more turf on, if she only knew what time it was. She could go to bed, but the hall was cold and the electric blanket was on a timer. Her grandson, Rory, had set it up for her. If she went upstairs, it might be toasty. Or it might not be turned on, not for hours yet.

The hall was painted autumn yellow, and under the yellow was wallpaper, with little posies of flowers, their leaves in gilt. If she opened the door she would see it now.

But she could not open the door. Because who knew what was on the other side?

Rosaleen felt the same swooping feeling and her feet were numb, somehow, under the table. She pulled a comic, small face at her reflection in the window – if her feet were dead, then surely the rest of her could not be far behind – but it was a mistake to make a joke of it and Rosaleen lost all control as she lunged for the phone. She dropped it on the tabletop, then she picked it up again and stabbed the fast-dial with her thumb, and held it to her ear, listening to the clatter of her heart. The phone at the other end started to ring, but no one answered. Rosaleen could hear it ringing, not just in her ear, but also nearby, somehow. It was real. The thing she had imagined was really happening. It was out in the hall.

Constance was coming in the front door. The ringing stopped.

'Hello!' Rosaleen said – into her handset or into the hall, she didn't know which.

156

Was that it? Was that the thing that was bothering her? The wrong thing?

'Hello!'

She had expected Constance, maybe, and Constance had not come. Constance was late.

'Mammy?'

Where she got the 'Mammy' from, Rosaleen did not know. When her children grew out of 'Mama', they had failed to grow into anything else.

'Call me Rosaleen,' she used to say. Until she realised that no one ever did, or would.

'In the kitchen!' she called.

Her grandchildren called her 'Gran', a word which made her skin crawl. And they called Constance 'Mum', which was worse, for being British as well as whiny: 'Mu-um.'

O my Dark Rosaleen!
Do not sigh, do not weep!

'Mammy! How are you?'

Constance was in through the kitchen door now, all girth and bustle. She had a couple of plastic bags she put down on the table. Even her bags were loud.

'I hope they're not for me,' said Rosaleen.

'Just a few bits,' said Constance. 'I was in Ennis.'

'Was that you on the phone?' said Rosaleen.

'Me?' Constance gave her a sharp look.

'What time is it anyway?' said Rosaleen, who could not keep the anger out of her voice, or the upset. Constance did not answer. She picked up the house phone from the table and made it beep, several times, checking something.

'You got your cards?' she said.

'Oh,' said Rosaleen.

'They're not too plain?'

'Where did you get them?' said Rosaleen.

'I kept the Santa ones for our house,' said Constance

157

who smiled and turned away from her, as though there was someone in the doorway – a child, perhaps – but there was no child there.

'How's my pal?' said Rosaleen.

'He's good,' said Constance. Rosaleen wanted to embrace the child that wasn't in the doorway. She put her hand out to grip the chair.

'How's Rory?'

'Good, good,' said Constance, and then, with a deliberate sigh, 'Actually, Mammy, he's in his room pretending to study, and he's on the internet. Twenty-four hours a day. I can't get him off it.'

'Oh dear.'

'If it's not on the laptop it's the phone. So I take away the phone and you would not believe it. The temper.'

'Rory?' said Rosaleen.

'He's nineteen. I can't be taking away his phone.'

'And could you not.' Rosaleen couldn't think what Constance might do. There was discussion once about his 'credit'.

'Could you not take away his credit?'

Constance looked at her.

'You know, I might,' she said.

'Go and give your granny a hug,' that's what she used to say. And Rory would walk over, very simply, and put his arms around Rosaleen, and lay the side of his head against her heart.

'Listen,' said Constance. 'I won't stay. Are you all right?'

'Of course I am all right.'

'Put the telly on,' said Constance, and she had the remote already in her hand. And on the telly came. 'All right?'

Rosaleen hated the telly. People talked such rubbish.

'For the news,' said Constance.

The sound came on to Angelus bells, and now Rosaleen

heard them outside too, coming from the church. It was six o'clock.

'It's very dark,' she said.

'Oh, November,' said Constance. 'I'll see you tomorrow. You'll come up to Aughavanna tomorrow, for your tea. All right?'

She had opened the door of the kitchen and was already moving through it, and there was the hall beyond her, painted a Georgian turquoise that Rosaleen always considered a mistake. Too acidic. Rosaleen was pulled after her daughter as she turned on the lights, and opened the door to the wine-coloured study, where Rosaleen slept now, because the room was small and easy to heat – an electric radiator, an electric blanket on a timer that only Rory knew how to control, a smoke alarm. And, tucked in under the stairs, a shining, white room with sink and toilet, all tiled and watertight, like the inside of an egg.

The stairs rose up into darkness. Rosaleen did not sleep up there. Not any more.

'See you tomorrow, Mammy,' said Constance, and Rosaleen said, 'You'll have a cup of tea?' hating, immediately, the sound of her voice.

'I won't,' said Constance. 'We'll have tea enough tomorrow.'

She was speaking loudly, as though Rosaleen were deaf.

'Why can't you, sure?' said Rosaleen.

'Mammy,' said Constance with a slight lift of her arms. There it was again, that stupid word.

'*Mammy*,' Rosaleen said. 'Grow up, would you?'

'I'll do my best,' said Constance.

And lose some weight! Rosaleen wanted to say. The woman would be dead before her. But Constance was already on her way down the hall.

It was very ageing – fat. It made her daughter look like an old woman, which was a kind of insult, after all the care that was put into the rearing of her. The coat didn't help. It was like an anorak, almost.

'Have a good night,' said Constance.

'I will,' said Rosaleen.

Mind you, the child always liked to sneak things. Down the side of her bed, a little nest of papers. Crinkle crinkle crinkle in the middle of the night.

'And lose some of that weight!' she said, after the door closed in her face.

Rosaleen waited a moment, listening to the silence, then gave a little two-fisted victory dance. She heard Constance crossing the gravel outside, the bleat of the unlocking car. Even her footsteps were clear.

She might have heard.

No matter. The woman was her daughter, she could say what she liked.

Rosaleen stood in the hall of acid blue, and listened to the car engine – a purring, expensive sound. She waited for the swirl of gravel, and for the silence after it, then she turned to face back into the house. It was November. The wind was from the south-west, slicing around the landing window, and into the house. Blue Verditer, that was the colour of the hall. Through the far door was the rose-coloured light of the kitchen, and in it, the blare and non-sense of the news.

Wah Wah Wah. The telly was a series of blanks and shouts. The light thrown out by the stupid box, thin and bright. Dim. Bright. Brighter. Gone.

It was all wrong. The wrong-coloured walls. The stairs she never climbed any more, and unimaginable things up there. Unimaginable.

Rosaleen reached for the curling end of the bannisters.

The wood was dark, the smell of the polish she used as a child so real she might catch it on a sharp inhale. A volute. That is the name of the curl. It unspooled and swept upwards to the landing and beyond that to the boys' rooms.

O my Dark Rosaleen,
Do not sigh, do not weep!
The priests are on the ocean green,
They march along the deep.

The abandoned bathroom, with its porcelain like ice. The girls' room. And the big bedroom. Untenably cold.

And Spanish ale shall give you hope,
My own Rosaleen!

And in those rooms: A print by Modigliani of a naked girl leaning on to her hand. A map on the wall of the whole world, as it used to be. And for the girls; a wall papered with posies tied with ribbons of blue. She pulled herself up the stairs, one two.

Shall glad your heart, shall give you hope,
Shall give you health, and help, and hope,
My Dark Rosaleen!

And then she came down again, to stand in the middle of the hall.

The big bedroom was directly above her now, its two windows facing the morning. And in the centre of it – just over her head – the double bed where her father lay dying, and then died. It was the bed where she herself had been conceived, and it was also her marriage bed. Not deflowered. That happened somewhere else. New mattresses of course. The same mahogany headboard, inset with a medallion of rose and cherrywood, the same dark iron frame with strong planks for cross-boards, and in it, all the pomp of her family life: kisses, fevers, broken waters, the damp of their lives, the sap.

The pair of them lying still and awake all night long and

Pat Madigan saying to her, some summer morning when dawn came, 'I don't know what I am doing here.' By which he meant lying alongside her, John Considine's daughter, a woman he had loved with quietness and attention for many years. Also patience, of course. And tenacity. He did not know what he was doing in this place – what he had been doing – if he had not wasted his life on her. He might have been with a different woman. A better woman. He might have been more himself.

Pat Madigan always knew who he *was*, of course, or who he *should be*.

Well good for him.

She only brought it up now to forget it. Rosaleen had married beneath her. There was no point fooling herself about that now. It was considered a mistake at the time. But she had flown in the face of public opinion, she had defied them all.

A love match. That was the phrase people used, but Rosaleen thought love had little enough to do with it, that it was an animal thing. Three weeks after her father's death. Not that she was ashamed of it. There were things country men knew that men from the town had no clue about. These young people with their little events below the waist, thinking they were just marvellous. Whatever it was Bill Clinton said about sexual relations, she couldn't agree more, because when they were young and in their beauty, which was considerable, Rosaleen Considine and Pat Madigan went to bed for days. That was what she called sex. Days they spent. It was a lot more than pulling down your zip while you were talking on the phone.

So what do you think of that?

'Hah!'

In defiance of the night, she said it out loud.

'What do you think of that?'

The bed was above her, ready to fall through the plaster, the place where her father died and her mother died, the place that later became her bed with Pat Madigan, when they moved into that room, and a kind of curse in it for the next while: no child conceived there except a few miscarried things, until Emmet was finally started and then Hanna. The bed where Pat Madigan himself finally died, his body wasted by the cancer until all that was left of him was the scaffolding. But, my goodness, he made a great ruin, for having been so well built, those big hinging bones, the joints getting larger and the cheekbones more proud, as the meat melted back and spirit of the man broke through.

He went on a Tuesday night, and they had the lid down by Wednesday afternoon: Rosaleen made sure of it. Planted on the Thursday in a terrible downpour and not one of the mourners allowed to care that they were soaked through. The days and weeks these people spent talking about the weather. Discussing it. Predicting it. The months and years.

It rained. They got wet.

How terrible.

Her father was buried in August, one hot summer, and of course John Considine was too big a man to be shoved into the earth, like a blown calf. They had to wait for priests and monsignors, not to mention his good friend, the Bishop of Clonfert. But something had gone off in her father, it spread through him in the days before he died, and it kept going off for the three or four days after, as men were summonsed from Dublin and from Liverpool; one couple, whoever they were, arriving, almost festive in their own motor car. Various nuns sat vigil by the coffin in the front room and one of them stroking her father's forehead as she talked to Rosaleen. Vigorously. Gazing at his dead face. Stroking it. Pushing it.

'Ah God love him,' she said. 'Ah, the crathur. Ah the poor man.'

Brushing his hair back, over and over. The smell of incense, of roses and lavender brought in from the garden, honeysuckle soap on Rosaleen's hands, and her father's nose, as the days passed, rising higher away from his own face, as though in disdain. Rosaleen thought the stroking nun was mad in the head. And she thought her own virginity was going off inside her, that her womb would rot, she had left it so long, turning one or other suitor down for reasons that were always clear at the time. A brace of young men, or wealthy men, standing in the room where her father lay now, adjusting their ties. She was much courted, John Considine's daughter. And in the end, she gave it away to Pat Madigan in a hayrick in Boolavaun; her body, later that night, alive and tormented by tiny prickles and welts because, Pat said, the hay was new to her skin.

Forty acres of rock and bog. That is what she got. And Pat Madigan.

The door to the front room was closed now. Her father's ghost was a cold twist of air turning on the broken hearth. Her father was a moment's anxiety, as she passed the study, *Hush hush! your father's working.* Fellow of the Pharmaceutical Society, Knight of Columbanus, Irishman, scholar, John Considine of Considine's Medical Hall. Rosaleen looked in at her own narrow bed and wondered, not for the first time, whether her father was actually important, or if these men, with their big thoughts about the world, were all equally small.

There was a dishcloth going off in the sink – she could catch the smell of it from the doorway – and the thing they put under the stairs, the new bathroom that looked so shining and so sanitary, was only another drain, really, opening into the house. The kitchen table was laden with grocery bags, the television blattering away. The evening was ahead of her, with maybe a book to pull her through it. Any book would do. She used to read while the place fell apart around her. And she still read. She liked it.

But first she went to the drawer full of papers. The guarantee form, never posted, for the washing machine before last. Old cheque-books, one end thick with accusing stubs, the rest slapping empty. Things to do with tax. Forestry stuff for the land at Boolavaun. She found the woman in the red room and then another postcard from Dan, a thing by Kandinsky with two horsemen against a background that was also red, and something about the stretch of the animals' necks that showed the wildness and difficulty of the journey they were embarked upon.

Rosaleen held it up to the light.

Beauty, in glimpses and flashes, that is what the soul required. That was the drop of water on the tongue.

The evening was just beginning. If she made a cup of tea now, she could have a little sandwich with it; something small to stop her waking in the middle of the night and wandering out into the hall, wondering where she was, though she was never anywhere else but here.

Where else would she be?

But there was something wrong with the house and Rosaleen did not know what it was. It was as though she was wearing someone else's coat, one that was the same as hers – the exact same, down to the make and size – but it wasn't her coat, she could tell it wasn't. It just looked the same.

Rosaleen was living in the wrong house, with the wrong colours on the walls, and no telling any more what the right colour might be, even though she had chosen them herself and liked them and lived with them for years. And where could you put yourself: if you could not feel at home in your own home? If the world turned into a series of lines and shapes, with nothing in the pattern to remind you what it was for.

It was time. She would doze in the chair by the range, tonight, she would not lie down. And in the morning she would walk down the town, over the bridge to the auctioneer's. She could get a price for it, apparently; the days when people were put off by the heating bills were gone. The auctioneer was a McGrath – of course – a brother of Dessie, who married her daughter. He had to wet his lips each time she passed; his mouth went so dry at the sight of her. Well he could have it. Let the McGraths pick over the carcass of the Considines, they could have Ardeevin and the site at Boolavaun, she would move in with Constance, and die in her own time.

They had all left her. They deserved no better.

The gutters falling into the flowerbeds, the dripping taps, the shut-up rooms that she had abandoned, over the years. The pity of it—an old woman.

Rosaleen took up the little stack of Christmas cards. She opened the first one:

My darling Dan,
I think of you often, and just as often I smile. I miss your old chat.
All my love,
Your fond and foolish Mother,

 Rosaleen.

She was an old fool, that much was true. There was no doubt about that.

'And by the way,' she put at the bottom. 'P.S Do, DO come for Christmas this year, it's been so long!!! And I have decided to sell the house.'

Part Two

COMING HOME

2005

Toronto

LUDO SAID HE had to do it, it was the last chance he would get.

'For what?' said Dan.

'To be in the house. To see your mother while she is still your mother,' Ludo said. He paused in his chopping and dicing and looked out at the yard. The snow outside was high to the windowsill, and the flat under-light made everything in the kitchen look drab and momentous. The blue of it took the money out of everything, Dan thought – all Ludo's cosy objects, and his middle-aged skin. The bell peppers on the chopping board, meanwhile, were a more thrilling shade of red.

'She is always my mother,' said Dan.

Which was Ludo's point exactly.

'Well make up your mind.'

'I rejoice in my contradictions,' said Ludo and he lifted the big knife, waving it high.

'Yeah well,' said Dan. 'I am not saying I came out of some other woman, I am just saying it was a long time ago.'

'This is not a lucky way to talk,' said Ludo.

'Lucky?' said Dan, as he opened the fridge, its interior green as a hanging garden with lettuces and leeks, the default champagne in the rack and imported gin in its earthen bottle, keeping cold. Ludo was, among other things, a rich man while Dan, for reasons that were never entirely clear to him, was not rich. Not even slightly.

'What do you mean, lucky?'

'Life is too full of regrets,' said Ludo.

A big-featured man with eyes of serious blue, Ludo favoured pinstriped waistcoats and leather jackets, with buttonhole and umbrella, and his house was full of stuff. This was new for Dan, who had woken up in a lot of beautiful white rooms in his day. A nice brick-colonial in Rosedale, Toronto, it had antique cotton quilts and a rocking chair in the bay window: there were three different kinds of maple in the front yard and behind the up and over garage door was a wide shovel for snow.

Ludo was interested in early American landscapes and Dan was surprised to find he was interested in them too. At least a little. They first met in New York over a sincere view of a river gorge that Dan was offloading for a friend. One thing led to another, of course. When Dan flew up with the piece they ended up in bed again, after which they discussed Ludo's growing collection, as Dan had hoped to do.

Sexually, Ludo was frankly masochistic and this appealed to Dan's chillier side. But you can never do these things twice. Besides, masochists were always boring in the end. Also – perhaps inescapably – in the middle. And Dan was slightly bored with being bored, though he still craved that little jolt of empathetic pain.

So perhaps it was *lucky* that, in Toronto, Ludo was off script; too baggy minded and curious to stay in role. Dan felt his age as he realised this was, in fact, what he had flown up for – for the chat, for Ludo's easy, good company. It did not take them long to hang up the leathers and settle into something else: mostly in Brooklyn, when Ludo was down lawyering in New York, then some skiing near Montreal, a winter break in Harbour Island, until Dan ended up in Toronto for six months because cash was so short, and Ludo so easy. He let out his place in Brooklyn and gave it a go.

Easy like a fox. Ludo handed Dan a credit card for household expenses with a rueful look that must have been useful to him in court. If Dan wanted to fuck him over, he seemed to say, then this would be a good way to do it, too. But Dan did not fuck him over. Or not much. And five years later, there they were, like a pair of sweater queens, sniping at each other about Dan's mother, because 'mother' was one of those words for Ludo, *She's your mother*.

Ludo's mother Raizie was back in Montreal. Eighty-three years old, she was on a kaffeeklatsch circuit with the escaped matrons of Mile End, over in leafy Saint-Laurent, where no one, it seemed, could believe their good luck, or their bad luck, because if their son wasn't buying a country place, he was in the middle of a terrible divorce. The daughters lost weight or they found a lump and one grandchild outshone the next. There were also disasters, of course. Men died. Women got depressed. Sons were seldom gay, it had to be said, but life was good enough for the escaped matrons of Mile End to leave some room even for this sad surprise and they were able to enjoy them both, Ludo and Dan, when they showed up. Dan was not the first man Ludo brought home but, as Raizie said, cupping his face with her dry old hand, 'You are the nicest!' There were no doubts. They went over to Montreal, twice, maybe three times a year, and Ludo came home each time more contented and capacious.

Dan liked to watch Ludo about his mother's house, a big man in a small space, the dinkyness of his hands as he washed her china cups, the unembarrassed way he sat in the old recliner, the way he said, 'Raizie, Raizie,' when she fretted about the past and all the things that could not be put right. It seemed to Dan that Ludo spoke many languages – even his body spoke them – while he, Dan, spoke only one. They went over to his sister's house, and her teenage children gazed at Ludo like they knew he was something belonging to them, but they weren't sure what, exactly. Or not yet.

Meanwhile, he, Dan, had not been home to Ardeevin for three years, maybe five. Donal, Rory and – what was her name? – Shauna – they were different people already. Those boys of piercing purity, with their beautiful country accents if they ever brought themselves to speak, and the mottled blush when they did because their uncle was a queer: no one told them that he was gay, they just figured it out for themselves. In this day and age. And he, Dan, maddened by the shame of it, carried a boner with him all the way back to Dublin and, one time, fucked a guy until he yelped in the washroom on the train.

The ground rushing under them in the crescent-shaped gap at the bottom of the bowl; a thousand flickering railway sleepers and the cold earth of Ireland.

Now that's what I call gay.

No, Dan could not go home. Or if he did go, it was not Dan who walked in the door to them all.

'Well, hello!'

It was someone else. A terrible version of himself. One he really did not admire. He might bring them out to Toronto, but they would not know where to put themselves or what to say. And their wretched mother, Constance, who disbelieved everything he said and did – every single thing. Dan could not eat his lunch without her doubting him.

'Oh my god that is so good.'

'What, the bread?'

Disbelieving the contents of his own mouth.

'Yes the bread, Constance.'

Anything other than 'white' or 'brown' was an affront to Constance. Food itself was an affront. She lived on bad biscuits, because there was no harm in a biscuit, and she had fat in places Dan had never seen before. That time in Brooklyn, she wore a sleeveless top in the heat and the flesh popped out in a globule between breast and armpit, which was a whole new place for Dan. It was like a new breed of arm. And now it was everywhere he looked. Walking down the street. Everywhere.

'I'm sure she's perfectly fine,' said Ludo, getting into bed beside him after dinner of stuffed peppers followed by a pomegranate and apple salad and a long evening talking about the Madigans.

'It's family,' he said.

And of course Ludo would love Constance, with her deliberate stupidity and her supermarket hair. That was not the problem. The problem, Dan realised, was that Constance would not love Ludo, as he loved Ludo. She just couldn't. She would not have the room.

'You have no idea,' said Dan.

'Go!' said Ludo,

'I don't want to go.'

'Stop off in New York on the way.'

Dan did not answer.

He loved Ludo. When did that happen?

Dan liked Ludo. He liked the familiar things they did in bed and he also found Ludo useful. As Ludo found Dan – useful. They made a good couple. Dan could put people together in three or four different towns, he knew how to make things beautiful and easy: everyone upped their game for Dan. So of course Ludo found all this wonderful and *enhancing* – as he liked to say – to be around.

And Ludo loved Dan, of course he did. From the very beginning Ludo had loved him. Totally. Abjectly.

Dear God I love you.

But that was four or five years ago. These days, Dan did not know if Ludo still loved him, or if Ludo was just nice to him all the time. What was the difference? The difference was the yearning he felt for a man who was within arm's reach. The difference lay in the fantasies of death and abandonment that happened in hypnagogic flashes as he turned to sleep by his side. If Ludo got sick, he thought, he would lie the length of his hospital bed, like Ryan O'Neal beside Ali MacGraw. Without him he was nothing. With him, everything. Wherever they were, the smell of Ludo's skin was the smell of home.

This was terrible, of course.

Dan did not believe in romantic love – why should he? – it had never believed in him. After Isabelle, he had pined for various beautiful and unavailable young men, but the word 'love', for Dan, was so much wrapped up in the impossible and the ideal, it was a wrench to apply it to the guy who was sitting up in the bed beside him, reading legal briefs in the nude. The half-moon glasses didn't help.

I love you, he wanted to say, instead of which: 'My fucking family. You have no idea how they go on at me. You have no idea what I have to put up with over there.'

Ludo said that getting insulted was a full-time job. He said he'd love to do it himself, but he didn't have a gap in his schedule, he needed his sleep, he loved his sleep, he did not want to spend the delicious hours of the night lying there, hating.

'It keeps me sharp,' said Dan. 'It gives me flair.'

'You hit forty, my love, these things are no longer attractive,' said Ludo, looking at him over the rim of his glasses. 'After forty, it's give, give, give.'

And the next morning, a FedEx guy called to the door with an envelope that had Dan's name on it, and inside was a ticket for the front of the plane.

Dan put the envelope on the kitchen table and looked at it while he drank his coffee and planned his day. He did not have a whole lot on. Ludo had stuck him in therapy once a week with Scott, a completely blank Canadian guy with a sweet and open smile. Now Dan talked to Scott in his head about being in love with Ludo, the unbearability of it. Scott seemed to indicate that unbearability was a good thing.

'Stay with it,' he said.

In fact he had been, for an anguished, tear-streaked fortnight, in love with Scott. He knew it wasn't real, of course, but now the damn stuff was out of the bottle, it seemed to be moving around.

Love.

Dan traced it around the house, a sweetness coating everything Ludo possessed, his gee-gaws and tchotchkes, the hideous paintings and the ones that weren't so bad. Everything full of meaning, throbbing with it: the little sherry glass of toothpicks in the middle of the table, Ludo's tube of shaving cream for a morning ritual that only stopped at the collar line.

'You know what this means,' he said to Scott-in-his-head.

'Yes?'

'It means I am going to die.'

And Scott-in-his-head smiled a sweet, Canadian smile.

In the event, Dan was sidetracked, in that week's session,

by the memory of his father in absurd, high-waisted swimming trunks. High also on the leg, they were the exact shape of the pelvic section of a plastic, jointed doll. Black, of course. It must have been on the yellow beach at Fanore. His father would join them there after a day working the land, the only swimming farmer in the County Clare. And one time Dan flung himself at his father's wet legs as he made his way up the beach and his father shrugged him off. That was all. Dan, who was weeping for some reason, hurled himself at the wet woollen trunks and was pushed back on to the sand. His shoulder was grazed by a rock which is why, perhaps, he remembered it, this utterly usual thing – his father moving past him to reach for a scrap of towel.

'I'm foundered.' That is what his father used to say, when he came in from the freezing Atlantic, shrunken, his muscles tight to the bone.

And Dan wept for his father. He could not believe this man was gone and his body – which must have been a beautiful body – destroyed in death. Because his father never felt dead, to Dan, not in all the years: he just felt cold.

Scott sat across from Dan, his careful face flushed with the effort of staying with him in his sorrow, while Dan threw one Kleenex after the other into the wooden wastepaper basket at his feet. He thought about all the discarded tears that ended up in it, from all the people who took their turn to weep, sitting in that chair. Many people, many times a day. The bin was made of pale wood, with a faint and open grain. It was always empty when he arrived. Expectant. The wastepaper basket was far too beautiful. The air inside it was the saddest air.

Dan told Scott about an afternoon in the desert, many years before – it was the first time he'd made a move on a guy, really wanted him, in this amazing place outside Phoenix. The house was built of rammed earth and set flat to the landscape, and there was no pool, just walls of glass in room after room built aslant to the sun and always in shade. Outside, the Sonoran Desert looked just the way it was supposed to look, the saguaro cactus standing with his arms held up, a bird flying in and out of a hole in his neck. The heat of the day was translated into night with a sunset of Kool-Aid orange, giving way, in streaks, to pink and milky blue. And Dan was stilled by the desert light that washed his lover's body with dusk and turned it into such an untouchable, touchable thing.

'Yes,' said Scott – who was, at a guess, straight as the Trans Canada Highway. And he followed the 'yes' with a silence that grew very long.

'It's just. I don't know if I am losing all that, with Ludo. I don't know if I am losing it, or if it's all, finally, coming good.'

'I see.'

Scatter cushions and oak dressers – in Toronto, Dan thought. *Here we go.*

The night before he left for Ireland, Dan told Ludo that he loved him. He told him because it was true and because he thought that, this time, the plane might fall out of the sky. Or he might get stuck in Ireland, somehow, he would get trapped in 1983, with a white sliced pan on the table and the Eurovision Song Contest on TV. He would never make it back to Rosedale, Toronto and to this man he had loved for some time.

This was why he had decided to go home, he said. Because he loved Ludo and Ludo was right, it was time to sort out his past, deal with himself. Time to become a fucking human being.

It was a mistake to tell Ludo all this, because Ludo immediately wanted to open the last bottle of Pommery and suck him off and get married. Dan had a flight the next day, but Ludo brought the champagne to bed and marriage would be a blast, he said. He found the sheer legality of it incredibly erotic. And very tax effective. If he worked it right, there was no telling how much they could save.

'I don't know,' said Dan, 'I don't know.'

'What?' said Ludo.

'I just.' He was talking about Ludo's money.

'Oh toughen up,' said Ludo. 'Talk to a woman, they've been doing it for years.'

'Yeah, yeah,' said Dan, who did nothing but talk to the wives of rich men. He talked to them about their husbands' paintings and their husbands' ghastly wallpaper. (*Take it down!* was his cry. *All of it. Down!*) Dan loved these women; their woundedness and their style; he admired the way they rose to their lives. But he did not want to be one. That would be a convergence too far.

'Don't be too proud for me,' said Ludo. 'Don't be too proud, is all.'

'Proud?' said Dan.

'Defensive,' said Ludo. 'OK?'

'OK,' said Dan. And he put his head on Ludo's chest, where it met the ball of his shoulder; in that dent.

'OK.'

'All you ever do is take!' This from his mother, some time, from the black and white movie of their relationship, *Whatever Happened to Baby Rosaleen.* 'All you ever do is take!'

Isabelle sending him a postcard, the year she moved upstate: 'I was going to send back all the presents you gave me over the years, then I realised – you didn't.'

And it was true that Dan stalled in the shop if he was ever obliged to buy a gift. Stalled, refused, could not calculate, drew a blank, was a blank. Walked away, as though from something terrible and, by the skin of his teeth, survived.

Another postcard, the next summer, from Dublin, a vintage thing with green buses going down O'Connell Street. And on the back:

'I am still alive.'

This was from an exhibition they saw together in Dublin, himself and Isabelle, when they were, maybe, eighteen. A book of telegrams by the Japanese conceptual artist, On Kawara, sent over the course of a decade to the same address and all saying the same thing: 'I am still alive.' The exhibition was a moment of complete excitement for Dan – it was a shaft of light that told him he had been living, all his life, underground. This was long before New York, long before he found conceptual work tiresome and even longer before he met the man, or thought he had, at a Starbucks around the corner from the Guggenheim, where the server called 'Kawara!' and Dan felt his knees weaken in his chinos. *I am still alive.*

Isabelle's last card was from Barcelona.

'Gaudete!' it said, and on the front those curvy balconies by Gaudi.

And after that, none.

There were tears in his eyes. Dan never cried until he started with Scott; now he was weeping full time, he was leaking into the slackening skin of his lover's arms.

'There, there,' said Ludo, who had a breakfast meeting at eight.

'It's not the money,' Dan said. 'I mean.'

'Fuck the money,' said Ludo.

'It's not the money,' he said.

And it wasn't. Dan thought of himself as more cat than dog. He did not need much, he could do as well without. So it was not the money that made Dan weep in the arms of Ludovic Linetsky, as he decided to marry him, for richer for poorer, all the days of his life. It was the sound of Ludo's wonderful heart, deep in his chest. Because Dan might make a good cat but he was a raging blank of a human being and he knew he would fuck this good thing up, just like he fucked up all the rest of them. He would look at Ludo some day – he could do it now if he liked – and just not care.

And where would that leave Dan?

Alone.

Useless and alone.

Normal life was a problem for Dan. He was beginning to see that now. Small things upset him. He would have a petulant old age.

'I'm not. I'm not,' he said.

'What?'

'I'm not.'

'Don't tell me,' said Ludo. 'You're straight.'

He was out of the bed and rummaging in a drawer now and he came back with a small hinged box of brown lizard skin and, inside, a pair of cufflinks: silver, inset with a fat little piece of amber. Dan took them out. They were lovely, and worth very little; the amber worn small and smooth as a butterscotch sweet in your mouth.

'Marry me,' said Ludo.

The cufflinks were his great-grandfather's, he said, all the way from Odessa. Dan rose to his knees on the bed and held the little box in his hand. He had no shirt to try them against. He was naked and shivering. He was getting married.

'I'm sorry,' he said.

'For what?' said Ludo. 'For nothing.'

They made love all night – two men, no longer young – and they talked it all out. He would grow old with Ludo, in a big house on the wrong side of a leafy street in Rosedale, Toronto. Dan stuck the tip of his tongue into Ludo's mouth, all night, into the chaos and mass of him. He took the malty sweetness of Ludo's body as a memory and a talisman, to keep him company on the journey home.

Dublin

IF ONLY SHE could keep it in a box, Hanna thought, or a jug, or a thermos, something sealed, to stop it crusting over where the liquid met the air. A Tupperware box might do. What she really needed was one of those plastic bags that they used in hospitals, vacuum sealed, the ones they hung from a drip stand. A bag of blood. She could put it in her new fridge – God knows, it looked like something you would find in a morgue – she could put her blood in a bag, any sort of bag, and squeeze down until the air was out of it and then just tie a knot in the top. Hang it from the wine rack. Close the door.

Hanna tried to lift her head, but her cheek was stuck to the floor. The blood was eye level, it was spreading and congealing at the same time. It was a race to standstill. But even though it stopped as it went, Hanna could not see the extent of it, because her eye was flush with the ground. The edges turned hazy as the blood oozed away from her, across the white floor tiles.

There were plastic bags in the high cupboard – which wasn't much use to her, down here. Hanna had put the bags up high so the baby couldn't smother himself. And there were safety catches on all the bottom presses, which is why she would not be able to kick one open, so there you go – sometimes safety was not what you needed most. Sometimes what you needed was a little plastic bag to put the blood in, so when the men came they would be able to put it back into you again. Or see, at least, that you had not meant to die.

She had slipped.

Hanna thought she had slipped on the blood, but actually the blood had come after. And she was still holding something in her right hand. A bottle. Or the neck of a bottle. The body of the bottle was no longer there.

Hanna didn't know how anyone could break a bottle and fall on it at the same time, unless they were very fucking drunk. Maybe she had been hit from behind. Maybe the attacker was going up now to the room where the baby slept, and he would do things to the baby. Nameless things. He would steal the baby or damage the baby and leave no mark, so no one could tell that he had been and gone.

The bottle broke, and then she sat down on the bottle and, after that, she was lying on the floor, looking at the spreading blood. Which must be coming from her leg. In which case, she was going to die.

The blood was dark, which was possibly a good thing. It was getting darker. It came quietly and then it stopped.

It was probably time to call Hugh though she did not want to call Hugh, she did not think she could. So unless the baby cried and woke him, he would not notice she was gone. And the baby was not crying, for once. They never did what you wanted them to. A little opposite thing, that is what came out of her. A fight they wrapped in a cloth. Push it, grab it, knock it away: she was feeding him once, and the spoon skittered away so she had to duck to retrieve it and the look he gave as she rose from the floor was one of pure contempt. It was as though he had been possessed – possibly by himself, by the man he would some day become – looking at her as if to say, *Who the fuck are you, with your pathetic fucking spoon?*

Good question.

Oh the baby. The baby. Hanna loved the baby and did not want to doubt him even now, drunk as she was and dying on the kitchen floor. But she did sort of think that, if she did die, it would be the baby who had killed her. It would be that fat, strong boy, with his father's ears and his father's smile, and nothing of Hanna in him that she or anybody else could see.

Hanna rested her head, and did not try to move it again. She was happy enough where she was. There was no need to get up, just yet. She would stay, for just a few minutes more, between things.

There was a tickling in her hair, a cooling unpleasantness at the back of her neck. The blood was coming from her head.

Hanna didn't sit down on the breaking bottle so much as crack her skull off something – the door of the press, perhaps – then break the bottle as she fell. If she put a hand to her head, she would feel an opening in her scalp, and inside it, her skull. The raw bone.

Hanna closed her eyes.

The kitchen floor tiles were new and she said to Hugh they were too shiny and too hard so everything would smash as soon as touch them, but Hugh wanted a kitchen that looked like an operating theatre or like a butcher's shop, with steel and concrete and metal hooks hanging off metal bars. In a tiny little semi-detached. Hugh wanted a man kitchen. A serial murderer's kitchen, with a row of knives pinned to a magnetic strip along the wall. Hugh cooked twice a year, that was the height of it. Every bowl and dish dragged out, the place covered in flour. The rest of the time he heated something up in the microwave or got in takeaway. Hugh was annoying and Hanna could not leave him. Not after she had died in the new kitchen, with the baby asleep upstairs.

But she was so cold, now, she got up to put something around her shoulders and she saw, as she rose, her body lying behind her on the floor, with blood browning on the tiles and then loosening around the broken bottle, where it was diluted with wine.

She would have to change her life. Again.

Hanna put her hand to her temple and felt the wound crusting under her hair. So much fucking blood. It did not seem possible. She felt light – gone, almost. She pawed her way along the counter, and lobbed the dishcloth on to the floor, then shoved the cloth about with her toe. Her life would have to change. Again.

Her life. Her life.

Upstairs the baby gave a strange, waking shout and Hanna stopped, waiting for the wails. But the baby didn't cry. The dishcloth made a streak like a brushstroke across the floor: it looked like she was cleaning up blood. Then she remembered that it was blood. It was her blood. She looked over and Hugh was there, standing in the doorway, holding the baby.

'What time is it?' she said.

'Sorry?' said Hugh.

'What's the time?'

And the nice thing – she could not forget it. The nice thing, or the horrible thing, was the way the baby took one look at her and struggled to be in her arms.

She would not go to Casualty, Hanna said, and she would not go to bed, she would sleep sitting upright in an armchair, she would get the blood off her face, and it would be fine. This is what she told Hugh. She headed out past her boyfriend and her baby, and sat down on the stairs.

'I am just going to the bathroom,' she said, and she leaned her head against the bannister.

There were coloured lights outside the door, and before she knew it, the place was full of men. Ambulance men, huge and bizarrely light on their feet.

'Jesus,' she said.

The paramedic was pretty relaxed. He crouched below her on the stair.

'What have we here,' he said.

'No,' said Hanna.

'Scalp,' he said. 'Oh, the scalp's a fright.'

'You are such a dick,' Hanna said over his shoulder, to Hugh. 'Why do you have to be such a fucking dick?'

'Look at yourself,' said Hugh, and he meant it literally. So Hanna looked down. She saw her T-shirt slicked on to her torso, the outline of her left breast perfectly stiff, like a sculpture of herself in dried blood.

The baby smiled.

And before she could refuse, they had her sitting up on a gurney, belted in. Before she could say, 'Where's my baby?' the guy said, 'He'll be in first thing,' and Hanna felt herself loosen and be relieved. Happiness slipped into her as she was pulled backwards up the ramp, and happiness tugged at her insides as the ambulance pulled silently away. All she lacked was a siren, to shout it. She was happy.

'It's a bit late for that, sweetheart,' said the paramedic. 'They're all asleep in their beds.'

In Casualty, they cleaned her up and put her in a gown, and though they snipped and shaved her hair back from the wound, Hanna did not even need stitches in the end. She was left on the trolley to sleep and woke with a filthy headache, and no offer of pain relief. The trolley was in a corridor. The woman who came along to check and discharge her did not ask about post-natal depression and this was almost disappointing. ('No, I've always had it,' Hanna wanted to say, 'I had it pre-natally. I think I had it in the womb.') All the woman wanted to talk about was drinking – which Hanna thought was a bit obvious, given the circumstances. She was also quite condescending. But Hugh was calm by the time he arrived in with clean clothes and the baby, who had stopped smiling now and defaulted to his usual screams.

'I think it's a tooth.'

'Did he sleep after? Did you put him down?'

In the car, they fought about the baby, and fell silent.

And that was it. For weeks, it was just, 'Hanna cut her head,' and once, when the buttons wouldn't fasten on the babygro and Hanna thought she might actually throw the baby away from her, she might hit the baby against the wall, Hugh took over the buttoning and said, 'See someone. Take a fucking pill.'

Meanwhile, he slept with her – he fell asleep in a normal way. And he also had sex with her – his erection was unaffected, that is, by the memory of Hanna encrusted in two pints of her own blackening ooze, and once he fuzzed his finger along the fine stubble around her wound and said, 'Oh, my love.' He reminded her to buy milk before he went out in the morning, and he mopped his butcher's counters last thing at night. He looked after the baby all the hours that he was home, although he wasn't home much. You could not accuse him of neglect.

Hugh was out at RTÉ working on a soap, which was brilliant – the work was brilliant, the soap was just a soap – but he was there all hours, talking to lighting and props, getting the right Ikea sideboard to set against a side wall.

Once all that was settled in, he would be home at a regular time, but he was also doing drawings for a pocket *Romeo and Juliet* and hustling for a thing about Irish Mammies in the Olympia called *Don't Mind Me I'll Sit In The Dark*. Retro was where Hugh was at. Normal with an edge. 'Just give me a litre of Magnolia matt emulsion,' he liked to say. 'And a place to stand.'

So Hugh was flat out. There was a mortgage to pay. Hanna pushed the buggy up to the Phoenix Park or along the quays into town and then she pushed it back to their little house in Mount Brown. Five kilometres to Stephen's Green and back, ten kilometres the long way around the Park. Seven months after the birth, she was back in her skinny jeans, but what was the point of looking good, when no one cared? She went to an opening night at the Abbey and flirted like crazy, but it was as though no one found that relevant any more. Hanna drank, that evening, until she could not feel her arse sliding off the high stool. No one noticed that either. Not even her.

It was true that Hanna got pissed as soon as she left the baby, but it was also true that she never left the baby, or hardly ever. She mixed up vodka in a fruit juice bottle to bring on a girls' night out and it was supposed to be a joke – the label said 'Innocent' – but she finished it on the way into town and didn't tell them about it, when the moment came. Hanna could not face the girls and their talk of diets and auditions, bitching about the state of Irish theatre and the many shortcomings of their men. The girls did not have babies, or not yet. They were really jealous. They thought having a baby would solve something fundamental in their lives.

The Innocent bottle was interesting. Hanna tried it in front of Hugh and he didn't notice it, either. It wasn't within his range.

Hugh was a very tidy person. He got upset if there was a scratch on something, or a mark, if there were used tea bags on the kitchen counter or a damp towel on the floor. Living with him put Hanna semi-permanently in the wrong. He told her to pick her knickers up off the stairs, in a tone of great disgust. Or he wanted to shag her on the stairs. One or the other. Sometimes both. It was as if he couldn't make up his mind.

They had, in the early days, enormous amounts of sex. It was not high-quality sex, but it was terrifically frequent. Then it just got terrific. Nothing outrageous, Hugh was a straight-up kind of guy – unless he plucked one of his cooking hatchets off the magnetic strip on the kitchen wall and stuck it in her, one fine day. There was no sign, anyway, of murderous intent. There was just this massive, penetrative intent that felt like murder, at least to Hanna. Not that she minded, being killed. And it was in the course of one of their happy little fuck-fests, tender, savage and prolonged – well done, us! – that the baby happened.

Happened.

The baby arrived.

Hugh made a baby in Hanna because he loved Hanna. In the middle of all that fury, a baby.

Hanna did not realise, of course. She thought her beer had gone off, the wine was corked, she got a pain in her back and there was a density to her coming that was muscular and new. She woke one morning utterly abandoned, wrecked. And, after a couple of weeks of this, she said, 'Oh.'

Hugh was delighted, ecstatic. He loved the baby both inside and outside of Hanna, and he loved the baby's clever mother. But he did not have sex with the baby's mother, after the baby came. He fought with her instead.

'What the fuck is this doing here?'

'What?'

'My script is under there.'

'Excuse me?'

'My script. I've been looking for my script and now its covered in . . . Jesus.'

Hanna shoved the buggy down the quays into town replaying the fights in her head. Push. Push. Shove. Shove. She was so lonely, she was horny all the time now. And it was a bit like sex, she thought – the fighting – but it really wasn't sex. Throwing Hugh's phone into a gorse bush up the mountains, or her own stupid cheap clutch bag into the River Liffey. There were long and impossible silences on the hard shoulder, there was the time she walked back down the motorway leaving the baby in the car seat, eating his crinkly toy. There was the broken front light and the deep scrape along the passenger door – Hugh really hated it when she pranged his precious car, because Hugh claimed to be calm but he really wasn't calm, Hugh was stony and white with rage.

The baby, meanwhile, turned red and shat. The baby opened his round, red mouth, and screamed.

And Hanna – of course! – ran around doing a million things for the baby: soother, spoons, blankies, books, Calpol, wipes, socks, spare everything, spare hat, lanolin cream, cream without lanolin, because Hanna loved the baby. Loved, loved, loved him. Cared, cared, cared for him. Worried and fretted and was in charge of the baby. Because oh, if the baby lost his soother, if the baby lost his spare hat, then a hole would open in the universe and Hanna would fall through this hole and be forever lost.

When she drank a couple of Innocents-with-a-twist, pushing the buggy in the sunshine, she found they could all coexist, Hanna and the spare hat and the missing hat, and the baby, who was looking at her, and also the hole in the universe. She could keep them all in different corners of her mind, and the tension between them nice. She could make it all hum.

The other great things about the plastic bottle with Innocent on the label were a) the colour, b) the amusement factor, c) it was hers.

One day in November, when the baby was ten months old, Hanna got a Christmas card from her mother with a note at the bottom to say she was going to sell the house.

She rang Constance to say, 'What the fuck?'

'Oh it's you,' said Constance, because Hanna never rang home.

'The fuck?' said Hanna, and Constance said, 'Don't ask.'

'It's not true, is it?' said Hanna.

'Oh, I don't know,' said Constance. 'It's not true, no. She's just getting old.'

'Any word from Dan?'

'Full house this year. He's coming home.'

The Madigans were never together, on the day. The girls always made it down, but the boys were wherever, either Claridge's or Timbuktu. So this Christmas was going to be a big one. It was going to be a doozie. And that evening, somehow, the baby got hold of her little Innocent bottle and spat the stuff out, spilling it all down his front and, never mind the hole in the fucking universe, when Hugh smelt the alcohol off the baby's Breton striped Petit Bateau, the world as Hanna knew it came to an end. Or seemed to come to an end. It was possible, like the time she ended up in Casualty, that when you have a baby there is no such thing as the end, there is only more of the same.

The thing was through the washing machine on the instant, so Hugh had no hard evidence. But he had the baby. He was sleeping in the baby's room. He would not

191

fight with Hanna, he said, but he would not leave her alone with the baby. And when it came to Christmas he would take the baby home.

Hanna said, 'That's a relief. No, really. Childcare. At last. Fucking fantastic.'

After two weeks of Hanna sober, they had sex in the kitchen, suddenly, they ended up on the floor – the same place as the night she cut her head, with the same view, when she turned to the side, of white tiles. Hanna was so wet between the legs she thought it was some kind of incontinence and later, in the shower, she wondered if there was something actually wrong with her, with her body, not to mention her mind. She went out and bought two bottles of white in the off-licence, because she'd got the drinking thing under control now and, after she opened the second one, the shouting started all over again.

'I need a job,' said Hanna. 'I just need a fucking job.'

After she left college, Hanna formed a fringe company with some like-minded souls, who failed to get funding after their second, slightly disastrous year. She broke through to the main stages with the part of a maid at the Abbey, and went straight from this to a sexy maid at the Olympia. She had a two-week break before touring a production of Hugh Leonard's *Da*, in which she played the girlfriend. Well. She played the girlfriend very well. After that, another maid, but this time on the big screen. There was a showing in the Savoy on O'Connell Street, a red carpet, Hanna, sitting in the dark with Hugh, their palms wet as they held hands, then her face a mile high, and Hanna blown back in her seat by the sight of her own opening mouth.

'I don't know, sir. She didn't say.'

A saucy look. Innocent. Irish. They all said, she should go to LA, she was like an Irish Vivien Leigh.

But she didn't go to LA. It was too late for Hollywood, she was twenty-six. And besides, Hanna wanted to do proper work, real work. She wanted the thing to happen, whatever the thing was, the sudden understanding of the crowd.

She did a Feldenkrais course and a Shakespeare workshop for schools, there was a fringe production of *A Long Day's Journey* that was best forgotten, and six months with a company who liked Grotowski too much ever to make it to an opening night. There was an ad for spreadable butter, a week here and there on a film; she got a whole four months on a mini series, and she was trying to break into voiceover work, for the money. Everything hustled for and flirted for. There was sexual humiliation. There was no path.

She had thought there would be a path, one that wound from the school musical all the way up to the red carpet at Cannes. But there was no path. No *trajectory*. No career, even. There was just *Theatre, darling*.

She still needed it.

Thank you. Thank you. Thank you.

At the age of thirty-seven, Hanna's dreams were rich – as was her drinking, indeed – with applause. Or booing, more often. Missed cues, lost props, stage fright. Hanna was wearing a pyjama top with a crinoline, she was in the wrong play and even in the right play, she had forgotten to learn her lines. That evening, with Hugh blank-eyed, slumped on the sofa, she pawed her way along the living room wall. She pushed her cheek against it and dragged her face along, not sure who she was playing this time. Some madwoman. Ophelia, undone.

Undone.

'Terrific,' said Hugh, who hated her and slept with her anyway, even that evening, with the smear of her spit drying on the wall downstairs.

Or loved her. Because he said that he loved her. It came out of him while he was fucking her.

I love, I lov, I luh.

The next morning, Hanna packed to go down home. She stood in front of the wardrobe and went through the hangers, trying to figure out what to bring. Her mother hated her in black, and Hanna had nothing but black to wear. She thought a few scarves might break it up, or some loud beads, though she could never tie a scarf, it always looked wrong. Hanna put one top against her and then another, checking in the mirror. She caught sight of her face and thought it was possible, it was more than possible that the theatre was finished for her now. Hanna had the wrong face for a grown-up woman, even if there were parts for grown-up women. The detective inspector. The mistress. No, Hanna had a girlfriend face, pretty, winsome and sad. And she was thirty-seven.

She had run out of time.

She dumped both tops in the suitcase, and threw the hangers on the bed. Hugh was standing there, against the wall of Prussian Blue, and when the baby fought for her she took him from his father. Just for a little while. As she brought him towards her, the skin of her chest seemed to sing; a clamorous want for the baby hit her everywhere the baby would be in her arms. And then she had him, and they were calm.

'Remember when we took him down to my mother's,' she said. 'That first time? Because the stupid bitch couldn't come up to Dublin, and "how many bedrooms did you say you had?" Remember we went down there and it was sunny all the way to the other side of Ennis, and then the heavens opened just outside Islandgar, and he liked it. The rain bucketing down, and I couldn't see through the windscreen. He didn't like the new car seat, or there was something wrong with him, until the rain came pelting on to the roof. You said, "Pull over, pull over!" and I said I couldn't pull over because I couldn't see where I was going in all the rain, there was just two inches of clear windscreen, after the wiper blade, this little slice, and even that just showed you more rain. The noise of it. And inside the car so silent, and I was still driving. I said, "It's like a dream." Remember?'

'Yeah,' said Hugh. 'Maybe.'

'I left myself, really slowly. It happens, sometimes. I do that. But this time it was really slow. It was so slow, it was like I caught myself leaving. I mean that was the first time.'

'Right,' he said.

'And I loved that. I just loved it. Going down to my mother's with the baby in the back. And all the rain.'

Shannon Airport

IN THE ARRIVALS Hall at Shannon the glass doors pulled open and the glass door slipped shut.

Constance watched as one after another passenger was ambushed and claimed. People were crying and laughing and Constance couldn't remember what she was looking out for, exactly. There would be some unchangeable thing about her brother to say he was her brother. Some glow. That is how she remembered Dan as a child and also, more surprisingly, from the last time they met – it must have been 2000 – a year when Constance no longer recognised her own reflection coming at her from a shop window and Dan was looking better than ever. She did not know how he managed it. Constance actually thought there might be make-up involved; or Botox, perhaps. It was as though the light had a choice, and it still chose him.

Maybe he was just fit. Though Dan never showed the effort of being fit, or unfit, she could not imagine him breaking a sweat. Handsome people did not move their faces much, that was part of the trick; her mother had it, and Dan had it too. It was the attitude, more than the fact of good looks. A sense of expectation.

Hanna was actually the prettiest of the Madigans but Hanna was all expression, all personality, and she did not photograph well – this, in an actress, was not a good thing. Constance gripped the steel rail in the Arrivals area and held her own face up like a plate for her brother to recognise, but it was, she knew, just a sad reflection of what she used to be. Her face was a shadow passing over the front of her head – like the play of light on the side of a mountain, maybe. For two seconds at a time, the old Constance was there. She inhabited the picture of herself. Everything fit.

And there was Dan – she knew him immediately – slight and alert behind his massive trolley: older than Dan should be, but looking absurdly young for his age. A gay man, as anyone might be able to discern. He checked the faces in the welcoming crowd with a nervous impeccability.

'Hell-oooo!' Dan threw out his hands, towards her, and stepped out from behind his luggage. More camp than she remembered. Every time a little more. It came up through him with age.

'Look at you!' He touched her lightly on the side of her face and then her shoulder, then leaned in, as though impulsively, for a hug. He greeted her like a friend and not a brother. He greeted her like no friend she ever had.

And he had too many bags with him. Far too many. Much of the luggage was matching. Dan noticed her noticing all this, as they walked across the concourse. They were fighting, before Constance had opened her mouth. They were doing it all over again. And Constance was utterly fed up with herself, suddenly.

I don't care!!! she wanted to say. *I don't care who you sleep with or what you do!*

Even though she did care. She checked the eyes of everyone who looked at him from the oncoming crowd.

'How are you?' she said to Dan.

'Good.'

'That overnight thing is a killer.'

Dan went to say something, but decided against it.

'I slept,' he said.

They were out through the main doors and in the fresh air; the beginnings of dawn to the east of them, and the lights of the airport trembling orange against the freshly blank sky.

'Hello Ireland,' said Dan.

He smiled, and she looked over to him. And there he was.

Dan was a year younger than Constance, fifteen months. His growing up struck her as daft, in a way. So she was not bothered by her brother's gayness – except, perhaps, in a social sense – because she had not believed in his straightness, either. In the place where Constance loved Dan, he was eight years old.

He stood beside her as she sorted out the ticket, then they walked across the car park together, almost amused.

This was the boy who ran alongside her in her dreams. Constance, asleep, never saw his face exactly, but it was Dan, of course it was, and they were on the beach in Lahinch coming round a headland to find something unexpected. And the thing they found was the river Inagh as it ran across the sands into the sea. Sweet water into salt. Constance had been there many times as an adult, and the mystery of it remained for her. Rainwater into seawater, you could taste where they met and mingled, and no way to tell if all this was good or bad, this turbulence, if it was corruption or return.

'You know what I want?' said Dan. 'I saw it on my way through and I can't believe it – because what I want, more than anything, is some Waterford crystal. Don't you think it's time? Some champagne saucers. I should have got some for Lady Madigan, she'd love them.'

'You think?'

'Or for me. I knew there was something missing in my life. I just didn't know what it was.'

'Champagne saucers?'

'Champagne saucers?' They were both, and immediately, imitating their mother.

'Oh go 'way now,' said Dan. 'I'm tired of you.'

'Actually,' said Constance, 'she's in good form.'

'How is she?'

'She's in good form. I mean, apart from all this stuff about the house. She's.' Constance could not find the word.

'Mellowed?' said Dan. They were at the car which, Constance remembered, was a Lexus. She did not know if she was ashamed of this fact or proud of it, but Dan did not seem to notice, as she popped the boot with the logo on it, and he lifted it high.

'More like mood swings, I'd call it.'

Dan said nothing to this, just worked the luggage into the boot, placing her shopping carefully to one side.

'I know,' he said, shutting the lid.

Though he had no way of knowing. How could he know? He had not been there.

Dan was ducking towards the driver's door, when he realised what country he was in.

'Wrong side!' he said, and they bumbled around each other. Constance touched his waist as they swapped over and he seemed smaller than he used to be. This was not possible, of course. It was just that everyone was fatter, these days, your eyes adjusted to it. Everyone was fatter except Dan.

He noticed the car, all right, when Constance put it into reverse and a video of the rear view came up on the dash.

'Con-stance,' he said. 'What is this thing you're driving? You're like the doctor's wife these days.'

'Ha,' said Constance.

'Mood swings,' he said. 'Is she serious about the house?'

'Yeah well,' said Constance. 'I think she's just getting old.'

'And. Not in a good way?' he said. Constance was searching through the gears for first and then reverse, and she could not laugh until she was straightened up. Then she laughed so hard she could not find the ticket for the barrier.

'Shut up,' said Constance. 'I am trying to get us out of here.'

It was seven o'clock in the morning. The sun over Limerick was fat and red, and coming in from the west, a shading in the air that was the beginnings of rain.

'You hungry?' she said.

'Mmmm.'

Dan slid down in his seat, and *Be like that*, she thought, because he made her feel so guilty all the time, hallucinating eggs and bacon.

In fact, it was the sunrise did for Dan. He was jet-lagged. The light brought that familiar sense of wrongness (Why did Constance buy this huge, stupid car? When did she even learn how to drive?) and Dan did not catch it in time. He thought it was the smell – something like wet dog, or cheese – this sickening sense that he would rather be anywhere else but here. Dan squeezed his eyelids, trying to keep out the insistent light of home, which was the same as any other light, it was just at the wrong time.

'Have you seen the others?' he said.

'Coming down tomorrow, if Hanna gets herself together. Emmet's working away.'

'Of course.'

'He has a new LayDee.'

'Does he, now?'

'Well yes,' said Constance, because that was always the case, with Emmet.

'And you?' said Dan.

'I beg your pardon?' said Constance.

'What are you up to these days?'

Constance tried to tease out the usual tangle of house, kids, mother, husband, mother's house, Christmas presents, dinner for ten or maybe thirteen, her children having sex, now, except for Shauna, who was too shy. What could she talk about? Looking up Pilates on the internet, trying to manage her own stupidity, a long weekend in Pisa on Ryanair, that was three months ago now. Constance was doing everything. She was 'up to' damn all.

'Oh, you know,' she said. 'Nothing strange or startling.'

And Dan closed his eyes, as though in pain.

'How are the kids?' he said.

'Oh!' she said.

'How's?'

'Shauna,' she said. 'You've got to see Shauna.'

'What age, again?'

'Beautiful,' she said. 'If only she knew it. Sixteen.'

Dan never really got a fix on Shauna, but Constance knew that this would change as soon as he saw her. Dan would take one look at Shauna, a girl who was as pale as he was, and with the same red in her hair. He would take this child, all knees and elbows, and he would fabulise her.

'Skinny legs,' she said. 'Shot up.'

'Mmmm,' he said.

His eyes were still closed. Dan watched the sunshine bloom on the inside of his eyelids, the way he used to as a boy but today, even this felt wrong. Purple blossoms that looked like bruises. Sick yellow clouds, with a black under-belly of shame.

Jet lag.

He opened his eyes to see tail lights, the cream and grey upholstery of his sister's car, the beginnings of rain on the windscreen. Ireland.

Great.

Constance was talking about the boys: Donal, who was the spit of his father, putting off uni for a year to work on a building site in Australia; Rory who was out every Saturday night.

'What about yourself?' she said, after a small silence.

'Toronto,' said Dan, as though the word contained all sorts of information, some of it surprising. 'Yeah.'

'I always liked Canada,' said Constance.

'Yes,' he said. 'I remember.' It sounded like he wanted to say more, but he didn't. And, when she looked over to check he was asleep.

He woke from a dream of the river Inagh entering the sea – loosely, endlessly – which made him think he was wetting the bed. Even as he blinked, Dan thought he must be pissing, he could almost hear it. A deep, intimate clunking sound startled him with the fact that they were on a garage forecourt, and there was petrol pouring into the tank behind him, and it would not stop. He looked over the back of the seat to see his sister standing at the tail end of the car, in her caramel coloured wool coat. Constance was looking into the middle distance, her cream scarf lifting behind her, the wind annoying her thin hair. Dan bundled his way out of the car, hitched his – completely dry – trousers up at the belt. The fresh air was a welcome slap of cold.

'I'll go into the shop,' he said. 'Do you want a packet of crisps?'

Crisps. Such an Irish word – years since he had the taste of it in his mouth.

Constance looked across the glossy black roof at him.

'Oh yes,' she said.

As they travelled towards home, the landscape accumulated in Dan like a silt of meaning that was disturbed by the line of a hedgerow or the sight of winter trees along a ridge. All at once, it was familiar. He knew this place. It was a secret he had carried inside him; a map of things he had known and lost, these half-glimpsed houses and stone walls, the fields of solid green.

The road was wider than the road of his childhood and the rain felt less and less real to him as they spun along it. So much water. They were held up by it, the tyres skating over a film of rain. Aquaplaning. Flying his sister's fancy car through the wet air. Touching nothing. Untouched.

If only he could keep his eyes open, Dan thought, everything would be all right.

Constance also dipped her lids as she spoke – they all did it, the Madigans, they blinked slow. They looked around inside themselves for a missing word, a feeling that was hard to catch or explain. They smiled into closed eyes, and shut their faces down.

'You happy?' he said, suddenly.

'Hmp,' she said.

'You should have an affair.'

'Oh, yeah?'

She drove on.

'Who says I haven't?'

'Constance Madigan,' he said.

'Just telling you.' She used to tell him everything.

'Who?'

'Years ago,' she said. He waited for her to continue.

'I thought, you know, it would be like jumping off a cliff,' she said. 'The big leap.'

'And?'

'It was like landing in a fucking puddle. A bit of a splash, that's all. It was like standing out in the goddamn rain.'

Three miles from home they saw her little blue Citroën.

'Oh look who,' said Constance, gearing down to tuck in behind Rosaleen, then paddling the brake as their mother surged and slowed ahead of them.

Constance flashed the headlights but there was no sign from the woman in the car in front. Forty miles per hour. Twenty. They could see the back of her little-old-lady head, low to the wheel, intrepid. The tail lights came on and the tail lights went off and there was no rhythm or reason for it that Constance could see, on the road up ahead.

'She walks a lot,' said Constance. 'She goes out for her walk.'

And, though Dan had not asked, 'Anywhere,' she said. 'It's the sea she likes. Along the beach maybe, or the pier at Doolin, up along the green road, or the cliffs, even.'

'What time is it anyway?' said Dan, with sudden irritation.

'Time?'

They both saw it: their mother might die in a ditch, she might be blown off the cliff top and carried out to sea.

Constance pressed the horn.

'Jesus, Constance.'

'What?'

'You want her to crash! You want to kill the woman?'

'Oh give over.' She bipped the horn again.

'Stop it!' Dan reached across her, as though to take the wheel.

'What?' Constance was bewildered by her little brother. 'What?'

'God, Constance!' Dan was eight again, shouting at his bossy sister. And it was all comical in its way, but it did not signify. Their mother, who would be killed at any moment, could not hear them from the other car.

Constance fell back to observe. Rosaleen was driving on the brake. It wasn't clear if she was stopping or accelerating. It was a problem with her eyesight. Or with her feet, perhaps. As if she had to use them both at the same time.

Co. Dublin

ON CHRISTMAS EVE, Emmet rang his mother from his house in Verschoyle Gardens, Dublin 24, where she had never been. There was no reason for her to come here, any more than she might arrive in the door of a Dhaka high-rise or a crumbling colonial in the middle of Ségou. There was, in fact, considerably less reason. A three-bedroomed semi-detached house on a housing estate off the N7 that Emmet was renting by the month, for an absurd amount of money. The sofa under the front window was a puffy leather thing, half marshmallow, half mushroom – his mother would hate it, but Emmet was indifferent to the house, he was pleased to find. It was insulated, it was new. Any freedom from Rosaleen, small or large, continued to give him pleasure.

Down in Ardeevin, the phone rang on.

Emmet looked out the window at the identical house on the other side of the road, alive with fairy lights. Since the money came in, Ireland depressed Emmet in a whole new way. The house prices depressed him. And the handbag thing, the latte thing, the Aren't We All Brilliant thing, they all depressed him too. But Verschoyle Gardens, in all fairness, did not depress him. Mateus, the little fella next door, would be out on his new bike tomorrow morning, his father holding the back of the saddle, running low and letting go.

A click. Silence at the other end. The electronic air of home.

She had a way with a receiver, picking it up as though it were a heavy object to be set with some precision against the human ear.

'Hay-lo?'

His mother still answered a phone like it was 1953.

'Mam,' he said and then winced. She hated when he called her 'Mam'.

'Emmet,' she said.

She would be sitting at the worn old table with the newspaper spread in front of her open to the easy cross-word. She might turn to look out the window at the garden, or let her eyes settle on the easel she had in the corner, with a landscape she was painting, long unfinished. Or she would look at the old chair by the range where his father used to sleep after dinner and before the news. It was hard to say, when she looked at any of these things, what it was she saw.

'I'm on my way,' said Emmet.

'You are?'

'I'm waiting for Hanna and then.'

'Oh good.'

There was a catch to her breathing; a difficulty or excitement. He could hear her rise out of her chair.

'So it'll be, three o'clock, maybe.'

Rosaleen was on the prowl.

'I see,' she said.

'Or a bit after, maybe,' he said, a little uncertain.

'Any time is good,' she said. 'Just so long as it is the time you say.'

She'd got him.

'Because that's the annoyance, really,' she said. 'Either people coming early and you have nothing done, or they say a time and then leave you hanging. That's what I hate. It's not about being early or being late, it's about telling the truth, really.'

'I know.' Emmet could not believe what he was hearing. 'I'm waiting for Hanna,' he said.

'Hanna?'

'Yes.'

'Hanna?'

'Yes.'

'Hanna's coming with you?'

'Yes.'

'Oh, well then, it's anyone's guess.'

It was true, Hanna was never on time. Emmet thought it was genetic.

'What about?'

'Hugh's coming down on Stephenses Day,' he said. 'You'll see him then.'

'Right.'

'Hugh and the baby. He'll bring Hanna back up to Dublin with him.'

'Oh the baby, what a pity. I suppose we don't have the beds, really. So it'll just be yourself? Lovely. And?'

'Saar.'

His mother always paused after a name she considered unusual.

'Yes. Saar is back in?'

'Holland.'

'Lovely. See you at three.'

'Maybe closer to four,' said Emmet.

'Right. Well tell Constance what time, she's the one with views on all that. Bye! Oh listen, are you bringing wine? I'm just saying don't leave it Hanna's end, unless you're happy to see it go down the plughole. Of course you're not the wine buff that . . .'

She paused.

'Oh Emmet, it would be lovely, now that Dan is home, wouldn't it be lovely to have something nice for once? I'd love – I don't know – are you bringing wine?'

'No.' He looked out the window. There was no sign of Hanna.

'It's just when Dan is back for once. I don't know. I just have this. You know. Champagne.'

'He's landed, then?' Emmet's picture of the kitchen reorganised around Dan; the sainted face, the slow-blinking eyes.

'He's asleep,' Rosaleen said, sotto voce. 'I must tell Constance to get champagne.'

'What about Hanna?'

'Oh stop it. We'll use the little glasses. The ones we got in Rome.'

Rome was 1962, an audience with the Pope, a man on a little Vespa, so handsome he would cut you, with a fat brown baby on his knee. Oh and Roma, Roma! The unexpected piazzas, the sprays of orange blossom, an old codger on the tram who stank of garlic so badly – Rosaleen should have realised that morning sickness was setting in. Dan was conceived in Rome. And Dan loved garlic! There was no end to the mysteries of Dan.

'Listen, Ma, I'll go.'

There was another small silence. *Ma.*

'Off you go.'

'See you soon.'

'Goodbye now!'

Emmet put down the phone, exhausted. Saar had baked biscuits for him before she left and the kitchen still smelt of cinnamon. Saar was terrific. Dutch, pragmatic, team-spirited. He put her on a plane back up to Schiphol, knowing that, next Christmas, he would be going to Schiphol too.

'I love you,' he said.

And she said, 'I love you.'

Then he faced back into the horrors of the Madigans – their small hearts (his own was not entirely huge) and the small lives they put themselves through. Emmet closed his eyes and tilted his face up, and there she was: his mother, closing her eyes and lifting her head, in just the same way, down in the kitchen in Ardeevin. Her shadow moving through him. He had to shake her out of himself like a wet dog.

Mother.

His stupid sister late, as ever. Over-packing, at a guess, busy forgetting things, locating her phone, losing her phone, shouting about her phone, messing, messing, messing.

Emmet climbed the stairs and tapped, as he passed it, on his housemate's door.

'All right?'

Denholm came out and followed him to his own bedroom, as Emmet pulled a bag out and set it on top of the bed.

'Shipshape,' said Denholm.

'Just checking you were still there.'

'Oh yes,' said Denholm, who did not have the money to be anywhere else and was, besides, always at the little desk in his room. 'How are you, Emmet?'

'Very well,' he said, turning to shake the man's hand – African style – there in lovely, suburban Verschoyle Gardens, Dublin 24.

'How are you?' he said.

Denholm was commuting to Kimmage Manor every day for a course in International Development. His mother had died a month after his arrival from Kenya and his sister, also in rural Kenya, was HIV positive, a fact she only discovered in the maternity unit of the local clinic that was run by the same nuns who got Denholm all the way to a housing estate off the N7 and to Emmet's spare room.

'I am very well,' said Denholm.

'The Wi-Fi working?' said Emmet.

'A little slow,' said Denholm. 'But yes.'

He had been talking to his brother on Skype, he said, before his office shut down. It was a big holiday in Kenya. They were all heading out of Nairobi, the same way Emmet was heading out of Dublin. They would get back to the villages in time for Midnight Mass, then a big party – all night – more parties the next day, and then on St Stephen's Day, which they called Boxing Day, a soup made out of the blood of the Christmas goat. Good soup, Denholm told him. Hangover soup.

Emmet went about the place, pulling open drawers, throwing some bits into a bag, which was a woven polyester conference bag with World Food Programme written on the flap. A couple of polo shirts, underwear and socks, a paperback from his bedside locker, his phone. He ducked into the en-suite bathroom to get his his toothbrush and deodorant.

'Sounds like the business,' Emmet said. He was slipping a hand under the mattress for his passport when he realised that he was just going down the road, in Ireland.

'Yes,' said Denholm, who could not keep the Christmas loneliness out of his voice.

And, 'Wow,' Emmet said, as he cast about him for nothing, trying to hide his sudden mortification at the fact that he was leaving Denholm alone. After all the hospitality he himself had been offered, in so many towns. Why did he not invite him home for his dinner? He just couldn't.

It was not a question of colour (though it was also a question of colour), even Saar was out of the question – Saar with her Dutch domestic virtues, who would clear the dishes and wash the dishes, and sing as she swept the fallen tinsel off the floor. Christmas dinner, for Emmet's family, was thicker than Kenyan blood soup, so none of the people that Emmet liked best could be there, nor even the people he might enjoy. The only route to the Madigans' Christmas table was through some previously accredited womb. Married. Blessed.

I am sorry. I can not invite you home for Christmas because I am Irish and my family is mad.

Hanna wasn't even bringing the father of her child.

High standards at the Madigans' dining room table. Keep 'em high.

'Is the tram running tomorrow?'

'Don't worry about me,' said Denholm, who would be trapped for Christmas Day on a housing estate off the N7, and he went downstairs, offering tea.

Emmet blamed his mother. You could tell Rosaleen about disease, war and mudslides and she would look faintly puzzled, because there were, clearly, much more interesting things happening in the County Clare. Even though nothing happened – she saw to that too. Nothing was discussed. The news was boring or it was alarming, facts were always irrelevant, politics rude. Local gossip, that is what his mother allowed, and only of a particular kind. Marriages, deaths, accidents: she lived for a head-on collision, a bad bend in the road. Her own ailments of course, other people's diseases. Mrs Finnerty's cousin's tumour that turned out to be just a cyst. Her back, her hip, her headaches, and the occasional flashing light when she closed her eyes – ailments that were ever more vague, until, one day, they would not be vague at all. They would be, at the last, entirely clear.

'I was going to bring my housemate,' said Emmet in the kitchen, a couple of hours later. 'He's having a rough time.'

'Oh?' said Rosaleen.

'His mother just died.'

'Oh no!' Rosaleen loved a good tragedy. Tears – actual tears – came to her eyes.

'And his sister and her baby are HIV positive.'

'Oh.'

Though perhaps this was not the right kind of tragedy, after all.

'I see.'

His mother seemed smaller than he remembered. Her skin was so thin, Emmet was afraid to touch in case she bruised. Not that anyone ever touched her – except Constance perhaps. Rosaleen did not like to be touched. She liked the thing Dan did, which was to conjure the air around her, somehow, making it special. When Hanna went to greet her, there was a big mistimed clash of cheekbones.

'Oh.'

'Ow.'

This was before they were over the threshold. Rosaleen opened the front door looking terrific. She had a crisp white shirt on, with a neat collar and her mid-length string of pearls. A slightly rakish pair of argyle socks showed between black trousers and tasselled loafers, her hair was a shining platinum from her special shampoo. And when Hanna reached up to kiss all this, their faces clashed at the bone.

'Are you all right?'

'I think so. Yes.'

Rosaleen's precision turning, as ever, into a kind of general difficulty for them all.

'Yes I am fine,' and then, 'Where's the baby?'

Even though Emmet had told her there would be no baby.

'He's with Hugh,' said Hanna, after a pause.

'What a pity,' said their mother. 'Oh well.'

And she looked at her daughter as though she, alone, would have to do.

Hanna had slept the whole way down in the car. The baby had kept her awake all night, she said – a little petulantly – and though his little sister annoyed him, Emmet felt sorry for her, freshly woken and bedraggled as she was, on their mother's doorstep.

'I told you,' he said to Rosaleen.

'Did you? Maybe you did.' And then, a little sharply, 'It doesn't *matter*, does it?'

She was an impossible woman. Emmet did not know why it was his job to keep his mother in line – he just couldn't help it. He could not bear the unreality she fomented about her. Emmet could not understand why the truth was such a problem to Rosaleen, why facts were an irrelevance, or an accusation. He did not know what she was skittering away from, all the time.

'A baby can't have AIDS,' she said, with some finality.

'They did the test at the maternity clinic – an Irish nun, actually.'

'A nun?' she said.

'Yes, in Kenya,' said Emmet.

'Oh.'

Rosaleen considered all this for a moment.

'And is he from Kenya?' she said.

'Who?'

'Your housemate?'

'He is. Yes, he is Kenyan.'

'I see,' she said and shifted her hips to one side on the chair.

'Are you making that cup of tea?' she said, suddenly, looking over her shoulder at Hanna. And Hanna, who was, in fact, spooning the leaves into the pot, paused for a micro rage with the caddy in her hand.

'There is a child,' Rosaleen said, turning carefully back to the table. 'On the autistic spectrum. He was born to one of the people who run the Spar.' And then, as a concession. 'She is an Estonian, would you believe. And the husband is very nice. From Kiev.'

But Emmet was already bored by the game. He was a grown man. He was trying to expose the foolishness of a woman who was seventy-six years old. A woman who was, besides, his mother.

'It's a long way,' he said. 'From Kiev to County Clare.'

He could see the next couple of days stretch out in front of them. There would be much talk about house prices, how well Dessie McGrath was doing, what everything was worth these days – more expensive than Toronto, Dan, yes, that cowshed down the road. Emmet would start an argument with Constance about the Catholic Church – because Constance, who believed nothing, would not admit as much in front of her children who were expected to believe everything or at least pretend they believed it, just like their mother. Hanna would have a rant about some newspaper critic, their mother would opine that these people sometimes knew what they were talking about, and on they all would go. It was, Emmet thought, like living in a hole in the ground.

Hanna put a couple of slices of bread in the toaster, and the smell of it rising through the house woke Dan and brought him downstairs. She heard his step outside the kitchen door and knew it immediately – she had kept the rhythm of his footfall inside her, all these years.

He came in; a handsome man who resolved himself into her brother as soon as he opened his mouth to say, 'I thought it was you!' His voice had an American inflection that Hanna remembered from the last time they met, some time before the baby, when she and Hugh took a week in Manhattan and Dan brought them to the Met and to an exhibition by Bill Viola, and they had a fantastic time: Hugh talking stage sets with Dan – a field of sunflowers, that is what Dan wanted, a lake, an expanse, and Hugh said, 'Put it on the vertical, turn it into the back wall.'

'Hiya,' she said.

They did not kiss, not in the kitchen, though they would have kissed were they up in Dublin or in any other town. Instead Dan pulled out a chair, and Hanna got up to fill the kettle again. She knew, as the water hit the crusted element, that this was the only place in the world where Dan would sit, requiring tea. In any other kitchen he would serve and smooth and tend.

'Tea?' she said.

'Perfect,' he said.

'You right?' said Emmet. And Dan nodded to his little brother as though they had seen each other quite recently, when the truth was, neither of them could remember the date, nor did they try.

Rosaleen, meanwhile, was smiling. Her face seemed almost translucent. She was happy to see them all. She was happy because Dan was home.

Or she was happy for no reason, Emmet thought. Her face was a kind of cartoon. It had always been like this. There was something out of kilter with his mother's happiness, as though a light had been switched on by a passing stranger, and left to illuminate an empty room.

He wondered about her brain. Rosaleen found it hard to keep still, in her old age. She was always out in the garden, out on the road, she was always walking; rendered ecstatic by some view. She was hopped up, now, and out of the chair.

'I could give you salad and some chicken,' she said to Dan. 'I have a bag of salad.'

'Oh, no,' said Dan.

'They're so easy.'

'They *are* easy,' he said. 'But, you know, you load up with healthy groceries, I find, and they go off as soon as you reach for the ice cream. Not that this is off.'

He was beside her at the fridge door, they leaned into the interior light together and he had the bag of salad in his hand. Hanna knew it was the first bag of pre-washed salad Rosaleen had bought in her life.

'It's very light,' said Rosaleen.

And Dan said, 'You know that looks sort of perfect, I just might.'

After which there was a kerfuffle about dressing; what vinegar Rosaleen had, or did not have, and would he settle for lemon juice. Emmet, during all of this, read the paper in a stolid sort of way, but Hanna did not mind. She sat at the table with an unlit cigarette between her fingers and she could not get enough of Dan, the way he had grown into himself, and grown also into some version of a gay man that she might recognise. Her knowledge of him came from two directions and met in the human being sitting at the table, who was saying, 'You know what I miss? Bread and jam.' Grown up, Dan was so inevitable, and yet so unforeseen.

He sat in their father's chair, the prodigal returned. He looked around him as though tranced by every small thing.

'This!' he said. He went to touch the little jug for milk

and paused, his finger a millimetre away from the china. 'I haven't seen it in.'

'Oh you'll find us very,' said Rosaleen.

'No!' he said.

'Rustic,' she said.

'No,' said Dan. 'That's what I mean. It's perfect. It's fine.'

'I like to use things,' said Rosaleen. 'Even if nothing matches. Not any more.'

'Absolutely,' said Dan, thinking how much Ludo would like his mother's table – how much Ludo would like his mother, perhaps, wondering if everything was going to be all right, after all.

Hanna saw Dan's small smile. They all saw it. The shadow of someone else was in the room. Rosaleen looked to the window, where her reflection was forming on the pane.

'Remember that Christmas,' she said to Hanna, 'you broke the Belleek?'

'I didn't break the Belleek,' said Hanna.

'The little Belleek jug,' said Rosaleen, 'Like a shell.'

'It was Constance,' said Hanna.

'Oh,' said Rosaleen, unconvinced. 'Remember that little jug?' she said to Dan. 'It was like a shell, what do you call that glaze, what it does to the light?'

'Lustre,' he said. 'Yes.'

'It was Constance, ' said Hanna.

'I thought it was you,' said Rosaleen, mildly.

'Well you were wrong.'

'Oh it doesn't matter,' said Rosaleen, as though it was Hanna who had brought the subject up.

'I Did. Not. Break. ThefuckingBelleek!'

'You can get it all on eBay now,' said Dan. 'And, you know, it doesn't price well.'

'God, the way you went on about it,' said Emmet. 'Mind the Belleek!'

'The Belleek!! The Belleek!!' said Hanna.

'How much is it, anyway?' said Emmet to Dan.

'Not much,' said Dan.

'We'll get you a new one, all right, Ma?'

And Rosaleen, stilled by the word *Ma*, decided to say nothing, except perhaps for one last, small thing.

'It was my father's,' she said.

Hanna went out to smoke her cigarette then, checking the rooms on the way through to the front door. But there wasn't a drink to be had in the house, she knew that already, apart from the bottles of wine lined up on the sideboard in the dining room for the Christmas dinner, and those could not be breached.

Back in the kitchen Dan was still romancing their mother, feeding her anecdotes about some woman who was too wonderful to be famous.

'She lives with just a housekeeper now, and someone to look after the dogs.'

'And he never came back?'

'He never came back.'

Hanna cleared some cups into the sink and signalled to Emmet, who was still stuck in the newspaper.

'Will you walk out the road,' she said. 'It's Christmas Eve.'

'Oh right.'

'They'll all be below in Mackey's.'

'I suppose.'

And in three minutes flat they were out the door, over the humpy bridge, and passing the bright forecourt of the Statoil garage, where there was, Hanna realised, cheap wine on sale in the shop, if she needed to get some on the way home.

'Jesus God,' said Hanna.

The wind was against them, and flecked with rain.

'I told her,' she said. 'I told her Hugh was taking the baby for the day.'

'*I* told her,' said Emmet.

'You think she's losing her grip?'

'What?' said Emmet.

'Just.'

'She's sharp as a tack,' said Emmet, because he could not countenance it.

The eaves of the houses on Curtin Street were draped with icicles that rained blue light on them as they walked beneath and the decorations continued tastefully into the main street where Christmas Eve was in full swing. It was taking your life in your hands, said Emmet, but it was more like passing your life on the road; some drunken geezer slapping you on the shoulder only to find – my God – Seán O'Brien from national school, who Emmet ran with and loved with the frank and unrepeatable love you have for another boy, when you are eight years old.

'Seán O'Brien, how are you?'

'Emmet, you langer.'

His eyes as blue and ironic as ever, in a scalded, red face.

Hanna, meanwhile, crouched low and flung her arms out, as a woman stumbled towards her – on to her, indeed – wearing gold sandals on bare feet, a golden cardigan, her hair gold blonde and leaping, fountaining, out of her head.

'Mairéad!'

'How are you, you good thing? How are you, my darling? Hanna Madigan.'

'My God, look at you. My God! Look at you!'

'You think?' She dabbed at the bright blonde hair.

'I thought you were in Australia.'

'We're home! We're up in Dublin. Home for good.'

Mackey's was jammed. They passed friends and the brothers of friends. Everyone was dressed, clipped, groomed; no beards, no stubble, no naked nails, some naked thigh, cleavage, muffin top. A pub that, in their youth, smelt of wet wool and old men was now a gallery of scents, like walking through the perfume department in the Duty Free.

Hanna stuck close to Emmet as they forced their way through the crowd. How was she supposed to recognise anyone, she said, when everyone's hair was dyed and all the same damn colour?

'They've all taken to the bottle,' she said.

Emmet caught his reflection in a bar divider and he saw another decade – not just the unkempt hair or the cheap shirt, but something about the ordinary, diffident look in his eye which made the others look a bit mad, he thought. He wondered how much cocaine was in the place. And then he wondered at the thought.

In Mackey's. Cocaine.

'How are you Emmet Madigan? I thought you were out on the missions. Will you have something, now, on me. A Christmas drink, on me.'

It was one of the McGraths, a nephew of Dessie's – and of Constance, therefore, by marriage – son of the real estate McGrath who was minting it these days. Michael or Martin. He was, as far as Emmet knew, a young lawyer beyond in Limerick. Not the worst of them, with the stubby McGrath thing. Walk through a wall for you.

'I will not, thanks.'

'You will.'

'I won't.'

'You'll take something anyway, for the good work. Keep up the good work.'

The man had his wallet out, and was thumbing through notes, half bent over, as though in humility. He could hardly see the damn things. Purple ones – five hundreds he had in there. He took out a wedge of apricot-coloured fifties and pushed it at Emmet.

'You will,' he said.

'I will not.'

'You will. Humour me,' and when Emmet backed away, there was a horrible pause. His hand pulsed mid-air, as though marking time with the money. Then he lifted his eyes slowly to say, 'It's for a special intention, all right?'

There must have been four hundred euros there. Emmet looked at the man and wondered if he had murdered someone. What shame or sorrow afflicted him so badly he had to get it off his conscience in this way? Nothing, perhaps. The shame of being rich. He couldn't hold on to the stuff.

'I'll get you a receipt for that.'

'Fuck the receipt,' said the McGrath nephew, and he loomed up into Emmet's face. 'Do you get me? Fuck the fuckin' receipt. All right?'

'I get you,' Emmet said. 'I get you. Fair play to you.' Thinking he'd never be able to get this through the system: they were a charity, not a money-laundering operation.

'We do have to keep things straight.'

The McGrath man leaned back and gaped at him then, as though to start a real fight, but Hanna, who had gone looking for a place to sit, was back by his side.

'It's bedlam,' she said. 'I went double.'

She had two dirty pints for him, encircled by thumb and forefinger. The other fingers held symmetrical small bottles of white wine, and in her right pinky, the stem of a glass.

'Hanna Madigan,' said the McGrath boy. 'It's well you're looking.'

'Ah, Michael,' said Hanna, with blatant insincerity. 'I didn't see you there at all.'

He turned away and, 'Why does everything feel so mad?' she said to Emmet. 'It's like. I don't know what it's like. Everyone's so.'

'I know,' said Emmet.

'Showing off.'

'It's the money,' said Emmet.

'Like everyone's a returned Yank, even if they're living up the road. Hiya, Frank! home for the duration?' She lifted a glass, then turned back to her brother.

'That fecker. People you ran away from, years ago. Then back to the house, for more of it, I suppose. No wonder they're fucking pissed.'

She was drunk herself, halfway down the glass. It happened all in one go, the shutters rolling up on a whole different woman. Emmet noted the transformation. Hanna's eyes clouding with a kind of mid-distance indifference, a twitching lift of her chin, a tiny smile.

Here's Johnny.

'Fucking baby this, baby that. Who knew she was so keen on babies? Why don't you have a baby? Take the onus off.'

'Yeah, well,' said Emmet.

'She's very worried about you.'

'You don't say.'

It was what Rosaleen said: 'I am very worried about Emmet.'

'God, you're cold,' Hanna said. 'You know that. You're a cold bastard, really. Does that Dutch chick know how cold you are? Does she know?'

It was a good question. Emmet ignored it.

'She always liked babies,' he said. 'It's adults she can't stand.'

'Puberty,' said Hanna.

'At least you didn't go bald,' said Emmet. 'She took that very personally. As I recall.'

'Anyway, she's very worried about you.'

It still got to them. Rosaleen never said it to your face, whatever it was. She moved instead around and behind her

children, in some churning state of mild and constant dis-
traction. 'I am very worried about Hanna.' It was her way
of holding on to them, perhaps. Rosaleen was afraid they
would leave her. She was afraid it was all her fault. 'I'm
really very worried about Constance, I think she might be
depressed.' All the things that were unsayable: failure,
money, sex, drink. 'I am very worried about Hanna, she
is looking very puffy about the face.' And, for a while, to
everyone's great amusement: 'I'm really worried about Dan,
do you think he might be gay?' to which Emmet had
replied, 'Don't ask me, I'm only his brother.'

'What about?' said Emmet, despite himself.

Hanna's face blanked and lifted.

'Fuck her,' she said. 'She just said she was worried about
you. That's all.'

'Well, she can relax.'

Hanna decided to leave it then, but it would not be left.
As soon as she tried to change the subject, it came back,
in a little surge of malice.

'Just if there was some little problem there, is all.'

She was now actually and improbably drunk, and this
distracted Emmet, for two seconds, from the fact that his
sister was talking about his sexual functioning, which is to
say, about his erection, first of all to his mother and then
to his face.

'*What?*' said Emmet, suddenly angry. Terribly angry.

'That's what she said.'

'What did she say? What, exactly?'

But Michael McGrath was back by Hanna's side. 'I hope
that's a Sauvignon Blanc,' he said, handing her another
little bottle of wine.

'Ah now,' said Emmet.

'Not at all,' said the McGrath boy, who had not, in fact,
brought a drink for Emmet. He stood there and settled

into his own pint, sank an inch or two off the top of it, feet planted.

'How's herself?' he said.

'Good,' said Hanna.

'She's fierce fit. I do see her betimes on the road.'

'Yes,' said Emmet. The man tilted his head.

'You'll be sorry, I suppose, to see the old place go?'

'Excuse me?'

The young McGrath clearly knew something they did not, and the intimacy of that was hard to handle. The glee.

'Great time to do it. Great timing. I had a house, now, we were doing the conveyancing on a house outside Kilfenora, handsome looking thing all right, rotten inside to the rafters, and they pulled it off the market on the Friday, put it back on on the Monday fifty grand up, and it went for over that again. Well over.'

'How much?'

'Ah now!' he said. He screwed up one side of his face, and bit off an imaginary large length of toffee. A wink. 'That'd be telling.'

'Right,' said Emmet.

Hanna drank with some intensity, looking directly at Michael McGrath, while Emmet thought about the hungry and the dead and about the man who stood in front of him now.

He should go back to counselling, Ireland was wrecking his head. He could feel a child's back under his hand; the amazing small bones, the acetone smell of his dying. Where was that? What day was that?

And, as though she knew what he was thinking, Hanna said, 'Would you jump into my grave as quick?'

'Drink up,' said Emmet. 'Let's go.'

'You go,' said Hanna. 'You fucking go.'

She blinked back some tears, gave Michael McGrath a

gammy, wet smile. An offer of some kind. It did not bear thinking about. As if servicing Stubby McGrath would make things better. His own sister.

'Come on,' said Emmet.

'I'm very worried about me, *actually*.'

'Oh for feck's sake,' said Emmet.

But he felt sorry for her, too, and did not object when she stopped off in the garage shop for a couple of bottles of Oxford Landing, the place jammed with people buying batteries, chocolates, alcohol.

The Hungry Grass

ROSALEEN TOLD CONSTANCE she did not want a present this year. She said it in a faint voice, meaning she would be dead soon so what was the point? What was an object – when you would not have it for long? Too much? Not enough? It was hard to say.

Constance thought she was immune to this sort of guff, but she also needed to tell her mother that she was not about to die so she went up to Galway and trawled through every last thing in the shops, until she found a thick silk scarf that was the same price as a new microwave and so beautiful you could not say what colour it was, except there was lilac in there and also pearl, all of which would be perfect for her mother's complexion and for her silver-white hair.

'Oh I can't remember,' she would say when her mother asked the price, or complained about the price. Times were good. Constance bought a wheel of Camembert, various boxes of chocolates, Parma ham and beautiful, small grapes that were more yellow than green. She got her hair done in a place so posh it didn't look done at all. Then she drove back home through the winter darkness in the smell of

PVC and ripening cheese, happy in her car. Constance loved to drive. It was the perfect excuse. For what, she did not know. But there was such simplicity to it: crossing great distances to stop an inch away from the kerb, opening the door.

The next morning she was back behind the wheel, picking Dan up from the airport, depositing him in her mother's, back in to the butcher's and a few things around town, a poinsettia for the cleaner, a trio of hyacinths for the cleaner's mother who was in hospital in Limerick and could not understand a thing the doctors told her. The cleaner was from Mongolia, a fact that made Constance slightly dizzy. But it was just true. Her cleaner – good hearted, a little bit vague with a duster – was from Ulan Bator. Constance left the presents with her money on the kitchen table, then back out to Ardeevin with the turkey and a quick tidy up while she was there: checking supplies, running a Hoover, though her mother hated the sound of the Hoover. After which, home to drive Shauna to a pal's house, her fake tan leaving a shadow on the cream upholstery of the Lexus.

'Ooofff,' said Constance, when she saw it and then chastised her temper. That all her problems should be so small.

The next morning, she went early into Ennis. It was 10 a.m. on Christmas Eve and the supermarket was like the Apocalypse, people grabbing without looking, and things fallen in the aisles. But there was no good time to do this, you just had to get through it. Constance pushed her trolley to the vegetable section: celery, carrots, parsnips for Dessie, who liked them. Sausage and sage for the stuffing, an experimental bag of chestnuts, vacuum packed. Constance bought a case of Prosecco on special offer to wrap and leave on various doorsteps and threw in eight frozen pizzas in case the kids rolled up with friends. Frozen berries. Different ice cream. She got wine, sherry, whiskey, fresh nuts, salted nuts, crisps, bags and bags of apples, two mangoes, a melon, dark cherries for the fruit salad, root ginger, fresh mint, a wooden crate of satsumas, the fruit cold and promising sweet, each one with its own sprig of green, dark leaves. She got wrapping paper, red paper napkins, Sellotape, and – more out of habit, now the children were grown – packs and packs of batteries, triple A, double A, a few Cs. She took five squat candles in cream-coloured beeswax to fill the cracked hearth in the good room at Ardeevin, where no fire was lit this ten years past, and two long rolls of simple red baubles to fill the gaps on her mother's tree. She went back for more sausages because she had forgotten about breakfast. Tomatoes. Bacon. Eggs. She went back to the dairy section for more cheese. Back to the fruit aisle for seedless grapes. Back to the biscuit aisle for water biscuits. She searched high and low for string to keep the cloth on the pudding, stopped at the delicatessen counter for pesto, chicken liver pâté, tubs of olives. She got some ready-cooked drumsticks to keep people going. At every corner, she met a neighbour, an old friend, they rolled their eyes and threw Christmas greetings, and no one thought her rude for not stopping to converse. She smiled at a baby in the queue for the till.

'I know!' she said. 'Yes I know!' The baby considered her fully. The baby gave her a look that was complete.

'Yes!' she said again, and got the curl of a sweet, thoughtful smile.

All this kept Constance occupied until the time came to unload the contents of her trolley on to the conveyor. The baby held itself so proudly erect, the young mother underneath it looked like a prop. She looked like some kind of clapped-out baby stand.

'You're doing great,' Constance told her. 'You're doing a great job.'

The bill came to four hundred and ten euros, a new record. She thought she should keep the receipt for posterity. Dessie would be almost proud.

Constance pushed her trolley on to the walkway and the wheels locked cleverly on to the metal beneath them, and she was happy happy happy, as she sank towards the car park. She thanked God from the burning, rising depth of herself for this unexpected life – a man who loved her, two sons taller than their father, and a daughter who kissed her still when no one was there to see. She could not believe this was the way things had turned out.

Her feet were swollen already; she could feel them throb, hot in the wrong shoes. Constance bumped the trolley off the walkway, set her trotters thumping across the concrete of the car park. It was half past eleven on Christmas Eve. In the pocket of her coat, her phone started to ring and, by the telepathy of the timing, Constance knew it was her mother.

'What is it, darling,' she said, remembering, as she did so, that she had forgotten the Brussels sprouts.

'He's still asleep,' said Rosaleen. For a moment Constance thought she was talking about her father, a man who was not asleep, but dead.

'Well don't wake him,' she said.

Dan. Of course, she meant Dan, who was jet lagged.

'Should I?'

'Or maybe do. Yeah. Get him straightened out.'

There was a pause from Rosaleen. *Straightened out.*

'You think?'

'Have you everything?' said Constance.

'I don't know,' said her mother.

'Don't worry.'

'It's a lot of work,' Rosaleen said, with a real despair in her voice; you would think she had just spent an hour in the insanity of the supermarket, not Constance.

'But I suppose it's worth it to have you all here.'

'I suppose.'

'I'll be sorry to see it go.' She was talking about the house again. Any time she felt needy, now, or lost or uncertain, she talked about the house.

'Right,' said Constance. 'Listen, Mammy.'

'*Mammy*,' said Rosaleen.

'Listen –'

'Oh, don't bother. I'll let you go.' And she was gone.

It was Rosaleen, of course, who wanted Brussels sprouts, no one else ate them. Constance stood for a moment, blank behind the crammed boot of the Lexus. You can't have Christmas without Brussels sprouts.

Sometimes even Rosaleen left them on her plate. Something to do with cruciferous vegetables, or nightshades, because even vegetables were poison to her when the wind was from the north-east.

'Oh what the hell,' said Constance. She slammed the boot shut and turned her sore feet back to the walkway and the horrors of the vegetable section. Then over to the spices to get nutmeg, which was the way Rosaleen liked her Brussels, with unsalted butter. And it was a good thing she went back up, because she had no cranberry sauce either – unbelievably – no brandy for the brandy butter, no honey to glaze the ham. It was as though she had thrown the whole shop in the trolley and bought nothing. She had no big foil for the turkey. Constance grabbed some potato salad, coleslaw, smoked salmon, mayonnaise, more tomatoes, litre bottles of fizzy drinks for the kids, kitchen roll, cling film, extra toilet paper, extra bin bags. She didn't even look at the bill after another fifteen minutes in the queue behind some woman who had forgotten flowers – as she announced – and abandoned her groceries to get them, after which Constance did exactly the same thing, fetching two bouquets of strong pink lilies because they had no white left. She was on the way home before she remembered potatoes, thought about pulling over to the side of the road and digging some out of a field, imagined herself with her hands in the earth, scrabbling around for a few spuds.

Lifting her head to howl.

Back in Aughavanna she unpacked and sorted the stuff that would go over to Ardeevin for the Christmas dinner and she repacked that. Then she went to Rory's room, where the child was sleeping off a hangover. Constance took off her shoes and climbed on to the bed behind him.

'Oh fuck,' he said.

'Your own fault,' said his mother, as she spooned into him, with the duvet between them and the wall at her back.

'Ah, Ma,' he said and flapped a big hand over his shoulder to find a bit of her, which happened to be the top of her head. But Rory was always easy to hold; easy to carry and easy to kiss, and there, in the smell of last night's beer and his rude good health, fretful, lumpy Constance McGrath fell asleep.

In the evening she brought Shauna over to Ardeevin with the ingredients for the stuffing and they put it all together right there at the table in the big kitchen. Dan knew exactly what to do with the experimental bag of chestnuts. They chopped and diced, the three of them, while the others were at the pub, and they put the vegetables under water for the next day while Rosaleen supervised happily from the chair by the range. Dan talked about Tim Burton with Shauna and they discussed the veins on Madonna's arms. He asked a couple of excruciating questions about pop music, she asked about an artist called Cindy Sherman, and this just knocked Dan for six. He kissed the child before they left, he piled her hair on the top of her head, saying, 'Look at you!' and Constance would have loved to stay longer, to be that thing, a grown-up child in her parents' house, but she had presents to wrap back in Aughavanna and she did not get to bed, as it turned out, until after two.

There was no dishwasher in Ardeevin so the next day Constance was at the sink non-stop, finding crockery, dipping through soaking pans and greasy dishes to prise out a bowl for the carrots, another side plate, a serving spoon. Hanna was too miserable to help and Emmet did not see the need for it – it was like he had a different set of eyes. So it was her and Dan, mostly, but Dan did not do dishes, Dan did food. And her mother did not like the scarf, of course she didn't. How could Constance have ever expected her to?

There was no pleasing her.

Rosaleen spent the early part of the day quietly enough. She walked into town for Mass and stopped for a cup of tea with the two elderly sisters who lived over the Medical Hall, because Bart and his wife were in Florida for the duration. She came back with the cooking in full swing, and she spent some time organising the table and making it beautiful, with pine cones sprayed silver and white baubles, which she scattered in an artful way around two pewter candlesticks: white candles, white cloth, a sprinkling of glitter, a squirt of artificial snow. She went out to the garden for greenery and a fading, freakish rose that bloomed against her sunniest wall. And this yellow rose she set on a corner of the mantelpiece, where it dropped petals as the day went on and the dinner was not yet served because – and you couldn't blame him – Dan did not get the bird on till nine. So Constance was grabbing the crisps out of Shauna's hand, saying, 'Wait', and then out of Emmet's hands, while Hanna leaned against the range, sipping sherry intended for the gravy, and nothing was on time.

And just as she had the gravy reducing in the pan, Rosaleen called them in to the front room. She was like a child, Constance thought, she waited until things were Completely Impossible, and then she went Beyond.

Rosaleen had the wrapped scarf in her hand. She held the parcel up and wiggled it from side to side.

'Wait, Mammy,' said Constance, wiping her hands on her apron.

'A scarf!' said Rosaleen.

But when the paper was off and the beautiful thing out in the light, Constance knew who had won this time around. The scarf was even better here in the living room than it had been in the shop and Rosaleen was almost put out, it looked so well in the winter light. She set it across her shoulders and picked at the fabric.

'Oh this is far too good for me.'

Rosaleen hated being upstaged by her own clothes. It was a rule. Vulgarity she called it, but the scarf was not vulgar, it was entirely discreet.

'It's lovely on you,' Constance said.

They had all drifted in to watch: Constance, Dan, Emmet, Hanna. With Dessie at the back of the room, looking at all the Madigans.

'Pink,' said Rosaleen, taking it off and setting it against the dark green and glitter of the Christmas tree. 'Very fresh. Though Lord knows, I'm probably a bit old for pink.'

No one answered, so she said it again.

'Long time since I wore pink.'

'I wouldn't call it pink,' said Constance. 'Maybe lavender.'

'Lilac,' said Hanna.

'Lilac shawl,' said Emmet. 'You know that's actually Sanskrit.'

'Is it?' said Dan, because there was no getting around Emmet when he had a fact, you just had to let him slap it out there, and admire.

'Yes. Both words. "Lilac" and "shawl".'

'Thanks, Emmet,' said Hanna.

Rosaleen bunched up the 'lilac shawl', annoyed by Emmet, or annoyed by the thing itself. She chucked it into the easy chair by the fireplace, and was cross with herself then, because her children were all looking at her.

'Oh I am tired of myself now,' she said.

And because it was Christmas, she started to cry.

'Oh, Mammy,' said Constance.

'My own children,' she said, as though they had ganged up against her in some terrible way.

'Your own children *what*?' said Emmet.

'My own children!' she said. Furious now. 'My own flesh and blood!'

And Hanna, who had done nothing all day except mope, said, 'Mama, Mama. Come on.' Leading her gently to the sofa. 'Would you like a little sherry?'

'No I would not like a little sherry,' said Rosaleen. 'Tell them, Desmond. Tell them what I want.'

Dessie was standing well back from them all.

'Sorry?' he said.

'Orange shampoo,' said Emmet. 'That's another one.'

'Oh shut up,' said his siblings, almost as one: Hanna inserting, 'the fuck' in there so ending a little late and off the beat.

'Tell them,' said Rosaleen, looking to Dessie, as though to her only protector, and Dessie (*the fool*, thought Constance) said, 'Well.'

235

'I'm putting the house on the market,' said Rosaleen. 'Dessie has it all arranged.'

There was nothing for Dessie to do now, except concur.

'Your mother thinks it's a good time – and it is a good time, it is a really good time – to realise this . . . asset.'

He waved his hand vaguely, as though talking about the wallpaper, or the carpet, a gathered handful of air.

'Excuse me?' said Hanna.

'She wants to get the money moving. Am I right? To divide it up a little. Now, rather than later.'

'Well none of you has any money,' said Rosaleen, perched on the edge of the sofa. She smoothed the cloth of her skirt over her knees and picked at a piece of fluff.

'I don't know whose fault that is. I mean, apart from mine. I don't know what I did to deserve that.'

And there it was. Her children were going to object. They wanted to say that they had money or that they did not need money, but their failure gaped back at them, and they just stood there, looking at it. It was true. They had no money. And yet, and yet. They each struggled to remember this, they had enough. Whatever they wanted, it wasn't this.

'Please don't,' said Emmet.

'It's too much for me,' said Rosaleen, her voice beginning to tremble. And this was also true: the house was too big for one person.

'So that is the way, I suppose,' Dessie said. 'That's where things are tending.'

'I am moving in with Constance,' Rosaleen said. 'I've had enough.'

Dessie stopped then, as though this last was news to him too.

And Constance said, 'Jesus, the dinner.'

The Brussels sprouts were burning. The smell of it had been getting worse for some time.

'The sprouts,' she said.

'Oh please don't fuss,' said Rosaleen as Constance squawked and ran out the door.

'Please stop.' She lifted her voice. 'No one likes them anyway.'

There was a silence in the hall. After a moment Constance came back in to the room.

'You like them,' she said to Rosaleen. The smell by now was quite intense.

'Oh I just. I don't know. Maybe I do.'

As they went in, at Dan's behest, to the dining room, where the smoked salmon and asparagus was set, they could hear Constance in the garden beating the saucepan on the ground outside, and a noise out of her like a heifer stuck on a barbed wire fence. She was weeping.

Dessie said, 'Maybe a little bungalow, Rosaleen. Maybe that's what you are looking for.'

He pulled his mother-in-law's chair out for her, and she sat down.

'Oh Desmond,' she said, picking up her napkin. 'And the price of them going up by the day. As you tell me, yourself.'

Donal was in Australia, which left two young McGraths, Rory and Shauna, to sit at the little fold-out table, and though they were the size of adults, they stuck like children to their mobile phones.

'Put them *away*,' Dessie said, as he passed, but they ignored him, and the Madigans sat in the tiny, demented sound of their electronic games. Hanna picked up the fork and set it down again. Constance did not come in.

They sat and looked at the food in front of them. It was half past two on Christmas Day, the weather outside was clear and fine; no traffic on the road, no wind to curl under the eaves or annoy the windows. The house was silent and large about them. There was no one to say grace – their father was dead.

It was Dan's job now. Dan the spoilt priest. He looked around him, then down at the table. He took a breath.

'Buon appetito,' he said.

Which gave the siblings a small jab of pleasure. They applied themselves to the asparagus, which was wrapped in smoked salmon with a lemon dressing. It was very good.

'This is very good,' said Emmet.

'Really simple,' said Dan.

Outside, Constance had stopped weeping.

'How's school?' said Hanna.

'Good,' said Shauna from the little table.

'Any word from Donal?'

'Surfing, sure. Byron Bay. There's a whole gang of them there from Lahinch.'

When the starter was done, Dan cleared and went into the kitchen where Constance was filling the Christmas plates. He brought them in two at a time; ham, turkey, three types of stuffing, all the trimmings. Then Constance herself came in – red-faced, sweating, the silk of her blouse flecked with grease.

'Ta-dahh!' said Dan.

There was a little round of applause for Constance and she sat into her accustomed place, and there they all were, girls facing the window, boys facing the room: Constance-and-Hanna, Emmet-and-Dan. Their mother sat at the foot of the table, Dessie at the head, and for a moment they pretended that nothing had happened, that this room would always be the same, and always theirs.

It was older, now, of course. The damp had crawled higher through the bamboo patterned wallpaper, leaving its tea coloured watermark, and the edge in the north-east corner was spotted with black and curled up from the skirting board. The Madigan children saw it with wiser eyes. The chandelier – so wonderful, long ago – was a cheap enough thing. The brown carpet was the best you could do in 1973.

The people inside the room were older, too. All of them so child-like still, despite the absurd grey hairs and the sagging skin in which their familiar eyes were set.

They worked the gravy and the sauces, passed stuffing, the salt, the water jug and the wine. They looked at the plates heaped with food and marvelled aloud at it, each of them silently shouting that she could not take it away from them, whatever it was – their childhood, soaked into the walls of this house.

And of course it could be sold. That was also true. The house was hers and she could sell it, if she liked.

'The turkey is great,' said Rory from the little table and Constance was proud of him; Rory, the peacemaker, working hard.

'Thank you,' said Dan.

'Very moist,' said Dessie.

Dan tried not to laugh at the word.

'You think?'

He looked up at stubby Dessie McGrath, there at the top of the table. He remembered a brief encounter with the alcoholic brother, Ferdy McGrath, when they were both still boys, playing by the river Inagh. But he never got near Dessie. Not even close. His brother-in-law was not so much straight as sorted. Dessie McGrath was a weapon.

'Yes it is,' said Dan. 'Surprisingly moist.'

Dessie did not blink.

'Hard to get right, at a guess,' he said and went back to his plate, shovelling the stuff into himself, while the

Madigan children chewed and chewed, and could not swallow.

The truth was that the house they were sitting in was worth a ridiculous amount, and the people sitting in it were worth very little. Four children on the brink of middle age: the Madigans had no traction in the world, no substance. They had no money. Dan, especially, had no money, and he could could not think why this was, or who might be to blame. But he recognised, in the silence, the power Rosaleen had over her children, none of whom had grown up to match her.

'I don't know how I'll eat all this.' She was a bit like a child, herself. 'My goodness.'

She forgot to tell us about money, he thought, and we forgot to make any, because the Madigans were above all that. The stuck-up Madigans, the Madigans beyond the bridge. Rosaleen thought money would fly to us, because we deserved it. She thought we would spend our lives giving it away.

Which is what Emmet had done, pretty much. Poured his life out, like water into the African sands. He felt it keenly – they all did – the lack of anything to show for it all. Twenty years saving a world that remained unsaved. If you thought about it, he was as much a fantasist as his mad mother.

The yellow rose gave up a clump of pale petals and they sighed as they hit the mantelpiece.

Hanna said, 'You know, Mammy, it's our house too.'

Rosaleen looked at her. She said, 'Beautiful. Beautiful Hanna Madigan.'

Each of them came back from the privacy of their own thoughts then, ready for the fight. The air cleared.

'What do you mean?' said Hanna.

'Nothing,' said Rosaleen. 'Just that you are. So pretty.'

'Thank you,' said Hanna.

'You have a heart shaped face, I always thought. An old-fashioned face. You were born to play Viola.'

'Yeah well,' said Hanna.

'No?'

'Sure,' said Hanna.

'Well you are an actress,' Constance said, trying to keep the inverted commas out of her voice.

'Yes I am an actress,' said Hanna. 'Yes that is what I am.'

'Well then,' said Rosaleen, in a soothing tone.

'I just don't,' said Hanna. Her hand was flat and she brought the edge of it down on the tabletop. 'I don't.'

'Work?' said Emmet.

'Darling, you have a baby to look after,' said Rosaleen.

'Hang on,' said Dan.

'Jesus Christ!' said Hanna, losing it.

'Can you please leave her alone?' Dan said, but Hanna was already building to a shout.

'I Just Don't Want To Play Viola.'

'I don't know how you can say that,' said her mother, sadly.

'I'm not sure anyone's asked,' said Emmet. 'In all fairness'.

'I have no interest in playing Viola,' said Hanna in a very deliberate voice. 'I am interested in process. That's what I do. New stuff. Viola is not where I am at, all right? It's not what I'm for. Anyway, nobody ever puts on *Twelfth Night*.'

'What a pity,' said her mother. 'I'd love to see you do it. Before I get too old.'

'Rosaleen, darling,' said Dan. 'Please stop.'

'Stop what?' said Rosaleen, but by some miracle she distracted herself into an old story about the night war was declared, when she was ten years old and Anew McMaster was playing Othello, naked to the waist and his beautiful voice, you could feel it on your skin, it was a force. Her father saying they were in for it now – because of the war, you know – and she had no idea what he meant. She thought it was something to do with the events on stage.

'What about your mother?' Constance said quietly and Rosaleen sighed.

'Oh, Mama.'

'Was she there, too?'

'That's a good question,' said Rosaleen.

'I mean, you know what I mean. What was she like?'

'Sorry?'

'Was she nice?'

'Well of course she was nice.'

'What kind of nice?' Hanna joined in, now. 'What style of a woman was she?'

'My mother?' said Rosaleen. 'Oh she was lovely. She was always beautifully turned out. She had to go to Limerick specially, or up to Dublin once a year, for a fitting. Always wore a hat. She had three of them on the go; a summer hat, a winter felt, and, you know, a thing for the races, or a wedding if there was a wedding. A dress hat, that is what I mean.'

'Right,' said Hanna. They were all turned towards their mother now. They were looking for something from her and Rosaleen did not know what it was.

'She always did things the right way,' she said.

Dan said, 'And was she – I don't know. Was she a happy type?'

'Well I think she was happy,' said Rosaleen. 'What kind of a question is that?'

To which there was no answer, really.

'It's a very hard thing,' said Rosaleen, finally. 'To describe your mother.'

'Yes,' said Hanna.

'Except that she is your mother,' Constance said, her voice full of disapproval, her face tucked down as she worked her plate. But the others did not know what she meant by that. And they sat for a moment, in silence.

'It's like there's some secret,' said Hanna. 'But there just isn't.'

And there they were. It was a Christmas like the ones they remembered from the old days – and how could they forget how the dinner always ended? It was traditional, you might say. Rosaleen got upset.

'I don't know why everyone is getting at me,' she said. 'The ungrateful children I reared.'

Tears coated her eyeballs; she blinked them back.

'Oh, darling,' said Dan in a voice that was almost bored. 'Rise above.'

'I gave you everything.'

Constance reached a useless hand across the tablecloth.

'And there is no end to it. I am still handing it over. I can see no end to it all.'

She was on her dignity, face averted.

'Whatever I did – whatever it was – it was not enough. Clearly. That's all. I just don't know.' The tears spilled over now. Rosaleen was a little girl. Rosaleen was a sad old woman. Their own mother. In a moment she would leave and go up to bed and Oh, they all loved her now, they were hopeless in it. They yearned to make her happy.

'Stop, Mammy,' said Constance. 'You'll make yourself sick, now.'

'No I am not talking to you, not any of you,' she said. 'Shauna, say your poem.'

'What poem, Granny?'

'Oh little Corca Baiscinn.'

But Shauna did not have that poem, or any poem. She had a song, said Constance. But she didn't have a song either, apparently.

'Did you bring your tin whistle?' said Dessie.

'No,' said Shauna. Then she changed her mind. 'I mean yes, I have it here.'

'Good girl.'

Shauna stood where she was, slender in a dress of black jersey that just about covered the beautiful S of her backside. She flung back her red hair and lifted the tin whistle, then she tossed her hair back again and stuck her hip to one side. After a quick, nervous smirk, she applied her lips and fingers to a tune that they all recognised, on the first four notes, as the beautiful 'Róisín Dubh'.

'Ah,' said Rosaleen, because it was her song, translated.

O my Dark Rosaleen!

Do not sigh, do not weep!

The sound of it sweet beyond reckoning and sadly heroic.

'Incomparable,' said Dessie, adoring his daughter openly, there in the middle of all the mad Madigans. 'Ye girl ye!'

And it was Shauna's job to light the pudding, because she was the youngest, so they turned off the lights and Dessie poured the whiskey from the cap of the bottle; two tin measures. The liquid fire spilled down the dark sides of the pudding, then the flames licked back up themselves, and they matched Shauna's eyes for blue, and her hair for orange. She shrieked at what she had done and, delighted, stepped back.

After which, Rosaleen rallied, as only Rosaleen could. She took up a spoon and struck it against her glass and, as if there had been no argument, no tears, she lifted her chin and made her Christmas speech:

'I look around me on a day like today and I can't believe how well you look, or that you are anything to me, or anything indeed, to the creatures running around my feet in this very room all those years ago. I can see them yet. The children you used to be. And how sad that your father is not here to enjoy you the way I still can. And maybe Dan could do the honours. Dan?'

Dan stood up.

'What is it again?'

'Go mbeirimíd beo,' said Constance.

'Guh merrimeed bee-oh,' said Dan

'Ag an am seo arís.'

'Egg on ahm shee-yuh a-reesh.'

'That we will all be alive this time again. Or this time next year,' Dessie translated, for the benefit of his daughter, and Shauna said, 'Ew,' making them all laugh. He pulled her into his lap, saying, 'Is that the way of it?' And Constance stood to clear the dishes, one more time.

'This time next year. Indeed,' said Rosaleen, in a wan voice. 'Wherever we may find ourselves.'

Constance, stacking the dishes, cracked a plate off the one below it.

'Mind the Belleek!' said Emmet.

'Any chance of a coffee?' said Dan.

'There's no coffee,' said Constance. 'Sorry. I forgot.'

'You forgot,' Hanna said, reaching for her cigarettes; the sloppy sarcasm perfectly pitched to undo her sister, who was heading for the door. Constance turned.

'Yes, I forgot. There is no coffee, except instant maybe. I forgot.'

'Just asking,' said Hanna.

'You can bring your own fucking coffee, do you hear me?'

'Oh, dearie-me,' said Rosaleen.

'Mind the Belleek!' said Emmet. 'Mind the Belleeek!'

Constance was holding the pile of plates, but instead of

dropping them or flinging them against the wall, she clutched them tight and screwed her face up.

'Oh God,' said Dan.

She looked altogether pathetic. She turned to leave then ducked back towards them again.

'You can't come,' she said.

It was a moment before they realised what she was saying. She was talking to Rosaleen.

'Sorry?'

'It's not fair. You can't come. You can't live in my house.'

'I can do what I like,' said Rosaleen.

'No, you can't. You just can't. There's about seventy little houses getting built around here, you can have one of them. You would love it. Everything new and clean. You can have your own little house.'

'You're not going to put me out on the roads,' said Rosaleen and Constance lowered her head.

'I just mean,' she said.

'Your own mother!'

'You can have your own little house.'

They thought they knew what would happen next. Constance would throw something (Mind the Belleek!) and Rosaleen would win. And when she had won, when she had everyone at the limits of themselves – Constance weeping as she brushed up the broken china, Constance begging to be forgiven – then she might decide not to sell the house, after all. She might not bother. And life would continue as before.

But in fact, Constance did not drop anything. She said, 'Dessie?' and she turned and walked out of the room. After a moment, Dessie lumbered after her.

'Tea will be fine,' said Dan. 'I'll make the tea.'

Hanna, who was drunk, lit up a cigarette.

'Fuck this,' she said. She took a couple of drags, then pushed back her chair and walked out too. After which, the men pretended to clear the table and scattered quietly about the house and no tea was made.

*

Dan went up to his old room to check his phone, and to text Ludo *OMG SOS*. He sat on the edge of the bed and even the sag of the mattress was familiar to him: taking his shape, as it had always done. There was no signal. He checked through old messages, that in their carelessness would remind him of his actual life – the one that happened far away from here.

If you can pick up some nice white fish, hake or turbot even I will give you a big kiss and a lick. xxl For like, four people?

Someone needs to tell Dale where to get off.

Hello from Atlanta airport. 2435 steps to gate C24 on the pedometer. Walking my way back to you babe.

Code for alarm is my birthday, figure it out! Don't forget to pick the raspberries. Enjoy!

The immersion cylinder next door made its usual hum: the high note of water thrilling through the pipes, a rolling chord of underboil, then the knock-back of an air hammer. Silence. Dan looked about the room where his young life was stored, his life before New York, not innocent so much as stupid.

Not innocent, at all.

The row of books: Man Ray, George Herbert, Gerard Manley Hopkins. Tennyson, even – how could he not have known? *Listener's Guide to Opera*. The anglepoise lamp he bought from his own pocket money in the local hardware store. The Modigliani poster on the wall a failed attempt to love some idea of a woman in the raw. Wrong painter. Wrong picture. Dan could not forgive himself all the misdirection of those years, as he told Scott, his portable therapist who

247

was back now in his head. He could not sentimentalise. All that withering and wasted time. He had failed to name the real events of his youth, or possess them as his own.

Even now, he wondered at the home movie of his memory. His father shrugging him away on Fanore beach – the slow motion feel to it. Who had pressed the mute button on his childhood? His father's hands were wet and cold. His mother was foolish. His grandmother had three hats. And, yet, everywhere he looked, the house held memory and meaning that his heart could not. The house was full of detail, interest, love.

It was a question of texture, Dan thought, a whiff of your former self in a twist of fabric, a loose board. It was the reassuring madness of patterned wallpaper under the daily shift of light. The sun rose at the front and set at the back of Ardeevin, wherever he was in the world, and when he came back, the house made sense in a way that nothing else did.

Downstairs, the sound of Constance hectoring her children about the washing-up. In the front bedroom, his brother Emmet, thinking his own thoughts. Dan could tell it was Emmet by the sound of his breathing almost. His little brother. He was fond of Emmet as a boy but, grown up, the man bored and frightened him. Balder now, Emmet always managed to look somehow undernourished, unfit. Unprepossessing. Dan did not know when their paths last crossed, then he remembered, with a jolt, the bones, under his hand, of his brother's shoulder as they carried their father's coffin down the aisle of the small church in Boolavaun.

That happened.

They carried the coffin. Six men. Sons at the front. In the middle, Dessie and their uncle Bart (queer as Christmas, Dan thought, how did he not guess?) A neighbour at the back, paired with a surprising American cousin, who was doing a course up in Dublin and had been dispatched west by a transatlantic phone call. It was a strange way to meet up. But the coffin – the coffin containing his father's body – was not so heavy. And it was such a practical thing to do. It was a task more than a burden. Once you have actually carried a dead man you are happy enough to leave him down, let them put the box into the damn ground.

Emmet had gone into his parents' room to find something, and he forgot, as soon as he entered it, what it was he was looking for.

It was a year or more since anyone had been in here. The wardrobe swinging open and half empty, his mother's pile of paperbacks on a little table beside the bed. Emmet glanced at the things on her dressing table, and it was as though she had already died. A couple of emery boards sliced with the residue of her nails. A tube of hand cream. Her little compact with a picture of a rose on the lid and – he knew the surprise of it so well – a mirror on the inside. There were bits of cheap jewellery in a crystal dish that might have been an ashtray once and rosary beads hung over the edge of the mirror. The rosary was his father's, last seen twisted about the dead man's fingers – she must have prised them off it again – when he was laid out in that same bed whose reflection was behind his own. Emmet almost expected his father's corpse to appear in the blank of the mirror, or to find him lying in the bed when he turned around.

His father was a Catholic. He was the real thing. Sinner and supplicant, one of the fretfully unredeemed.

Hail Holy Queen, Mother of Mercy,
Hail our life our sweetness and our hope.

To thee do we send forth our sighs
To thee do we cry poor banished children of Eve
Mourning and weeping in this vale of tears.

The beads were made of some translucent material gone grey inside, like poor man's pearls. Emmet reached to touch the thing and then couldn't, it made him feel slightly sick.

He looked, instead, at the postcards Rosaleen had stuck into the frame, between the wood and the glass: a minotaur by Picasso, the Annunciation by some Renaissance Italian, a version of the Nativity by Gauguin. All of them, he presumed, from Dan.

That mirror had seen enough action over the years.

It didn't bear thinking about, the things that happened in that bed. But also from Rosaleen, sitting in the little chair applying lipstick, tweezing, dabbing, checking and improving. She had such a demanding relationship with her own reflection. Rosaleen challenged her looks, and they rose to meet her.

He wondered where she had hidden herself, the passionate woman he had avoided and adored when he was a child. The woman who quoted poetry at them and the Bible. *I would you were cold, or hot. But because you are lukewarm, neither cold nor hot, I will spit you out of my mouth.* The woman who knelt down on the floor in front of him, and took him by the shoulders on the morning of his First Holy Communion, and said, 'Remember who you are. When you take the host, say it in your heart: Hello Jesus, my name is Emmet Madigan.'

This is what pushed him, from one country to the next. This energy. A woman who did nothing and expected everything. She sat in this house, year after year, and she *expected.*

Emmet caught sight of himself in the empty glass, and he took his disappointing face out of there. He had to get away from his mother, somehow. He had to step to one side, let the rush of her wanting pass him by.

He would marry Saar, that was one way to do it. He could follow her to Aceh in a few months' time, and after that he would follow her wherever she wanted to go. But when he tried to locate Saar in his mind, he found only Alice. Foolish Alice, with her helpless goodness, her idiotic lack of guile. He wondered who she was sleeping with now, if she would be at the big FAO bash in Rome, what would happen if he fell at her feet and wept, would that make any difference? He had an image of himself as Gabriel, offering a lily to a white-skinned Madonna who had Alice's downward glance and her slight, sad smile.

Outside, a jackdaw was bashing a snail on the roof, its feet scrabbling against the metal guttering. And *Sell sell sell*, he thought. Give the money to the poor. Burn the fucking place down.

Because Emmet was still trapped, always would be trapped, in some endlessly unavailable, restless ideal.

O clement, O loving,
O sweet Virgin Mary.

And he laughed a little, at the ironies of all that.

Downstairs, Constance did not know where to put herself. She was shaking after the confrontation in the dining room. She was so worried about Rosaleen, she was desperately worried about her mother, also cross with her, and cross with herself for buying the stupid scarf. And she was in a rage with Dessie, for taking the woman at her word. Rosaleen would never sell the house. It was just the kind

251

of thing she liked to say. Because Rosaleen never *did* anything. This maddening woman, she spent her entire life requiring things of other people and blaming other people, she lived in a state of hope or regret, and she would not, could not, deal with the thing that was in front of her, whatever it was. *Oh I forgot to go to the bank, Constance, I forgot to go to the post office.* She could not deal with stuff. Money. Details. Here. Now.

Rory came up behind her at the sink and he put his arms round her, the way Dessie sometimes did, though Rory was taller than Dessie and he also lacked – it went without saying – Dessie's sexual intent. He bent to lay his cheek against her shoulder and he swayed from side to side, humming a little.

'Happy Christmas,' he said.

'That's one way of putting it,' she said.

He lingered there another moment.

'Can I have some money?' he said.

'What do you want it for?'

'I just need, like, thirty.'

'Ask your father.'

He did not leave. He said, 'I love you anyway,' and he planted a kiss on the nape of her neck.

'I'm sure you do,' she said. 'Now go ask your father.'

He let go, but turned to prop his handsomeness against the counter and look at her for a minute.

'Next time, you could throw in a couple of beers.'

'I might,' said Constance.

'If you remember.'

'Hah.'

'God, Mum, she's really stiffed.'

'Don't talk about your auntie like that.'

'I mean really, though.'

'Shift.'

It was a secret thing for her – it wasn't a big deal – but

just the fact of her son made Constance entirely happy. He could do what he liked, she would not mind. He was a good guy, and he loved his mother, and not even his laundry offended her. Or not much.

'Out of my way now. Move your big spágs.'

*

Hanna came into the kitchen, and looked at the pair of them as though she knew they had been talking about her. She stubbed out the cigarette on the top of the range, and poured herself a glass of white wine. She lifted the glass to her mouth, and felt the baby at her lips, warm and baby-smelling, an unexpected yearning, as she drank, for his frank gaze, the damp interior of his hand.

The house was disappearing around her.

Hanna pushed away from the range and wandered away, before there was a fight with Constance, who was, clearly, in a snit. She went back into the hall and wondered where she could set it down, this hurt that sloshed around inside her. She glanced into the dining room and saw her mother gone from the Christmas table. She turned in to the good front room, with the cracked hearth, and walked all the way to the front window, where she set her hands on either side of the frame, facing north. The glass was as old as the house. It was her favourite thing, a fragile survivor, slubbed and thickened to gather and distort the light. Hanna tipped her forehead briefly against it as she looked out into the gloaming.

The house was disappearing around her, wall by wall.

It came to her at dinner, and she could not let it go. The knowledge that if she walked out of it now and kept walking, she could reach the famous Cliffs of Moher and there she could, unfamously, die. She looked about her, at the faces moving, the food, the candles, the glassware, the yellow of the white wine and the brown of the red. She thought about the cold outside, wondered how far the fall, how long the drop. She had her baby in her arms and they twisted slowly in the black air, drifting towards the sea, and then hitting the sea. The water was hard and the baby bounced up out of her arms and they were swamped and sank, both of them, and even that sinking was just a slower fall, as they turned and found each other, and lost each other again. It was a soft and endless death – at least in her mind. The baby astonished by it, the way it was astonished by escalators, lifts, the wonder of gravity, the baby looking to Hanna and Hanna looking to the baby saying, 'I have you. Yes!'

She heard Dan come in behind her, recognised him by the squeak of his shoe. This is how they knew each other, the Madigans, they knew the timbre of a voice, the rhythm of fingers tapping on a tabletop, and they didn't know each other at all. Not really. But they liked each other well enough. Apparently.

'I am getting married,' he said.

'Oh God Dan are you?'

Hanna turned.

'Why?'

Dan could not find an answer to that. Not immediately.

'Oh come on,' he said.

'Sorry. Sorry, I mean, who is the guy?'

'Well that's the why,' Dan said. He tried to say Ludo's name but couldn't, the room wasn't ready for it yet.

'It's someone in Toronto,' he said.

'That's brilliant,' she said.

'Clearly.'

'No I am. I am really pleased for you. Of course I am. I just thought that you got away from all that, you know? That great institution called marriage.'

'I did get away from it,' he said. 'And now, I can do what I like.'

'Absolutely.'

They heard Rosaleen's little car coughing into life outside and the wheels chewing the gravel. The driveway was full of cars – the Lexus, Dessie's BMW, the battered tin can that Emmet affected, these days. Hanna glanced out the window to see her mother's Citroën up on the grass, head-lights washing the trunk of the monkey puzzle tree, before she bounced across a flowerbed and sliced, at an angle, through the piers of the gate.

'Nice one,' she said.

Rosaleen was indicating right, away from the town and towards the sea. The inside light was on and everything was very yellow in there. It looked, Dan thought, like some kind of artwork, he could not think by whom – the dirty, electric look of the lit box jouncing out of the dim garden, Rosaleen, inside, in a purple woollen hat and a teal coloured coat.

Did the coat have a hood? Yes it did have a hood, it was one of those waterproof things for hikers that everyone wore these days. Did the hood have a fur trim? No it did not.

He remembered every detail. She left the inside light on. She was wearing a purple hat and a North Face three-quarter-length jacket in a blue-green. The light still lingered in the western sky. They all heard her leave and none of them thought anything of it. Except that it was Christmas Day and there was no place in particular for her to go. For the first long while after the sound of her engine faded, they did nothing.

'Where's she off to?' said Emmet. 'With no bell on her bike.'

He was passing the front room and the others followed

him down to the kitchen, where the kids had turned on the TV. They were happy to leave the front of the house to its festive, empty business. They dipped into the wine and stood about. Constance would be moving on soon, and they did not want her to go.

'Is there some nun?' Dan said. There used to be a nun – a sip of sherry and MiWadi for the kids, who all came back from the convent parlour laden with miraculous medals and little prayer cards with their names on the back.

'Sister Jerome? She's long dead,' said Constance, who was packing up, or trying to, because she had to drive her gang across town for the Christmas evening gathering of the McGraths.

'Tell them,' said Hanna.

'No,' said Dan.

She picked up the remote and turned the TV down.

'Dan has some news,' she said.

'Tell them what?' said Dessie.

Dan looked at his brother-in-law's broad face, pink with Christmas wine and well-being. He lifted his hands up suddenly, to clack non-existent castanets.

'I'm engaged!'

There was a small silence. Dessie's pink intensified.

'Congratulations, man,' said Rory. 'Legal! Hey.'

He loped over to his uncle and hugged him, right there and then. A big wraparound hug, complete with back pat. So no one had to ask the obvious question – the one to which they all knew the answer. Of course it was a man. Of course.

'Oh I am delighted,' said Constance.

'Congratulations,' Emmet said.

Hanna raised her glass. 'Safe at last.'

And Rory said, 'So who's the lucky guy?'

So that took another half-hour of their day, because Dessie went to the boot of the BMW and liberated a bottle of champagne intended for his mother's house, and they popped it and had an awkward glass. Then Constance was barking and squawking as she tried to get her brood out the door, and with Constance gone, there was no one to worry about Rosaleen.

The house was silent. They left the TV on and watched people singing and dancing for a while.

A phone call came in from their uncle in Florida. Emmet picked up and, after a few pleasantries, Bart said, 'Will you put your mother on?'

'She went out for her walk,' said Emmet.

'What time is it there anyway?'

Emmet looked at his mobile.

'It's nearly five,' he said.

'Listen I'll catch her in a bit,' said Bart. 'I'll ring at seven.'

Emmet put down the phone.

'Should we ring Constance?' he said.

And Dan said, 'What for?'

The Green Road

ROSALEEN WAS OUT on the green road, and she was cold. She was going for her constitutional. As she did after lunch, most days. She was getting out for a bit of air. She had left it a little late. Lunch was late. Even so, she had not thought it would be dark, not yet, the way the Atlantic sky held the light for so long after the sun was down, something to do with the height of the heavens out here on the green road. The west was still open and clear but the ground under her feet was tricky enough. All the colour was going from things and nothing was easy to see. You could not tell grey from grey.

The little Citroën was parked where the tarmac stopped, back at Ballynahown, and Rosaleen was out on the dark road under a deep sky. There was no moon. There was the sound of running water, quite loud. One of her feet was wet – the front part – and the path was uneven. Rosaleen found the strip of grass in the middle of the road and stuck to that, and, *Lift your eyes*. There it was. She stopped to look. The stone wall that was the remains of a fort keeping watch on the Aran Islands and the far distant mountains of Connemara. The mountains were purple and navy blue, the three islands black against a silver sea. The sun was gone below the horizon, but the light from it still bounced up off the sky. So the sea was dark in the distance and light close to. It was all a question of the angle. Because the world was round but the light was straight.

There were no more people.

The houses were far behind her. The last two on the left hand side were dark and deserted, their blank windows looking out over the valley. And then a farmhouse on the right, with an arthritic collie who herded her along her way, in sprints and crouches, its belly scraping the ground. Old people in there. Who knows what kind of Christmas in that house.

The sea was on her left, while the slope, she knew, rose on the right, the boulders, grey and humpy in the darkness; the few sheep standing behind them for shelter, their heads drooped and shoulders slumped, foursquare on patient feet.

There was no wind but the air was cold. Her eyes smarted with it, and *Where did it begin?* That was the question that went through her, though it was more a cadence than a question, it was another scrap in a life full of scraps, some of them beautiful.

O my Dark Rosaleen!
Do not sigh, do not weep!

She was sighing now, she was weeping now, she was feeding the wind with the little shards of her tears, that the wind blew back at her, hurting her own face. Hard to know if they were tears of sorrow or of cold. She was so frustrated. *Rosaleen, Rosaleen* someone was calling her name, but when she listened it was no one, not even the wind.

Rosaleen was tired of waiting. She had been waiting, all her life, for something that never happened and she could not bear the suspense any longer. Rosaleen was in a hurry, now. She thought she might find a cliff edge and throw herself down it from purest impatience. She might kill herself just to get something done.

But she was not going to kill herself. She had never been interested in that sort of palaver. *Where did it begin?* And where was the end of it. How long would she have to continue, being like this. Being herself.

O my Dark Rosaleen.

And why was there no one to love her?

She was a small thing under a big sky, and being tiny was not the same as being dead. It was quite the opposite. Rosaleen spread her arms wide and flung her face up.

'Hah!' she said.

In the middle of nowhere, on Christmas Day, when no one was out, not one person was walking the roads.

'Hah!'

Old women were not given to shouting. Rosaleen did not know if she still could, or if your voice went slack like the rest of you, when you got old.

'Oh, don't mind me!' she said. She roared it. She stuck her fists down straight by her sides. 'Don't mind me!'

There was no problem with her voice, that is what she discovered. Old women do not shout because they are not allowed to shout. Because if they shout and roar then there will be no dinner.

And let that be an end to it now.

'Don't you worry about me!'

The mountain took her on. Knockauns was to the right of her and it sent her voice back her way, and there was mist, she saw, coming down for her too. So she quickened her pace and stumbled on a rock, but she did not fall.

'Hah,' she said.

Rosaleen was on her own. And that was the way she wanted to be. That was just great. She got in her little car and she drove away from the lot of them. The big faces on them. She left them to it. Such selfish children she had reared. She left them to get on with it, whatever it was – their lives – and she came out to walk off her dinner and take the sharpness of the air inside herself. To get the sea air.

Rosaleen opened her lungs and filled herself up.

It hurt her chest. It hurt the inside of her. The air was cold and she was cold so Rosaleen thought hot thoughts – driving up over her own lawn. Yes! And out the gate. She was so cross, the car drove itself. They went for miles down familiar roads until they found her own stands of dark pine. They bumped past the house where Pat Madigan was born, the little door painted in flaking layers of green over red over blue. They drove right past all this, Rosaleen and her little car, through another stand of trees that were her trees, horrible and dark. On and on they went, until they came to the edge of things. Then the car stopped and Rosaleen got out.

The sea was huge for her. The light gentle and great. The fields indifferent, as she walked up the last of the hill. But she got a slightly sarcastic feel off the ditches, there was no other word for it – sprinkles of derision – like the countryside was laughing at her.

Presences.

At the gate beyond the last house, where the tarmac road turned into a green road and the sheepdog turned for home, she looked back on the valley of Oughtdarra. Solemn and dark now, with the Flaggy Shore at the sea edge of it, graves and dolmens there, and ancient roads and gateways to nothing, from nothing. A couple of houses were lit up for Christmas, the blink of the lights a glimmering from this distance. There was a little ruined church down in that place, with a curse in the name of the man who built it too terrible to speak aloud. This she knew from Pat Madigan who took her walking along these uplands with her little dog in the late summer of 1956. He talked more in those days and weeks than he ever did after, about curses and the like, *piseogs*, the fairies on the mound of Croghateehaun and the people lost in the scrubby, treacherous ground below it. He talked about the foxes behind Knockauns mountain, the seventeen ancient forts between here and Slieve Elva, and the goats that lived in the hazel scrub. He told her the depth and beauty of the cave called Polnagree, the two Englishmen who went down it with ropes and lamps. He pointed to the place where the three townlands met, Oughtdarra, Ballynahown and Crumlin, a gap in the cliff that belonged to none of them called Leaba na hAon Bhó, The Bed of the One Cow. There was a story, he said, about that cow and the end of the world.

Then he laughed, and told her about a heifer he had once, who came into heat with her head stuck in a big bucket – a tub almost, made out of blue metal – the handle was up over her poll, whatever way she managed it, and the bull was working her, the pair of them walking the field with the bucket swinging and banging until she came into a standing heat and he mounted her. 'And the sound out of her then', he said. 'I am surprised she didn't deafen herself, in the bucket.'

There was no stopping him.

He pointed to a house where a man killed himself by hanging and a rock overlooking the sea where the ghost of a hungry man was said to sit, turning to stare at passersby. He talked of a place – miles away – where a woman kept her daughter chained in the hen-house, and a woman whose house was full of money sent by her sons in America. He said there were babies born in one house that never saw the light of day. He said that the women of one family in particular took their babies back into themselves like cats did their kittens, and it was important always to marry out, in a place like this, if you got the chance. And she was his chance. He did not say that he loved her. He said that if she would have him, a fine woman like her, unencumbered and free, with her own money and no one to stop her, if she would make her choice and choose him, that he would worship her with his body, and with his entire soul, until the day he died.

Foolish but true.

That is what he said.

And that is the way he saw the land, with no difference between the different kinds of yesterday. No difference between a man and his ghost, between a real heifer and a cow that was waiting for the end of the world. It was all just a way of talking. It was the rise and fall in the telling, a rounding out before the finish. A flourish. A shiver. And it was for her. He had saved every detail up for her alone, as though every rock and tree awaited her coming for its explication.

And when she laughed at him, he only agreed with her.

'If I am a fool,' he said. 'Then let me be a great fool and not a small one.'

There was no turning him down. And when he entered her – that first time and every time subsequent – it was a sacred kind of pleasure he took. She was sure of it.

My own Rosaleen!

Pat Madigan worshipped her. And he did not tell a lie. He wanted her for the money she had, for the fine house and the children he could get out of her. He laughed at her talk and then he ignored her talk. But there were times, even in his last days, even at the very end, when he looked at her with a pride so keen it was sinful.

My virgin flower, my flower of flowers,

Somewhere along here, that is where the first kiss happened between them, her little dog sitting down for them to finish, looking out to sea. She had married beneath her. Even the dog seemed to indicate it, by the indifferent set of her head.

My life of life, my saint of saints,
my Dark Rosaleen!

And, 'Hah!' she said, because she'd had the pleasure of Pat Madigan for forty years, and 'Hah' because he was dead and she was still alive, up here on the green road. Years since she had been kissed on the mouth. Years.

Rosaleen missed her little dog, a little grey pompom of a terrier cross, with a red tartan bow between her ears. Milly. She could feel her almost running along beside her, could feel her brush against her shins. Rosaleen lifted her foot not to tread on her and saw the blackness of the road underneath. If it was the road – it might as well be a river. Whatever it was, she was sitting in it. And there was no dog, of course there wasn't. She was plonked like a fool on her wet backside, and it was time to get up and sort herself out. It was time to get on with it. Her walk on this road which was the road of her youth.

There was no rain, but everything was wet. Sopping. A deep liquid sound in the ditch on her left, there was a cave somewhere near and Rosaleen was afraid of caves. She was afraid of heights, too. She did not know what she was doing up here – when she thought about it she was afraid of the dark and it was getting dark now, though the afterglow lingered over the western Atlantic; a sky too big for the sun to leave.

It was old age, of course – the fear. Passing cars, children on bicycles, plugs and sockets, escalators: she was afraid of things that beeped, or hummed, she was afraid of looking like a fool, of wearing the wrong stockings, wearing the wrong clothes. She put something on because she liked it and then a while later she realised it was all terrible. Rosaleen was terrified of losing her mind, of saying things or snapping in public – if she hit at a stranger, if she said something rude or obscene, that would be unbearable. She took the precaution of saying very little, any more. Even here on the mountain she kept her own counsel. But she was afraid the stone wall would fall on her and her leg would get trapped, she was afraid of getting raped, and what were the chances of that? On Christmas Day of all days. Who would even rob you up here on the green road?

'Hah!'

This is why Rosaleen had come up here, to this wild place. She had come to cleanse herself of forgetfulness and of fury. To shout it loud and leave it behind. To fling it away from herself.

'You see!' She wanted to roar it out, but her throat didn't like her mouth opening and the rasp of the cold.

Rosaleen could not see the top of Knockauns or the walls on either side of her. It was truly dark now. There was no moon. The sea was glittering under a black sky and Rosaleen could not tell black from black, except for the sense of motion from the distant water and even that was going dark and still.

She might as well be dead. She might as well be underground.

Except for the movement of her legs, one in front of the other, and the sense under her cold feet, of the rocks and earth and tussocks of grass on the green road.

It was here she walked with her lovely dog, Milly, and with Pat Madigan when they were courting. She cycled out to him, with her little dog in the front basket, and they left the bike against a ditch. It was here they kissed, and more.

Pat Madigan grew silent with the years. After that first

rush of talk he said less and less. Towards the end of his life, he said little or nothing.

And that was her fault too.

What did it mean, when the man you loved was gone? A part of his body inside your own body and his arms wrapped about you. What happened when all of that was in the earth, deep down in the cemetery clay?

Nothing happened. That is what happened.

Rosaleen held her hand up to verify it in the black air. She pulled off her glove to see the living whiteness of it, but there was something around her legs – the dog, perhaps – and she was crawling, she was on her knees, with one gloved hand and one hand naked. The cold was in her hand now.

Each breath hurt. She pulled the air into the tiny parts of her lungs. Her flesh was pierced in microscopic places by the air of the vast world as it pushed its way into her blood.

Rosaleen's head was hanging low like an old horse, she was on all fours and the stones hurt her knees. She wanted to go back and find that glove, but she couldn't turn back, she had no confidence in the road, she thought it might be disappearing behind her. Because there were gaps between things, and this frightened her. This is where Rosaleen was now. She had fallen into the gap.

BART RANG FROM Florida at seven o'clock.

They sat another half an hour. Dan flicked channels. Emmet read an old newspaper. But they must have been thinking about her, because they each said, when the time came to go out and look for her, that none of them were sober enough to drive.

At half past seven, Emmet walked into town to check with the old ladies above the Medical Hall while Dan went through the phone numbers she had at the front of the phone book, but most of the people listed there were either in the kitchen, or dead. No one wanted to tell Constance, but she had to be told, so when Emmet came back they made the call and, seven minutes later, they heard her car sweep through the gate.

Constance was frantic. And it was all their fault. She was crying and blaming and fretting, she did not know where to sit herself down. She took out her mobile and scrolled through the numbers, despairing at each one. She rang a neighbour, asked them to ring another neighbour. She left the house, still talking, to drive around and look for her mother. Half an hour later she was back with her husband in tow, and he said, 'Have you contacted the Guards?'

The Madigans looked at him.

Dessie had been drinking. Of course he had – it was Christmas Day.

'Let's not panic,' said Emmet.

The men sat in silence, in the stillness of Rosaleen's stopped kitchen clock and the sound of Constance making instant coffee through her tears.

It was the nine o'clock news stirred them, the thought that Rosaleen might be a news item herself, by the morning. Or some memory of their fathers, perhaps, saying, 'Shush, now,' their mothers saying, 'Turn on the news for your father,' the ritual observance of an outside world that had entered the kitchen and filled it, silently, on this night. It was already here.

'We have to call the Guards,' said Constance.

Dessie waved his mobile.

'I'll try Maguire,' he said and made a call. He listened a moment and said, 'Christmas.'

'Oh for goodness sake,' said Dan, who picked up the house phone and just dialled 999.

Hanna sat with her hands over her face, for all that followed, pressing down on her eyelids, feeling the flick of her pupils beneath her fingertips as her eyes moved from side to side. She thought about the cliffs. She saw, in her mind's eye, her mother's face washed over and again by dark water, her limp body bending with the curve of the waves; the cold, unfeasible weight of her, pulled on to dry land.

'This guy's in Ennis. He says it's the third missing person this evening, Christmas is a busy time. He says to ring everyone, check the outhouses. He says we need a bunch of people to drive around and look for the car. He told me to check the graveyard. He asked about her mental state.'

'The graveyard?' said Constance.

'I said it was fine?'

All of this came out of Dan with a rising inflection at the end of each sentence, as though he was in an American movie, with a camera in front of him, and a future audience of millions. His siblings watched him. They waited for the moment the drama of his life became his actual life – for that shock.

'She never goes to the graveyard,' said Constance. 'She doesn't do the grave.'

Dessie said he could get twenty men with cars in half an hour through the local hurling team, and Constance said on a day like today it's not hurlers you need but alcoholics, by which she meant the dry variety, because they were the best bet, also women like herself, maybe, the ones who were too busy doing the dinner to bother with wine. There was a world of blame in this sentence, if anyone chose to hear it, but what she said was also true. Dessie was already walking out in the hall and talking quietly into his phone.

'I have that sorted for you now,' he said, and twenty minutes later half the membership of the local AA meeting (or so they were to assume) was convened in the dining room, Ferdy McGrath chief among them. Six men and one woman, they introduced themselves to Emmet and to Dan, and then generally, as though innocent of each other's sorrows and abjections. A mixed bunch, Hanna thought, eyeing them with careful contempt. None of them carried a sign.

Constance went out to the pantry with some empty bottles, trying to make the place look decent, and she knew this was a bit mad but it was also allowed. Constance was *allowed*. She felt almost light-hearted.

The passageway beyond the kitchen was very cold. There

was a cardboard box against the wall and Constance put the bottles into it. The place smelt the way it always had: musty, with some creosote in there, and the sweetness of old apples. As she straightened up, she remembered her mother standing at the back door, looking out at the summer rain. It must have been when Constance was a child.

She could see it still: her mother's silhouette in the doorway; beyond her, the red of poppies, the green of the garden, the air golden with shining rain. Rosaleen standing, looking out at it all, waiting to leave.

It was nearly ten o'clock on the evening of Christmas Day; a still enough night, with no rain. Emmet had a map spread out on the table and he marked out sections and roads with bold arrows and circles. He took mobile numbers, checked for torches; he was on the brink of doling out malaria pills.

Three cars to the cliffs, one to the car park at Lahinch, another along the coast roads between Doolin and Liscannor, a phone call to a guy in Doolin to check the harbour car park, another car along the coast from Doolin to Fanore, the last to the high road from Ballinalackin to Ballynahown.

The house was filling up with people from the town. Dan saw men he had not seen since school. They eyed him carefully and then they touched him, a deliberate hand on his arm or shoulder, saying, 'All right, Dan? Anything I can do?' Down in the kitchen, four women were wiping the kitchen table, setting out bowls and plates of food covered in cling film. Dessie's sister Imelda brought, among other things, two bags of coffee, and Constance had a weakness, she had to be helped to a chair.

'Oh, oh, oh,' she said as her legs gave way from under her, and she sat with her feet planted and a bag of Colombian grounds in her lap.

'Oh,' she said again, taking the blame for it all, the forgotten coffee, the hissy fit, her mother now wandering the night. 'Oh.'

'Oh, yeah *what*,' said Hanna, who was leaning against the range with her arms crossed, and there was nothing to be done with her except put her in one of the cars, she was no use to anyone at home.

'Go,' said Dan, so she stumbled out with Ferdy McGrath, a twist in his eye that said he would be able for her.

'God, Ferdy, remember you used to coach me at camogie?'

'I do,' he said. 'You had a great burst of speed.'

'I had,' she said. 'That's true. I did.'

And he put her in the passenger seat of his drinker's jalopy and closed the door.

The cars put on their indicators and left, one after the other, heading west. Dan followed the sound of them out to the gate, and then went along the deserted road, looking for a phone signal. As soon as he got one, he rang home to Toronto, and when Ludo picked up he said, 'My mother's gone. She drove off. She could be anywhere.'

It was pitch black. Dan had walked away from the house and when the light went out on his phone, the night blinked and swallowed him. The darkness shifted, not to a place five feet away, but right up to his face. It stole his breath. He turned one way and then the other, and was not sure of his direction. Twenty yards away from the house and he did not know where he was, or how to return. He found the grass verge and shied away from the ditch beyond it, felt his way back by the sense of vegetation against his shoe and by the promise of a distant street light around a curve in the road. It took an unconscionably long time. He felt, at every step, as though he was walking into something, and he flinched away, taunted by the black air.

ROSALEEN STOPPED WHERE she was. Head low, swaying from side to side. She could not feel where the ground began and the flesh stopped, it was all one pain.

She had lost her glove. And that was a nuisance.

Rosaleen was a nuisance. Her children thought she was a nuisance because it was true. She was. A nuisance.

Rosaleen was a nightmare. She was very difficult. She was increasingly difficult. She made her children cry.

They'd be sorry, to find her gone. They would be very sorry. These people, who spent their entire time leaving her. Not ringing, not writing. They told her nothing, spent their lives getting out of there. Get out and keep going! that was the cry. Don't turn back! If you turn back you will see your mother turned into a pillar of salt.

Well two could play at that game.

Rosaleen had two feet, she had a car. Rosaleen could also walk out that door and not come back. And how did that feel? How did it feel when your mother left you?

Hah!

The same, the same. It felt the same.

Rosaleen put the old head down, one knee in front of

the other. She was on all fours and the stones were very sore under her. There was a shooting pain also in the flesh of her palm, a nerve thing. She took it up and shook it, but she could feel nothing of the hand itself, just the shooting pain, and a burning in her fingertips. She wanted to go back and find her glove, but she could not go back into all that – the pursuing darkness and the night.

She took the glove off her right hand and squeezed the cold hand into it, with the thumb twisted around the wrong way. There was a little ruin of a house up here, and she would be safe inside it. A little famine cottage she had passed many times, but whether it was near or far she could not tell. Everything was taking such a long time. Rosaleen did not think she would make it. She would die on the side of Knockauns mountain, they would find her cold and still in the morning light, and then they would be sorry.

And she was sorry too.

Her lovely children.

Why she could not be nice to them, she did not know. She loved them so much. Sometimes she looked at them and she was so flooded with love, she just had to go and spoil it. It made her angry in the after-wash. They were so beautiful. They used to be so beautiful. They were so trusting and good. It made her feel not good. Unappreciated. It made her feel irrelevant. That was it.

What about me? she said.

But Rosaleen did not exist. Oh no. Rosaleen did not matter.

Hah!

Rosaleen wanted to say it out loud but she couldn't. She was stuck in the sound of her own breathing, dragging and rough, an immense clattering in her teeth when she pulled the air into her.

Fuh fuh fuh fuh fuh

The cold was inside her. It was in her bones, making its way into her flesh, it was wrapped around her innards, seeping into her stomach, her body tried to shake it out again. A deep trembling took hold and her arms and legs grew comical and stiff, she had to swing them high and down. After an endless long time of this, she realised the person beside her was Pat Madigan, it was his was the voice urging her on. And a great sense of peace spread through her then, followed by a jag of irritation.

Where have you been, all this time?

A MAN CALLED John Fairleigh walked in to the dining room in waterproofs and hiking boots. Young, black haired, weatherbeaten; he introduced himself and went straight to the map on the table, pushed away the silver and white baubles – but carefully – and said there were more on the way, the team would be here soon.

'Any word?' he said. And Dan looked at him.

'No.'

'Is this where she liked to go?'

Emmet looked at the map.

'Somewhere on the coast. Somewhere. Walking in circles.'

John Fairleigh said he did not think so. Their mother was not walking in circles.

'A woman of that age, she will be moving in a linear way. She will be near the car, definitely within a kilometre of the car, probably within a hundred metres. So the first job is to find the car. And when we find the car, it's a hundred metres, a kilometre max.'

'Right.'

'Not that easy, not necessarily,' he said. 'It's dark. Your

mother may be cold. She's looking for shelter. A building, a barn. That's the only thing she is thinking about now, is where to hide herself away from the cold, which means she could end up hiding from us too – behind a wall, under a bush, an old fertiliser bag. She could make herself hard to find.'

Constance was weeping.

'But we will find her,' he said. 'Don't worry.'

'No, no,' she said, waving him on.

'How was she in herself?'

'Sorry?' said Emmet.

Constance flicked a glance at her brother.

'Hard to tell,' he said.

'She went for her walk. Our mother is absolutely fine,' Constance said. 'She went out for her walk.'

'She's just a wonderful person,' Dan intervened, in a pathetic, upbeat kind of way.

'*Wonderful*,' said Emmet.

'It's a word,' said Dan.

'Yeah well,' said Emmet. 'Wonderful in your prime is a bit mad when you're older, is bipolar in your fifties, maybe, and by the time you are – what age is she? – seventy-six, well by then it's more your brain, isn't it? It's plaques or what have you. It's hard to tell.'

'She was never bipolar,' said Constance, utterly shocked.

'No?' he said.

'Not even close.'

'Well,' said John Fairleigh. 'It's hard. Old age is hard, emotionally. It just is.'

'I don't know how you can say she was bipolar,' said Constance.

'I suppose what I am trying to ask is,' said John Fairleigh. 'Was she in any way despondent?'

Constance gave a small cry.

'Please don't take my brother's word about this,' she said. 'Please don't.'

But John Fairleigh ignored them. Dan had the brief idea he was some kind of impostor.

'Don't worry. We had an elderly woman out for two nights running, September two years ago. And she wasn't fantastic, in all fairness, but she was absolutely fine.'

The siblings were quiet then.

'It's a good clear night,' he said, and looked at the map again. 'Talk about Christmas.'

ROSALEEN WAS BY the little house, that was tucked into the side of the mountain. A famine cottage of tumbling-down stone, with one door one window, no roof. She could see it by starlight. She was surprised how much she could see. She could go into the little famine house and look up at the stars, there were so many of them, but first she had to cross the hungry grass in front of the doorway. There wasn't much, just a few blades of it, and once she was across the hungry grass she would be safe from the weather. Of course, after she crossed the hungry grass then she would be hungry for ever. That was the curse of it.

Sometimes the grass was on a grave where no priest came to say prayers, because the priest was too busy, or the priest was fled. Sometimes the grass was on the threshold of a house where all the people died, with no one left to bury them, and the house fell into ruin after.

But it did not matter if she crossed the hungry grass, because she, too, was going to die. This she knew because her dead husband Pat Madigan was beside her on the road. He went so quiet when he was alive. He stopped talking. He stopped liking her. But he always loved her. And when he was young he walked that road like it belonged to him. He was king of everything green about him, king of the hedgerows, king of the sky. He picked up a stone and he flung it into the broad heavens. He flung it into the sea, where it grew into an island. Grew and grew.

Fuh fuh fuh fuh

If she bared her teeth, they clattered against each other like a pair of joke dentures, so she tried to press her lips together, to stop them cracking and breaking in her skull. The expense of it.

Fuh fuh fuh fuh

Her husband Pat Madigan was a little bit cross with Rosaleen now because Pat Madigan was a saint but he could be cranky enough, betimes. He wanted Rosaleen to crawl over the hungry grass and get in out of the cold.

'Would you stop your romancing,' he said. 'Go on!' he said. 'Hup!'

And Rosaleen swung her arm up and put her hand down, and then the other, and she dragged her old legs through the ruined doorway of the little stone house. No roof, but a gable wall to protect her against the slice of the cold. Two little rooms, the first had something in it – she could see the pink of it in the darkness and it was toilet paper. Rosaleen backed away in fright and then crawled carefully to the left, into a second tiny room, where she turned about slowly and keeled over, curled up on the ground. She lifted her top knee a little, and put her hands between her thighs.

The ground was fine.

There was no sign of Pat Madigan. He was gone now.

After a while, she felt very good. Her brain cleared in a way that was marvellous. There were pains in her wet knees, but they did not matter. The cold was hard in her left hip and she was shaking in a way that was new to her. But the stars were lovely, she could see a piece of the heavens out of the corner of her eye, framed by the stones of the cottage wall.

If she slept now, she thought, it wouldn't be the worst thing.

There was a medicine her father used to spoon into her when she was a child. Very pink, whatever it was. And as soon as she swallowed it – out like a light. Asleep. She often wondered what that medicine was.

Her father gave her Kaolin and Morphine for her stomach. There was great company in morphine, he used to say, it is hard to pull yourself away from it. They put Pat on it, at the end – Fentanyl patches that she stuck on his thigh. It made him happy. The morphine made him love her again, and then it made him constipated and cross. And then he died.

Rosaleen was shivering. Her body was shaking her loose, she was just holding on. She had to remember as much as possible, now, she had to be sensible. There was no such thing as hungry grass. And Pat Madigan was long dead. She had to remember everything. The names of the tablets and the names of the diseases, the names of the parts of the body that was trying to leave her now. But she had no intention of going, or of letting it go. She had no intention.

Rosaleen saw a satellite moving through a delicacy of stars above her, and it was as though she could sense the earth's turning. She felt fine. She was out of the worst of the cold. She would have a small sleep and make her way home before morning.

She was woken by a wrenching and a ripping sound, the end of the world. The thump of something. A huge noise like a plane taking off in her ear. The plane reversed, and then it went forward again. Reversed. There was a cow on the other side of the wall, breathing, tearing a few mouthfuls of midnight grass. The jolt of it lasted a long time in her blood.

I'm awake, she said. *I am alive.*

FERDY MCGRATH WAS driving along a back road on his way to the sea when Hanna said, 'Stop!'

It was the house at Boolavaun.

'Did you see something?' said Ferdy. 'Did you see a car?'

'No, just,' said Hanna. 'I just need to check the old place.'

He looked over to her.

'I don't know. My father's house. I just think we should.'

He got out of the car and followed her over to the black mass of the house. She shone the light of her phone on the door and he added the light of the big yellow torch, a useless tub of a thing, with a wide, weak beam.

Hanna peered in at the window, that still had a half curtain of white net. She did not see anything inside. The door showed all its colours in flakes and blisters, bright red, a blue that was bright and profound – azure or gentian blue – it reminded her so strongly of her Granny Madigan she went to touch it; and over all of these an ordinary green.

'She might have gone in the back door,' she said.

'We should be looking for the car.'

The bottom of the door was rotted away and covered with boards of thin plywood. Hanna bent down and pulled one away and, 'Hold your horses,' he said, but she was already crawling through it, into the little porch, across lino that was multicoloured, like a scattering of sweets. This was the floor she remembered from her childhood. She stood up in the little space and opened the door into the kitchen.

She cried out. 'Ferdy!'

She called out for his help, even though she did not like the man much.

'Ferdy!'

His wide torch flashed at the window and the place was weakly illuminated. An old table, cupboard doors hanging open, the rusted hulk of the range. Hanna saw it all in shapes and shadows, the floor crackling with grit beneath her feet. So many things had happened in this place, and nothing much happened. People grew up and moved away. Her granny died.

Passions. Impossibilities.

The push of it.

'Are you right?' The torch left the window and she heard Ferdy walk along by the wall of the house. A long silence then the loud jiggle of the latch on the back door.

'She's not here,' she said, and she backed slowly out, hunkering down. 'She's not here.'

When they got back in the car and Ferdy looked across at her in the passenger seat.

'You have her eyes,' he said. 'You know that. She was a powerful woman, a great woman, your grandmother. She was a cousin of my mother's – but you know that too, sure.'

Hanna thought he might touch her then, but something

queered the impulse and he shoved up the lever beside the steering wheel instead, indicating to no one his intention to pull back out on the road.

A mile further on, they saw Rosaleen's car, beached on the ditch, with the front door hanging open and the inside light still on.

The call came into Ardeevin, just before midnight. The car was found.

Hanna was calling for her mother. Emmet could hear her down the line, a tiny pathetic sound.

Mama, Mama.

Ferdy put a muffling hand over the phone, in order to shout, 'Hang on!'

'Don't let her go,' Emmet said, thinking Hanna would be the next one lost.

Constance drove the rest of them up there, the expensive car tight to the bends of the road and when she reached the spot, she pulled in behind Rosaleen's little Citroën with sad precision. Emmet jumped out to walk around it, he pulled open the front door and checked, for no reason, under the front seats. Then he switched on the headlights and the hazard lights, and they stayed in the blinking urgency of all that, willing their mother to appear.

Rosaleen's children stood peering and calling into the black air. She was somewhere out there, and it was unbearable. Their concern was also a concern for themselves, of course. Some infant self, beyond tears. Dan felt it like a whiteness inside his chest. A searing want.

'Rosaleen!'

Even Emmet was surprised by the force of it, this huge need for a woman he did not think he liked, any more.

'Mam! Mam!'

283

Constance ran to the nearest wall and looked over it, as though her mother was a dropped wallet or a set of keys.

'Mammy?' she said.

The comedy of it was not lost on them, the fact that each of her children was calling out to a different woman. They did not know who she was – their mother, Rosaleen Madigan – and they did not have to know. She was an elderly woman in desperate need of their assistance and even as her absence grew to fill the cold mountainside, she shrank into a human being – any human being – frail, mortal, old.

They stood, facing north, north-west, west, their shadows swapping on the road in front of them while Hanna's voice came, in a wisp of sound, across the land.

'Mama!'

There were headlights making their way up the valley from the turn-off at Ballinalackin. The cars took a long time. They drew up, and parked, or failed to find a space, blocking each other and doing three-point turns on the narrow road. Emmet knew this well, the provisional feel to large events, even when – especially when – lives were at stake. This time, however, the life was something like his own: this was the disaster he had been avoiding, in the midst of all the disasters he had sought out. This was real.

John Fairleigh walked up, glued to the phone, one arm beckoning everyone together.

'No need for the lifeboat, now,' he said, and the vertigo dropped through them again; their mother falling down the massive cliff face.

'Lifeboat?' said Constance.

'Listen, lads,' said John Fairleigh, generally. 'I am going to hold you here, for a minute, all right? I don't want anyone falling into a bog-hole, or what have you. All right? You're going to check the road and the sides of the road.

You do not go off the road. That's what we are doing at this particular point. We are all staying on the road.'

They moved away from the frantic lights of her car, a clutch of heroically recovering alcoholics and the children of Rosaleen Madigan, while more car headlights made their slow way up from the valley. The gate was closed behind them – everyone minding their country manners, though you could barely see the surrounding countryside, you might as well have been on the moon, for all the fabled beauty of the green road.

They walked together, torch beams criss-crossing. People tripped and cursed in low voices, or they blinded each other with the glare of the lights.

'Keep them low, lads. Give your eyes a chance.'

Constance stopped and turned off her torch, to let her sight adjust, and in a while, she could see everything. A haze of light gathered in the sky above Galway, in the far distance, but Knockauns was dark and the night above her open to an endless depth of stars.

She had been left behind, now. She was alone – Constance, who was never alone, whose mind was always full of people – and after the first pang of it, she allowed the darkness to have sway. She lifted her hands a little to test the air.

A call came through to Emmet's phone from Ferdy McGrath, and when the line broke up they all heard him hallooing in the distance, and saw the signalling light of his torch. They picked up the pace, saw after a while the little ruined house where she must be.

Hanna was already there.

She went in through the doorway and stumbled in the rocks and rubbish in the small main room, before she looked into the smaller second room and saw the dark heap that was her mother lying on the ground.

Afterwards, neither of them could remember what they had said, except that Rosaleen kept apologising and Hanna kept reassuring.

'Oh I am sorry.'

'Are you all right?'

'Oh I am sorry.'

'You're all right. You're all right.'

And so the two of them continued, in a kind of bliss, as Hanna opened her coat and spread it on her mother, then laid herself down beside her, drawing Rosaleen's hands in under her own clothes to get the heat of her bare skin, rubbing along her arms and back, and they stayed like that heedless of everything that happened around them.

Outside the house Ferdy McGrath gave the cry, while inside, Rosaleen whimpered at the pain in her hands, that were burning in the heat of Hanna's skin.

'Oh no!' she said.

Hanna should have been more careful, she thought later, she might have done the wrong thing entirely, but the only thing that was on her mind was to stop the rattling in her mother's body, so she pushed Rosaleen's legs straight with her knees and lay alongside her, lifting her shoulders to complete the embrace and pressing her close, holding tight and then tighter as she tried to still the trembling.

'You're all right. You're all right.'

They stayed like that for a long time. Hanna used everything she had. She used her breath, hawing it out on Rosaleen's neck, sighing on to her closed eyes. She did not notice Ferdy run his coat up under her mother's legs and wrap them in it, she did not notice the others, stumbling in the litter and overgrown rubbish of the house floor, or the foil blanket that was put over them both by John Fairleigh. She noticed nothing until he cradled her mother's head from the other side, ran a mat under her shoulders, and brought a flask of tea to her lips.

'Good woman,' he said. 'Good woman.'

It was the kind of phrase their mother hated.

Hanna had the comical idea that Rosaleen would be cross, she was far from cross. She looked at John Fairleigh with unblinking eyes. The tea slopped out of her mouth, and she just kept looking, as though nothing but John Fairleigh existed in the wide world.

Outside, people stood around for a while, waiting for the ambulance, wondering if it would not be better to lift her down the mountain and drive her out of there. They felt the cold. Everything took a long time. A few went back to open the gate and give directions. Another man with a head torch arrived. 'Anyone with a car down there, can you move the car?' And it was like a fleadh or a gymkhana for a while, with a guy in a hi-vis jacket directing cars into a field. No one went home, though they knew she was found. People sat into their cars and waited, they switched the radios on and listened to Christmas carols, broadcast from deserted studios, until – a long time later, it seemed – they saw the far distant blue light turn up the road from Ballinalackin.

'She only went for a walk,' Constance said to Dessie, as though objecting to all the fuss.

Dan, who had stayed by the little famine house, lingered in the doorway of the inner room and did what Rosaleen loved him doing best. He talked to her.

He said, 'You know you left the light on inside the car?'

He said, 'I think it's time to hang your Ecco boots up, darling, don't you?'

He said, 'Honestly Rosaleen, you have no idea. Half the O'Briens are down there in the kitchen with buckets of coleslaw and left-over potato salad, and Imelda McGrath came over with real coffee, because real coffee is where the McGraths are at these days. You know what Dessie had in the boot? He had Bollinger in the boot. I kid you not. *Where will it end*, that's what I say.'

He said, 'Oh. The moon.'

Because the moon was rising in the north-east over Knockauns mountain. A sliver of a thing, the pale light lifted the landscape to his eyes, and there it was, the most beautiful road in the world, bar none. Where else would you go?

'You know?' he said. 'You could be anywhere.'

He watched the slow progress of the paramedics as they wrestled the gurney over the rocks and grass: the chrome glinting and the business of it clanking as it dipped and rose.

She had never gone very far, he thought. A week in Rome. A fortnight in the Algarve. Another time, Sorrento, and The road! she said. It was taking your life in your hands. But oh! the coast was very beautiful coming down into Amalfi, she would never forget it, and the little restaurant right out over the ocean, where she had a glass of limoncello, free at the end of the meal.

Waking Up

SHE SOLD THE house anyway. This was a surprise, but it was not the biggest surprise. Rosaleen woke up in Limerick hospital on St Stephen's Day and she looked around her, at the buff coloured walls and the handmade decorations, and she smiled.

There was no problem getting a bed, she said. She wondered at that; the things you hear on the news about people on trolleys for days.

'They're all home for the Christmas,' said the nurse, who was Tamil at a guess, with a name so long she had an extra inch on her plastic tag. Rosaleen looked closely at her face and eyes.

'So pretty,' she said.

The nurse took no offence.

'I feel, I don't know how to describe it, I feel much better.'

'That's good.'

'I didn't feel well at all,' she said. 'But now I feel much better.'

'Yes.'

Emmet, who was sitting in his conscientious way at her bedside, saw all this and did not quite believe it.

'You were up a mountain,' he said.

Rosaleen turned her head and rested her gaze on him. She looked a little puzzled and then she smiled.

'Yes.'

'Do you remember?'

'Oh, I remember the mountain, all right,' as though this was not what she was talking about at all. 'Oh yes, the mountain.'

She was looking at him very intently.

'You rest now, Rosaleen,' said the nurse.

'I mean before the mountain.'

She nestled her cheek into the hospital pillow and looked at her son.

'Oh darling,' she said.

Emmet did not know how to reply to her, but she did not seem to want a reply.

'Oh darling. I am sorry.'

'No need,' he said.

'I put you through it.'

'You're all right.'

'I put you through the wringer.'

She closed her eyes, slowly, gazing at him all the while, and when she was asleep Emmet went down to the metal clipboard at the end of the bed.

'What's she on?' he said.

'Drip,' said the nurse. And then, after a moment's thought, 'She is happy.'

And indeed, Rosaleen was happy. She continued happy for some time. Not just happy at the fuss that was made of her – the visits, the journalist spurned at the door, the priest sounding his thanks for her deliverance at morning Mass, *Yea though I walk through the valley of the shadow of death* – she was happy with other small things, the light as it thickened on the hospital floor, the clever controls for lifting the bed, the flowers Pat Doran the garageman brought in to her, though they were – to coin a phrase, she said – *petrol station flowers*.

'What lovely colours, Pat. You shouldn't have.'

Rosaleen was delighted to be alive. This is such an obvious thing to be, Hanna wondered why everyone was not delighted, all the time. She brought the baby in to see her, and they sat, her mother and Hugh and *the puddin*, as Rosaleen called him, 'Oh the puddin!' insisting they hoist the baby on the bed for her to hold. Rosaleen loved babies, she said, and it was, for a while, easy to believe her. She wanted to *eat him*, she said. Hugh took pictures on his phone and they admired them as they happened: Rosaleen thin and the baby fat in front of her, the baby putting his hand into Rosaleen's mouth and pulling her jaw down.

'Ya ya ya yah,' said Rosaleen, and the baby laughed.

She was delighted. And the baby was delightful. Hanna tried to hold all that, so she could remember it the next time the baby screamed, the picture of her mother, handing the baby back to her saying, 'Oh, how I envy you now.'

As if life was always worth having, worth reproducing, and everything always turned out well in the end.

Emmet saw what he had not seen in many years: his mother being wonderful. She regaled them all with descriptions of the ambulance, the doctor's cold hands, the cow on the other side of the wall when she fell asleep on the mountain.

'It was like a plane taking off in your ear,' she said.

When Dan came in, the pair of them laughed at everything and Emmet was not jealous. He watched Rosaleen for deterioration of some kind but her brain was fine – or what the world called her brain: short term, long term, the current Pope, the days of the week. It was just her mood that changed. It was just her life that had changed.

She looked on her children as though we were a wonder to her, and indeed we were a bit of a wonder to ourselves. We had been, for those hours on the dark mountainside, a force. A family.

There followed a time of great kindness and generosity, not just from neighbours and from strangers, but among the Madigans. There was no talk of bringing Rosaleen home to Ardeevin, 'That cold house,' said Constance. She had the room all made up, she said, and Rosaleen's things brought over, so she could stay as long as she needed to, out in Aughavanna.

A Face in the Crowd

DAN FLEW BACK to Toronto and found that Ludo had posted an alert for Rosaleen on his social media page, saying, 'If anyone has anybody in Ireland, especially on the west coast, then please spread the word about this missing woman.'

'That was a bit previous,' he said, scrolling through the responses and best wishes, including one from a psychic in Leitrim offering his dowsing skills. He paused at a line from a guy called Gregory Savalas and clicked through to his homepage, which showed mountains and lemon groves. Dan thought it must be in California, but his address was listed as Deya, Mallorca, and there were pictures of a dog, another guy, a small pool, and 'Greg' himself in a faded denim baseball cap and cutoff jeans, a blue neckerchief, boots, his face sticking a little strangely on to his bones. He also had a little paunch and a glitter in his eye, to tell you he was not clear – how could he be clear – but he was damn well alive, he was inhaling, exhaling, swimming, drinking Rioja and looking at the lemon grove, enjoying the lemon grove. He was inhabiting a life and he was living the hell out of it, because it was his life to enjoy.

Greg.

Dan checked the photograph again. There he was: that sardonic, slow-moving, slightly fey guy who had died, Dan was sure of it, in the mid nineties. Greg who was once dead, and was now alive.

The page was quite the lifestyle statement. There was very little you might call 'real' – a slight intensity to his expression perhaps, in a world of aged stonework, bowls of lemons, stunned blue skies. But there, under a photograph of an under-lit palm tree, with a comet streaking across the Milky Way were the lines: 'Had I the heavens' embroidered cloths/ Enwrought with golden and silver light,' which was Dan's party piece, all those years ago when he played at being 'Irish' for them all.

Dan checked the friends list: some of them were linked to Ludo but there were none that he recognised from the old days, not even Arthur who seemed destined not to die. He searched and searched, remembering Billy, remembering Massimo and Alex, the loft on Broome Street. His heart was busy with the cohort of the dead: men he should have loved and had not loved. Men he had hated for being sexy, beautiful, out, dying, free. It was not his fault. He had forgiven himself, as he told Scott-in-his-head, or he had tried to forgive himself, years before. But now – look – Gregory Savalas.

The relief he felt was close to love. The fact that this human being, among so many human beings, should have survived.

Hi Greg,
You won't remember me, but I remember you from
way back in the day, when you had that tiny gallery
on the Lower East Side with, like, one perfect thing
on the wall. I was a friend of Billy Walker before he

went – you know I still turn a corner and see him and have to give myself a shake, he was such a beautiful boy, a beautiful person really. Anyway, this is Irish Dan. I am still alive. I see that you are still alive. Enjoy the lemon groves. Enjoy. Enjoy. Just sending you a little wave.

The Eyes of the Buddha

EMMET WAS EXHAUSTED when he got back to Verschoyle Gardens. Again. He was not burnt out, he just needed to talk to someone. He needed to read. He meditated for an hour each morning and, when he was done, stretched his hands out, giving thanks for the people sleeping in the rooms on either side of him, Saar on one hand and Denholm on the other. This was the way relationships went for him now. The sex with Saar was important, of course it was, the sex with Saar was an intimate thing. But he also knew it was something other than sex that moved him along his life's course. It was a kind of tension and it was here, in this configuration.

Emmet would never fall in love. He would 'love', he would, that is to say 'tend'. He would cure and guide, but he did not have the helplessness in him that love required.

Denholm slapped his shoulder and said he should have children. Every man should have children.

'You think?' said Emmet.

'No question,' said Denholm. This was a guy who had been educated in a mud room to speak convent English, write in Victorian copperplate: Denholm could, at eight, recite the

Kings and Queens of England and the life cycle of the tsetse fly. Back in Kenya, he would often hold hands with his male friends, and here in Ireland he did so too, once, walking home with Emmet after a few drinks in Saggart. He had forgotten where he was and who he was with, and Emmet went to sleep that night, smiling like a fool.

One evening in February, he got an email from Alice in Sri Lanka:

> *You know when they are making a new statue of the Buddha, they do the eyes last. They use a mirror to paint by, and afterwards the artist is blindfolded and led outside where he washes his face in milk. They call it Opening the Eyes of the Buddha – wood into flesh, or at least, presence. I go every morning to the Temple of the Tooth and then work until dusk, living by the light, have not woken in proper darkness for months. From here back to the UK in March and then, who knows. If you hear of anything coming up, let me know.*

Emmet sat and meditated, but it did not help. He shifted on his sit bones, and did not know what to do with this holy hard-on he had for a woman he had failed to love some years before. He let all the psychic rubbish of sex clatter through his mind, to enter and leave at its own chosen speed – which was pretty fast, as it happened: flashes of breast and cock, the movement of pink tongue behind (a surprise this) Denholm's (but that's all right, that's fine) white teeth. He let it all barge through him and when it was gone, there he was, back with Alice.

> *Dear Alice*
> *Lovely to hear from you. I was thinking of you just*

297

recently, at the malaria forum we are setting up here, and actually that's not a bad place to consider if we ever get to the stage of looking for applications. Hope- fully in the next three months. Rainy Ireland, eh? But you'd be in the field a fair amount. Malawi, mostly. I'll let you know, if you like. Don't want to blather on. Hope you and Sven (??) are thriving. Lots of love, xEmmet.

He sent this and regretted it. Wrote another one, that was also, in its way, a bit of an untruth.

I think about you all the time.

He sent this too, and listened to his life opening.

Property

HUGH WAS BETWEEN jobs and he came back with Hanna in the New Year to help sort and pack and get Ardeevin on the market. He brought an old Polaroid camera and some last rolls of film and Hanna heard him about the place the first day they were there, silently looking, then the click-whirr-click as the photograph was extruded, another silence as he shook the thing dry and a little piece of her childhood rose to view. She looked through them later: the spiral at the bottom of the bannister, the squat taps in the upstairs bathroom, the vivid ghost, on the wallpaper, where a wardrobe had shielded its own shape from the sun.

'Research,' he said.

When the baby took a nap, they went upstairs and made love in her childhood bed, releasing all her scattered selves into the room: Hanna at twelve, at twenty, Hanna here, now.

The baby was walking, and into everything, Hanna followed him around that afternoon and it was all murderous: the broken greenhouse, the stream at the side of the garden, where he might drown. But it was simple too: the pleasure of the door knocker she hoisted him up to lift and drop, the textured granite stoop and the door that gave under his pushing hands to expose the vastness of the hall.

They ordered a skip, bought paint. In the evening, she washed and went over to Aughavanna with the baby, leaving Hugh in his painter's overalls, blanking out the bamboo grove on the dining room wall.

Hanna thought that once the house was gone her thirst might go too, but the house was not gone yet. And neither was her mother, who made such a fuss of the baby – *Hello, you. Yes. Hello!* – from a slight distance, of course, because of the baby's sticky hands but loving him, nonetheless, and getting all his smiles.

It was a long day. Back in Ardeevin, Hanna succumbed to a bottle or two of white from the garage shop, and there was such a bad fight, Hugh threw her out of the house. Physically. He pushed her into the garden and closed the door. Hanna bashed the knocker and yowled. She stumbled back and around to the kitchen window where she saw Hugh pouring the last of the wine down the sink. He went from room to room, turning out the lights and he left her there for a very long time, looking up at the blank house, weeping in the cold.

The next morning, after they had kissed, made up and all the rest of it, Hanna lay and looked at the ceiling and remembered looking at the same ceiling, as a child. She wondered what it was she had wanted, before she wanted a drink.

A life. She had wanted a life. She lay in this bed as a child and she thirsted after the great unknown.

The baby slept and woke and rolled off the mattress they had set for him on the floor. Then he was off again, pulling books on top of himself from off the shelves and laughing.

'Ben, stop it, Ben, no!' But she did not really mind. He

could break the Belleek for all she cared, in a couple of weeks it would all be gone.

Over in Aughavanna she said to Constance that maybe Dublin was the problem, the baby was in much better form.

'Boys!' Constance said.

Her own screamed for the first year, there was no consoling them. Then once they got on their feet, that was it, they never cried again.

'Run them and feed them,' she said. 'That's all you have to do with boys.'

'And what do you do with girls?' said Hanna. 'Drown them at birth?'

'Yeah well,' said Constance. 'There's a rain barrel round the back.'

They both glanced over to Rosaleen, but she had not heard, or pretended not to hear.

With all the running around supermarkets and cold mountainsides and overheated hospital corridors, Constance actually lost weight over the Christmas. When she looked at herself in the mirror, the ghost of a former self looked back at her and Constance thought it was trying to tell her something, even as she turned to the side and smoothed her stomach with a smile. Something terrible would happen, she was sure of it, because her mother had courted chaos and found it up on the green road. She had made some deal with death, and Constance did not yet know when it would fall due.

It was a good thing Hugh painted the place because half of County Clare trooped through the house on the first Saturday, it was busier than a wake. The house sold in three weeks, closed in eight. By the first of March the Madigans had shut the door for the last time. Whoever bought it did not move in – a developer, by all accounts – so the place stayed empty while Rosaleen's bank account filled up with money. Pucks of it. No one took her Christmas promise all that seriously: she had always been very private in these matters and never exactly open-handed, so it was a great surprise to each of her children to find themselves so much the richer. They had money, a significant amount of money, and that felt fine.

Rosaleen did not bother going over to Ardeevin. 'Oh I don't think so,' she said and Constance did not pressure her. It was an emotional time. They looked at smaller houses in the newspaper and Rosaleen said, 'Lovely,' but it was a bit of a reach after all she had been through. When they went to view, she drifted from living room to kitchen to bathroom.

'Oh Mammy, look at the insulation on that hot water tank.'

The new houses in their neat estates seemed only to confuse her, and indeed it was difficult to imagine her there. Constance set her heart on a little gate lodge, a sweet house with high ceilings and big Georgian windows, but the garden was far too small and it was slap bang up against the main road.

'What about this one, Mammy? You just need to put a kitchen in.'

'A kitchen?'

Besides, the market was turning. According to Dessie, the market was in a massive state of denial. Better to wait than to buy.

But the price came plummeting down on a place in town; an old stone house covered in Virginia creeper, tucked in behind the church, refurbished inside, everything to hand.

'Is that limestone or granite?' said Rosaleen. 'It's a very dark grey.'

Then she saw something rustling through the foliage. A

rat, she said later. Or she thought it was a rat. She fumbled her car keys and dropped them in a bed of hydrangeas, she pulled at the collar of her blouse, and took a turn. Constance got her checked out, over and back to the hospital again, it took three weeks for tests and waiting for tests, and by the time she was given the all-clear, the little house was gone.

Constance drove her home one last time from Limerick Regional and their path took them up over the humpy bridge, past Ardeevin. The front windows were boarded up and the gate hanging open, but Rosaleen did not seem to notice the house, it was as though the place had never been. That evening, Constance went to pick a few roses from the wreck of the garden and she came back hugely tired and alone.

There would be no perfect house, how could there be? Because Rosaleen was impossible to please. The world was queuing up to satisfy her, and the world always failed.

It was a trick she had learned early, in the front room of Ardeevin, perhaps, when one suitor or another would be sent off with a flea in his ear for thinking he might be good enough for the daughter of John Considine. Or earlier than that – it was hard to tell. Rosaleen was difficult to psychologise, a woman who never spoke of her childhood until she was in her sixties, and then in a way that made you wonder if she had ever been a child at all.

The remarkable thing was the way Rosaleen's children spent such enormous amounts of energy getting themselves, in one way or another, turned down by her too. Even the money she gave them felt like a coldness, once the house was gone.

Emmet, who had seen so much injustice in the world, had to remind himself as he checked his bank account – and then pulled back from the screen to check it again – that his mother never killed anyone. And yet, her children thought she was 'terrible'. Her eldest daughter, especially, felt, as she tended her, supplicatory, rejected.

'Mammy would you like a biscuit with that?'

'A biscuit? Oh no.'

Rosaleen, who was so needy, was always telling you to go away. So when she was, for those few wonderful months after the green road, easy to love, her children were utterly beguiled.

Paying Attention

EMMET WALKED IN to the house on Verschoyle Gardens one Saturday afternoon in November, to find his mother sitting in the kitchen with Denholm.

'How are you, Emmet?' said Denholm. 'Your mother has arrived. I made a cup of tea.'

'Mam,' he said.

'You wouldn't believe the traffic on the N7,' she said. 'I thought I would run out of petrol.'

'But you didn't.'

'Evidently,' she said. 'Would you check the handbrake? I am always afraid that thing will roll away on me.'

'You drove,' he said. Her car was in the driveway. Emmet had seen it, he realised. He had noted it in passing: *There's Rosaleen's car.*

'Yes! My goodness. And the fields flooded everywhere. I saw two swans paddling into a barn outside Saggart. But the roads are all very different these days. You know I haven't done that journey in so many years, I can't think when I did it last.'

She laughed, towards Denholm, a light little trill of hilarity.

Emmet put his bags of shopping down on the counter and took his phone out of his pocket. Right enough, the thing was jammed with missed calls and text messages: Hanna, Dessie, Dessie, Dessie, Hanna.

Nothing from Constance.

'I should have been up before, you know, I have been very remiss.'

'Rosaleen,' he said.

His mother turned to Denholm.

'I never liked Dublin.'

'Really?'

'It was always so dirty. Dear dirty Dublin, that's what we used to say. But Hanna too, you know,' she said to Emmet. 'I should have been up here, for the baby. I do love that baby.'

'You are the grandmother,' said Denholm.

'Well indeed,' she said. And the little laugh was back again, her body light and tiny in the chair as she rocked forward to touch Denholm on the forearm.

There was a pause then, as she considered what she had just done.

'Your sister's baby. How is your sister's baby?' she said.

'The baby is very well, thank you.'

She's here, Emmet texted to them all, and could not think what else to say. His mother was exerting the full of her charm on a Kenyan, in his kitchen.

'You're here,' he said.

'Yes!' she said, and there was a slight manic gleam to her eye. 'I came to see you.'

She looked at her son, she looked him straight in the eye, and for a moment, Emmet felt himself to be known. Just a glimmer and then it was gone.

'And it is such a nice house. Such a nice road. I didn't

realise there were houses like this, just off the motorway. You never know what is behind the trees.'

'I am sorry we only have tea,' said Denholm.

'Oh. Sorry. Yes,' said Emmet, turning to the shopping bags. 'Biscuits! We're not really a biscuit house except for Denholm, he is addicted to those Belgian things with the chocolate.'

'Not for me! I never had a sweet tooth.' She put her hand on Denholm's forearm again and this time, as though surprised, she let it rest there. The veins of her old hand were purple under the thin white skin, and the surface of Denholm's arm very opaque by comparison. Rosaleen reached for Denholm's hand, quite slowly. She held it up off the table and ran a curious finger along the side of it, where the dark brown of his skin gave way, in a line, to the lighter shade of his palm.

Emmet nearly died, he said later. *I nearly died.*

'Oh,' said Rosaleen.

Denholm pulled his hand gently away, and curled it into a loose fist on the tabletop.

'Why have I not seen it before?'

'Rosaleen,' said Emmet.

'Why have I not seen that before?' she said. She was quite fretful now. 'Why do you think that is?'

'I have no idea,' said Emmet.

And Denholm, in a rush of compassion, held both his hands out to her and turned them palm up and then palm down.

'Please don't listen to my mother,' said Emmet.

Rosaleen gathered herself then and glanced down at her lap.

Her car keys were on the table in front of her and she picked them up, in a decisive way. Emmet thought she was about to leave again and he started forward from his place at the counter, but she just clicked the remote. An electronic squawk came from the car outside.

'My bag is in the boot,' she said.

Emmet stopped where he was.

'Right,' he said.

And his mother reached for her cup of tea.

'Everyone is looking for you, Rosaleen. Constance is beside herself.'

'Oh Constance,' she said, in a tone of great exasperation.

And it occurred to Emmet that Constance had not, in fact, phoned.

'What do you mean, *Constance?*'

His mother looked terrible, suddenly. There were shadows like bruises under her eyes, and the eyes themselves all pupil; black as black glass. Tears came. She leaned in to Denholm.

'Constance threw me out,' she said.

And Denholm said, 'Your daughter? Oh no. Oh no. That is pretty bad.'

For a long and amazing moment, Emmet thought it was true.

Later, he rang his sister's phone in Aughavanna, and Dessie picked up. She could not be disturbed, he said. She was in bed.

'OK,' said Emmet, moving into the living room, pacing about.

Constance wasn't well.

'Right.'

Dessie's voice trembled a little. She's *had a diagnosis*, he said. They would operate pretty much immediately and get the lot of it in one go, but it was major – Dessie paused at the word – *major* surgery, and when she told Rosaleen this morning, Rosaleen took it all the wrong way. She lit out the road and Constance was frantic, she was more concerned about her mother than she was for herself. She was under the doctor now, pumped full of Ativan. And it was typical of Rosaleen, Emmet could hear a slur in his voice, whiskey perhaps – *chypical* – to cause the maximum bother at just the wrong time.

'It's all about her,' he said, as though he had a right to say such a thing. 'It's all about her.'

Emmet had a sharp urge to defend his mother.

Dessie fucking McGrath.

'Oh, God,' he said. 'Oh, Constance. Oh, no.'

'Can you hang on to her?' said Dessie. As if Emmet had an option.

'Of course. Of course,' as he rolled his eyes and walked the living room, wondering what he had to cancel at work – the hundred thousand people on the side of a road in Aceh, perhaps – and if there was a set of clean sheets to be had. His mother sleeping in his bed. It was an odd thought.

But please come down, Dessie went on. Please come. When Constance is up and about again. There were plenty of beds in the house God knows, they were coming down with bedrooms. Stay a while, when you bring her back home.

But that was yet to come. For the moment, Emmet looked at his mother sitting in his pathetic, chipboard kitchen and he was strangely pleased to see her there.

'I don't know where I am to sleep tonight,' she told Denholm. 'Though I don't sleep much, you know. Not any more.'

'No.'

She sat there, very small.

'I am sorry I touched your hand.'

'Oh. Please,' said Denholm.

'No really,' she said.

And, in all fairness, Emmet thought, she looked pretty bad.

'I have paid too little attention,' she said. 'I think that's the problem. I should have paid more attention to things.'

Ballynahown – Bray – Sandycove

ACKNOWLEDGEMENTS

THANKS FOR INFORMATION used and cheerfully misused in this book are due to: Seamas Collins, Mary Healy, Barbara O'Shea and Catherine Ginty of Trócaire; Rohan Spong and Trent Duffy; Fintan O'Toole, Tom Conway and Gary Hynes of Druid Theatre Company; Sinead Dunwoody, Paul Gallagher, Louise Canavan and Tom McGuinn of the Pharmaceutical Society Ireland, and Alan Carr, Leader of the Galway Mountain Rescue Team. Thanks also to Declan Meade, Fawad Qurashi, John Stack – and to Siddharth Shanghvi, for afterwards.

A NOTE ABOUT PLACE-NAMES

The green road of the title is a real road that runs through the Burren in County Clare. I have used some of the actual place-names along that beautiful coastline and these are spelt according to various maps, old and new. I have also made some names up or stolen them from other townlands – especially for places associated with the Madigans, the Considines and the McGraths. The town where they live is not named. This is to underline the fact that this is a work of fiction, populated by fictional characters. Any resemblance to the good people of West Clare, or to anyone else for that matter, is entirely coincidental.

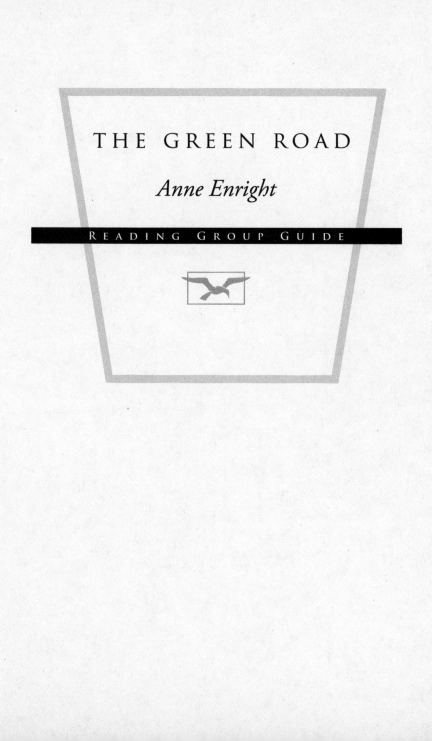

THE GREEN ROAD

Anne Enright

THE GREEN ROAD

Anne Enright

DISCUSSION QUESTIONS

1. All of the children move out of Rosaleen's orbit and establish their own lives elsewhere. How does their homecoming affect them?

2. Rosaleen writes distinct Christmas cards to each of her children. What does her card to each child tell you about their relationship? What do the cards tell you about her?

3. After Dan announces his decision to become a priest, Rosaleen says, "I made him. I made him the way he is. And I don't like the way he is. He is my son and I don't like him, and he doesn't like me either" (p. 34). What role does dislike play in her relationship with Dan?

4. Enright writes, "Emmet . . . was drawn to suffering—it was, after all, his job" (p. 106). Is his interest in suffering heroic or self-absorbed?

5. Dan, Hanna, Constance, and Emmet all have aspects of their private lives that they do not share with one another. What do they hide from one another, and why?

6. Emmet is described as not having "the helplessness in him that love required" (p. 296). From Dan during the AIDS crisis in New York to Rosaleen on the green road, how are helplessness and love portrayed as related in the novel?

---

7. Toward the end of the novel, Enright describes Rosaleen on the green road: "there were gaps between things, and this frightened her. This is where Rosaleen was now. She had fallen into the gap" (p. 266). What does this "gap" mean for Rosaleen and her relationship with the green road?

8. Pat Madigan is largely absent throughout the narrative. How does his absence shape the novel?

9. When the children return home, they come back to a country that looks quite different than the Ireland they grew up in. How has it changed?

10. Anne Enright has said that a major theme of *The Green Road* is compassion. How do members of the Madigan family show compassion to one another?

11. Of Rosaleen, Enright writes, "her life was one of great harmlessness" (p. 149). Do you agree?

12. The house in County Clare is the most prominent home in the novel. How have Rosaleen's children chased, established, or resisted establishing their own homes?

Barry Unsworth   *Sacred Hunger*
Alexi Zentner   *The Lobster Kings*

*Available only on the Norton Web site